THE BIG CLEAR

A NOVEL

CHRISTOPHER HARRIS

ASPHALT
HOUSE

The author is grateful for permission to use a brief excerpt from:

"Rhinestone Cowboy," Copyright 1975 by Glen Campbell.

Asphalt House paperback edition September 2018

Cover design by Dillon McGaughey

ISBN: 0692128305
ISBN-13: 978-0692128305

ACKNOWLEDGMENTS

Thank you to Craig Clark, for friendship above and beyond.
Also thanks to Chris Walsh, Rachel Vogel, Bill Childs and
Tony Catania.

PROLOGUE: 1996

Even at night, this place was saturated with color. The moon was a small sun, and cast them all in bright relief. It wasn't the kind of night targets eat bullets. It was the kind of clear night everybody digs in and prays for a little cloud cover. A little obfuscation from above.

But tonight they didn't have such luxury.

A few of them were present on New Year's Day in '91 when 281 diplomats evacuated from the American embassy, not even a klick north of here. A couple of them were on the ground in '93—the days of Gothic Serpent—and knew the men who died. But motivation, hell, it didn't work that way. Hokey but true: the only motivation anyone needed was the next man. You had your part of the smoothly functioning whole and you executed. One-upsmanship and bravado were for other platoons. These men were selected by the major himself for their quiet as much as their fearlessness. They came out of the night and cut your throat. They were each fingers of a silently strangling hand.

But no matter how tough these men were, it would be suicide to drop into the outskirts of the Medina neighborhood, rally in the forest south of the airport, and slink up through several blocks of squat desert houses unless you had help. They saw curious faces inside windows. They saw lights flicker off as they approached.

The furthest-forward American was a first lieutenant with an M24 strapped to his back. His name was Storm. He was flanked by four men, two on each side, who swept for impediments while they continued north and became more upright as the scope of this betrayal came clear. It might be three a.m. local time but they'd been seen a dozen times over, and nobody made a sound. Night vision wasn't necessary. Storm continued his intricate hand signals—eyes on that corner, cover me as I explore this alley—but he felt sinister suggestions in the air around him, found himself believing they could just as well communicate by radio and no local would budge. It was a weird, awful, indebted feeling. It smelled like ambush.

A native sentry stood against a wall, yawning and holding his stomach. Lieutenant Storm took him silently. He squatted, hand on his combat knife, duckwalked his first few steps barely breathing, eyes fixed on the sentry's face, watching for signs of recognition and when none was forthcoming Storm sprinted and dove, hit the man's ankles, felt them crack, then kicked up and his boot struck the sentry's face and they tumbled to the soft earth together. Storm's knife was out, he held the blade against this soldier's mouth as coins of blood fell from his broken nose, he saw the man's jugular in this phosphorescent moonlight and began the simple cut, then somebody above him said, "Ssht!" and Storm heard a cotton-rip of silenced small arms fire, one of his platoon-mates was close by and a bullet thunked into this wall above him, a rifle muzzle was in his face, it was this sentry's mate or superior and he had the drop on Storm, but one of the Americans had the drop on *him*, everyone had the drop on everyone else and this was a moment either Storm finished the job, killing the man wheezing beneath him and setting off a daisy chain of close-in combat, or he took a chance by dropping his knife and explaining who he was. Orders were never specific enough to account for every contingency.

He relinquished the knife and said, "Atto," which in the parlance also meant skinny.

Everyone waited. Then the man beneath him rolled over groaning, cupping his nose, and Lieutenant Storm let him up.

They spoke to Storm in Northern Somali. They asked if he was in charge. They asked if he knew where he was, who they were. He answered, lowly, in their language: the fact of his fluency registered on their dark faces. He sheathed the knife. Four other Americans fidgeted, and other platoon members were scattered behind them, waiting. The sentries offered to take him in, only him. The others would have to wait behind. *We are not so many*, they told him. *There are only one or two other men.*

He knew this was a lie.

They conducted him down a side street that was half sand. A mosque squeezed between two white buildings was dark and quiet, and these sentries gave no deference. They were small and they swaggered, a comfort and cool that belied this occasion. Twice they approached a lighted doorway and Storm sucked in his stomach, felt his organs draw tight and slop together. But twice they strode past and that urgency—of a curve taken too quickly, of a roller coaster's apex—dropped out of him. He half-smiled grimly; the further they took him, the less likely was his survival.

Finally they came to a covered porch where two men bearing Uzi pistols flanked a lighted doorway. Storm felt his heart get away from him, felt his pupils go huge, so that the light in this entryway hurt in the back of his head. They didn't bother taking his weapons, another very bad sign.

Inside, men were seated at a table, smoking cigarettes and tearing apart beef sambuusas. They were drawn and tired-looking; they watched him enter but didn't react. One man said a few words in a language Storm didn't know, probably Maay. The sentries pressed him forward, further into this house, into an empty room with stains on the wall that were either rust or blood. They left him alone and his fear was intense. He knew the American brothers he'd just left behind were suffering for him. He knew they were suppressing the urge to follow him in, guns blazing. His toes curled, his bladder ached. He was alive.

Someone limped in behind him: one of the men who'd been eating at the table. He fit the description—mid-fifties, hair close-cropped and receding, well-kept mustache, quite thin—but in English he said, "I am not him. You will not see him. You will discuss with me."

"And who are you?" said Storm.

"There is no time. The sun will rise in less than three hours and it will be impossible to kill the president."

He said this word, *president*, with some irony. He withdrew a pencil from his shirt pocket and began drawing directly on the grimy plaster wall.

"You," Storm said. "You're an arms dealer. You're a drug trafficker. You blackmail the entire region with the gasoline you run out of Kenya. You sell machine guns mounted on flatbeds. You've killed thousands of your countrymen." The man kept sketching. "Even now you're getting ready to shell your own people. If I shot you right now, I'd be saving hundreds."

The man stepped away favoring his right heel and folded his arms behind his back, admiring his work. "No no," he said. "He is always a friend to America."

"You make me sick, asshole." Truthfully, Storm was relieved, and emboldened by that relief. If he hadn't been ambushed yet, it probably wouldn't happen.

"We are here. The target is here. We attack with small guns from the west. We will make noise, shoot at the house where he sleeps. But there are many guards with him, and we will not be close. Very good security, but he will walk out of the house. And you will be here." With a smooth, young finger he tapped a new spot on the wall. "Up above."

"You have good rifles," Storm said. "You can get any

equipment I have.”

The man scratched his nose and made a *tut-tut* sound. “This is a long distance. This is six hundred meters. More. We will distract him, and you must make this shot.”

“I won’t do it,” said Lieutenant Storm. “I have the authority to abort. You’re just too fucking evil.”

This businessman, this traitor, this patriot: he grinned. He was handsome and charismatic, like a film actor. A silence in the heavens roared: that absence of celestial piloting in whose void the clever rise and dictate terms. He wouldn’t dignify Storm’s outburst with a response. Details had been negotiated, or the platoon wouldn’t be here. As a young man, he’d been a chauffeur for American oil executives, wormed his way into a few small deals, bought a stake in an aviation company, acquired an oil drilling outfit….

So Storm said, “You won’t be president. You’ll never be president. We’ve got a man picked out.”

He shrugged. “Progress is progress.”

“And once it’s over, what stops my men from shooting all of you?”

He sucked his teeth. “They are not your men.”

The absence of adornment in this room now seemed menacing. The floorboards bowed beneath their feet. Two exposed bulbs with pullchains, an empty table scarred by cigarette butts, a bundle of garbage emitting a faintly antiseptic smell, an overall nightmare shroud of internment and interrogation. Most galling was the way this small man rubbed his palms together, tiny motions, not actual rapacity but a pantomime thereof, a self-aware little act.

“Not the head,” said the Somali. “Do not shoot his head. We must take photographs. What ammunition do you use for such a job?”

“M118LR,” Storm said. “175-grain 7.62×51mm Hollow Point Boat Tail.”

“Yes. Ah, no. He asks: please not the head.”

“You’re weak. Calling on the Great Satan to do your

work."

"Weak?"

"I know what we did to you. I mean you personally. We arrested you and shipped you off like a dog to a prison on that island. And we locked you up and you whimpered like a dog. You couldn't clean yourself. We had to wipe your little ass for you."

"Weak." The Somali no longer smiled.

"So how humiliating is this? Make a phone call, bring in the tall powerful American to change your country's history."

"No. No, let us see," a dead-serious shine in his eyes, "how strong is this tall powerful American." He stepped near Storm—who momentarily raised his hands—then across to the table. He stooped to one knee and put his right elbow on the table, a universal challenging posture. "Come," he said.

Storm snorted. This little man wanted to arm wrestle.

"You're kidding me."

"If I am so weak."

Storm shook his head. The Somali's pant leg hiked up when he kneeled, and the older man's calf was pitiable, almost hairless. Storm wore combat fatigues, shaded light for the desert. Many years doing this, many missions whose morality he didn't always understand. But this was the first time he wanted to walk away. Politically speaking, the major didn't keep his men in the dark, didn't want them to feel like robots blindly executing commands. Tonight, knowing he had no choice, feeling his vital role in exchanging one rat-king for another, Storm craved a little blindness.

So he kneeled, too. He flattened his belly against this table, felt sand slide and crunch beneath his leg, hooked his thumb against the Somali's thumb and took hard hold of the man's hand. *This is satisfaction I can derive.* Their faces were close. The older man's dark skin looked pore-less, and he showed his teeth.

They began to pull. The stupidity of this filled the room.

Then the Somali smiled, began to give way, his elbow

still anchored to the table, his arm bending backwards, Storm pushed to end this quickly as the Somali smiled in his face, locked on his eyes, evincing no worry, because then there was a click and pressure on Storm's right thigh, it was an automatic weapon that the Somali pressed hard against Storm's leg as their arms stabilized, there was victory in the older man's grin as he gave out every message he had to give, but then he looked down at his own person, down his own torso, past his waist, to the spot at his groin where Storm had shoved his knife blade, not cutting yet but pressing hard against the Somali's crotch.

"Do it," said Lieutenant Storm.

FRIDAY

"That's him humping it around South by Southwest…wait…where's that button…I promise things get better…as they, y'know, progress."

Beep.

"Okay sorry, the first few are just…" *beep* "…I'll just keep scrolling, man…" *beep* "…all right, here's your brother at Auditorium Shores…" *beep* "…it's a little out of focus, I think that's his elbow…" *beep* "…okay, here we go. Here's where he meets up with your wife."

Aesop Savakis wrests the camera from Dub Storm's hands and makes a shrill sound Dub interprets as mournful. The late-March sunlight floods Aesop's office, a detonation of dust motes like asterisks referencing all that's unseen.

Dub watches Aesop. This is always a moment of high emotion; Dub knows it's stupid to hand over the little digital Minolta because the client might smash it against a wall, resulting in bad feelings over a bigger tab. But whatever response lurks in Aesop's face as he forwards *beep beep beep* through photos of last weekend's escapades, there's no more outward hint. He's a charcoal briquette in an expensive shirt and cufflinks.

"This it?" he finally asks.

"Well. They get a little more…familiar. I followed them back to the Heart of Texas down on 290 and as you can see they left the blinds partway open."

"I mean this here's all he did? This is all it was? Fucking my wife?"

Aesop looks up from the camera and laughs.

Dub says, "I'd have sworn it was you, Mr. Savakis, maybe playing a fast one. I bet you have all kinds of stories. Standing in for one another in second grade and whatnot."

"This here's a goddamn *relief*."

"Glad to hear it, I guess. If you told me what I was supposed to be looking for…."

"No no," says Aesop, "I didn't want y'all going in with any expectations. But sure as shit I thought he was selling me out to Monumental Concrete. Figured y'all'd come back with pictures of him getting his face stuffed with food by the competition." He looks back to the camera. "Instead, oh lookit, I suppose it's Miriam getting stuffed."

This isn't how these things go. Dub pulled up to Aesop's crappy office park on Bee Caves steeling himself for tears or fists. Matrimonial work rarely ends well. Here are snaps of the twin brother committing biblical transgressions, and this is good news? There's a black-and-white TV in the corner depicting a dark sky occasionally filled by manmade lightning.

"Y'all followed him how many nights now?"

"Three others," Dub says. "He, uh, met your wife again Wednesday. Otherwise, he stayed home."

Aesop flops into his vinyl desk chair and sighs like a release valve. "One thing I can't afford right now," he says, "is lousing up any bids. We're going after some major contracts." Dub squirms a little here on the badly-laid wall-to-wall of this one-room office. "Sorry, Mr. Storm. This here's excellent work. Let me write y'all a check."

Aesop signs and dates a check and tears it from his ledger book, but doesn't hand it over. Instead he looks at the television for a moment, then returns to the Minolta, again beeping through the most lurid photos. "The real difference between my brother and me," he says, "is I guess he's hung like a damn cashew. These pictures surely are the shit, Mr. Storm. So close up, and there's no telephoto on this thing. Like maybe it's y'all pulling a fast one on me. Maybe they pay y'all to take these, and then to ignore my brother meeting with Monumental?"

"That would be clever," says Dub. "But in my experience crossing clients is pretty unhealthy for business."

Aesop gives him the check and the camera. "But then how the hell did y'all get so close to those two half-wits?"

Dub taps his temple. "Trade secret," he says, then goes outside to his '89 Accord and fires up a blunt of Northern Lights. He putters back east with the window down listening to the Toadies' underrated second album and when he stops at a light, he hides the blunt and watches a lady taping a "Save Zilker" flyer to a mailbox. He chuckles at the perfect 75-degree day.

*

Back at the brick house on Johanna Street—the house he grew up in, the house he inherited—Dub checks his answering machine and is relieved to find no messages. He lays half-a-bag of Cool Ranch Doritos on a plate, covers them in Velveeta, sets the microwave on nuclear. There are ant traps on the aqua linoleum, little black octagons of doom, and he invokes his telekinetic powers to force an ant to trudge into one. But they don't heed him, and besides the traps have maybe been there since the millennium. There's no sadness in any of this. Everything is all right.

Dub's cell phone rings. "Red alert!" says Kid Collins, Dub's friend of thirty-odd years, occasional legman and weed connection. "I'm stranded downtown looking up at a 600-

foot crane and it's freaking me out. Weak sauce."

Dub says, "What a coincidence, Kid. I'm flush and I'm dusted."

"Oh, man, all I wanna do is go out to the Free Side and swim and smoke, and then go someplace and watch the 'Horns tonight. I got Dutch Passion Blueberry. I even got Silver Haze. Come get me, dude, and let's soak up a little sun."

Dub puts on his camouflage swim trunks and eats. Then the doorbell rings. He has no peephole and is still moderately stoned.

"Hi there. Remember me?" It's the bearded Latino guy in his same gray suit. He came around a couple times before South by Southwest. "I'm Raphael. I'm redoing the place across the street. Can I talk to you, Mr. Storm?"

Grackles screech in the magnolias overhead. Dub hears tinkly chimes a few blocks away playing Brahms' Lullaby: a retrofitted ice cream truck that roams South Austin selling roasted corn on a stick. It's only two o'clock but it's a Friday, and the workers who are supposed to be tearing down the old house across South 2nd are sitting around listening to a boombox and yelling about the weekend in Spanish. Johanna Street is gap-toothed with former aging shacks in various stages of deconstruction, the vanishing backdrop for Dub's childhood.

"Um," Dub says. "Not really interested right now."

"I know you own the house outright," says this Raphael. "And I know you still haven't paid your property taxes, and they were due February 1."

"Okay, man, that's just some creepy stalker shit."

"You got assessed at, what, half a million? Hard to keep cash enough to pay taxes on that. Especially when…what's your line of work again?"

Dub inhales and touches the bridge of his nose, knowing this conversation will pass, knowing this little man is but a moment from departing. The boombox over there says something in Spanish about Baghdad. "Oh, I train jockeys. Got a couple horses in the garage, jockeys come by and race 'em around the city. Best thing for both of 'em, really. The horses and the jockeys."

Raphael grins and nods to show how good-natured he is. "My point, Mr. Storm, is if you're having difficulty with this year's taxes, it might be a good time to sell?"

But now Dub is only half-listening. He's looking across his burned-out front yard, east down the sidewalk, in the direction of Polvos. Walking this way is a skinny blonde, waifish in a white t-shirt and jeans. She strides alongside the waist-high fence Dub shares with the next-door neighbor, doesn't smile, and lifts the latch on his front gate. She's very young and not exactly beautiful, is probably just this side of slatternly, but it's difficult to look away. Dub sees Raphael's slack jaw and feels his own.

"I'm Angela Easley," she says. "And you're Mr.…?"

"Storm."

"I knew your name," she says. "It's a tactic. A way to gain advantages." She laughs, crushed and miserable. "I need your help. I'm here to…hire you." She blinks several times behind insectile sunglasses, doesn't know what to do with her hands. Her arms are so thin and uniformly tan that they lack depth, and Dub sees them as boneless doodles poking out from under her rolled-up t-shirt sleeves.

"Well," says Dub. "I don't get much walk-up business. This here gentleman was just leaving," giving Raphael a throat-slash gesture. "Won't you step on in my parlor?"

The house is a perverse museum, Dub knows: the same Sixties Scandinavian furniture his parents proudly installed, only now with burn holes and three shades dingier. Lime green is now the color of mildew, lavender is slate gray. And for some ridiculous reason there are four rocking chairs scattered around the living/dining area, which Dub registers only now. Angela sits on a wing chair of padded naugahyde vinyl and the motion tightens her jeans, plus presents a rather lascivious view of her midsection in one muscled half-inch stripe. Her sunglasses are still on, and she's obviously trying not to cry.

"It's all right," Dub says. "Whatever it is, I'm sure I can fix—"

"Do you know the world's greatest phoniness detector?" she says.

"Let's see. I'm afraid I do not."

She inhales thickly. "An old dog. I have an old dog named Barney, I got him when I was nine, and now I'm 24. He's still sprinting around, he's still fun, but he's got a gray face. When I walk him, I swear more than half the people we run into are like, 'Oh, how old is he?' 'Oh, look at the old soldier.' 'See that, honey, that's an *old* doggie.'"

Dub is digging for a story behind this story, trying to pull it out of her with his eyes. But he's still stoned, and so also kind of just taking it all in.

"Like it never occurs to them," she says, "it might not be the happiest thing in the world for me, to be told my dog looks like he's going to die soon, this family pet I've known practically my entire life. Seriously, this happens *all the time*. At least three times a walk. If I was wheeling around my grandmamma, would they come up to us and go, 'Oh, look at this old woman, how old is she? Boy, she must be really old.'"

Dub squints a little in the sun that halos her, and grins.

"You'll have to forgive me, Mr. Storm. I'm very...." Behind the sunglasses, she's looking at the wood-paneled wall, at a print of an awful Navajo watercolor hanging over the couch, depicting Texas in its primitive age. She swallows, frowning.

"I don't mind," says Dub. "Anyway, I'm a little...headachy. I think I might have scotch back there, or some juice."

"Camellia Kane says you helped her."

"Mrs. Kane. She had a pretty airtight situation."

"She says you're trustworthy. She says you don't take as

much work as you could. You could do ugly jobs for eviction lawyers, but you don't, and you don't advertise."

His phone rings: Kid again. He clicks away the electronic chirping. "It's very flattering."

"I'm going on and on."

"There's nothing to be nervous about," says Dub. "I'm a peach."

Finally, she cries. Her body shakes and she reaches up under the sunglasses with bite-ravaged fingernails to pinch her eyes. It's like someone stifling a sneeze. She curls forward, lips quivering, sighing into the back of her hand, fighting the horrible thing that's happened. After a minute of desperate little gulps and sniffs, Dub realizes the conventional thing would be to fetch her a tissue. He pats himself down, then walks into the bathroom and realizes the best he can do is wadded-up toilet paper. She accepts, finally removing the sunglasses, and blows her nose.

She says, "Why don't I…." Her eyes are slightly too close together. She doesn't wear mascara. "I'm not… I'm not well. Why don't I go on talking, and eventually I'll come around to it."

"Absolutely."

She frowns. "My father was having a barbecue out in Westlake last night, and my dog and I stumbled in on it. Old Irene Stein was sitting there with her teeth stained red by the wine, and sure enough she goes, 'There's the furry old man. Oh, how old is the poor thing, sweetheart?' Do you know what my therapist told me last week?"

"No."

"The world has provided me with a way to spot narcissists. They see Barney and think he looks old, and it makes them think about the unpleasant facts of aging—time marching on, leaving them behind—so that they feel the pain of the childish self, and they need to hurl those thoughts out of their tiny *fucking* little heads, so they say something insensitive." She says it *in-sin-sitive*. "Apparently I have a severe problem dealing with narcissists."

"Hm."

"And that's what they all are. All my father's developer pals, putting up skyscrapers and paving over watersheds to hurl the bad thoughts away."

"Wait," says Dub. "The Easleys of Westlake. You wouldn't happen to be related to Heather Easley."

With a perfect band of teeth, Angela bites her bottom lip, hard. "She's my big sister."

Heather Easley. Dub feels sharper, less high. His instinct—the human instinct—is to ask about Heather, to weasel his way into catching a glimpse of her. But this is against Dub's drama-free code. The thing to do is embody cool; nothing good comes any other way. So he says, "Oh. High school pal of mine."

"Really. You don't look that old."

This makes Dub laugh.

"Sometimes I think *I'm* a narcissist," Angela says. "I can't think of anything worse to be. But so I went to sleep, Mr. Storm…and, oh, here it is then," and she sobs anew. "I woke up this morning, and my ex-husband called and said our son is missing." Revealing this, Angela dons her sunglasses again, becoming the socialite Dub now knows she is. "Hunter. He's three."

"…"

"Apparently there's a note. Of course we called the police. They were at our house this afternoon, I just came from there. Wyatt, my husband. He lives in New Braunfels, but when the police got down there he wasn't…. They can't find him."

"…"

"He won't answer when I call. He gets Hunter on the weekends but he picked him up last night. I'm supposed to go to this *thing* and I asked if Wyatt could take him early. But he won't call me back and I *don't know where my little boy is.*" Tears roll out from under the sunglasses, she digs one hand into her thigh until Dub hears the denim scratch.

He finds his mouth incredibly dry, but says, "What's your relationship like with your ex, Ms. Easley? Would he deliberately do something like this just to be cruel?"

"No. It's the first thing the detective asked. Wyatt knows I…. He wouldn't do that to me. We're on good terms."

"I don't mean this to come across the wrong way. But usually once the police are on a case, that's my cue to get out. There isn't a lot of friendly overlap."

"But you find people," says Angela. "Camellia told me you track people down. They're just waiting. That's what the police said, all they can do is wait for Wyatt to show up. They broke into his house and they didn't find any note, and I have a feeling they don't really *believe* me, Mr. Storm. I have a feeling they're not really even looking for him, which means nobody's looking for Hunter. And I told them: Yes, I'm sure I wasn't dreaming. No, I'm not so far gone I can't tell the days apart. Yes, I'm on…medication, but not the kind that makes you mondo bizarro. I'll show you my phone. He called. Wyatt *called* me."

Dub takes the phone, a significantly more expensive gadget than his own, and dutifully reads the screen: Wyatt Parsons called at 11:50 a.m. He nods because she wants him to. Angela is unsteady and so young, slightly entitled-seeming within this rocking package of distress, if only because things are not typically withheld from her. She'll collapse right here if he doesn't say something. "My professional opinion is it'll be all right, Ms. Easley. And I would be glad to help you look for your boy."

She forces a small grin, reaches up under the sunglasses to wipe her eyes. "I never know what to do," she says. "I'm not used to people believing me."

"Does your family know you came here?"

She shakes her head.

"I'm sure they're worried. Why don't I take you home."

Angela stands up and shakes his hand. "No, thank you.

But unfortunately I don't have any money to pay you, Mr. Storm. You see, the poor little rich girl doesn't have a bank card, or credit cards, or a single penny's worth of cash. They took it all away. So you *will* have to come meet the checkbook holders."

"I'll follow you in my car."

She takes back the phone and steps out into his front yard, stands with one hand dangling from the wrought-iron flowers that adorn the supports for his front stoop. She makes a call. Dub walks away, feeling for his keys, doing the genteel thing and pretending not to listen. Truthfully, though, all he can hear is Angela's voice throttling up again, growing more distressed. He watches as she turns away, he sees the fine rump, the curves of her back. He thinks about Heather, the big sister.

"They aren't there," she says. "They'll be there at four. Can you be at 4201 Michaels Cove at four?" She withdraws a gold pen from her pocket, looks around his yard for something to write on.

"It's all right," says Dub, tapping his temple.

She nods and puts the expensive pen in her mouth and tries to smoke it.

*

There's nothing else to do before four o'clock, so he decides to go swimming.

By the time Dub picks up Kid downtown, Pete Bellingham has horned in on the afternoon. Pete's maybe 23 with sewage-smelling dreads and a perpetual sunburn. He crashes on various couches around the city and to all appearances owns a single shirt: a sky-blue number on which he long ago spattered darker-blue paint, giving him the appearance of someone who's always just come in from the rain. Dub pulls up at the old Paramount at 7th and Congress, where a marquee just ahead reads *Mrs. Warren's Profession.* "Dude, my friend is in that," Pete says, clambering into the Accord's back seat.

"You don't have any friends," says Kid from the passenger's side. "We're your only friends."

"Naw, she's Irish. Everything she says is like a question, even when it's not. Deirdre or something. I met her at Guitar George's house. Everyone getting all spiritual, man, and she's walking around asking questions. But I liked her. She's got a real devil-maker attitude."

Dub bangs a U-ey, eliciting angry honks from uptight state government types. He says, "What do you mean, 'devil-maker'?"

"No no," says Kid. "C'mon, man, don't ask Pete explanations for shit that comes out of his mouth."

"You know," Pete says. "Devil-maker. Like she just don't give a shit."

Dub scratches his forehead. "You mean, as in, 'Devil may care?'"

Pete says, "Whatever, ooh la la. You say it in a French accent, I say it like a goddamn American."

Kid pulls a face like he ate something sour, and they laugh. Dub zooms back south across Town Lake and hangs a right on Barton Springs. They park in one of the Zilker lots and walk down to the jogging path. It's leafy and sun-dappled in here and Kid hands out pinheads. Sitting within a tree's exposed root structure—ropy and twisted and complicated—Dub smokes and watches a dozen turtles who've found a log out in the placid stream, sleeping and dreaming of soup. Dub tastes earth and sugar in this here weed.

"Them fucking suckers with real jobs," says Pete. "Am I right?"

"Might be getting paid for a trip down to New Braunfels," Dub tells Kid. "Maybe I could use some company."

"Another unfortunate marriage coming to an end?" Kid says. His teeth belong in a much older man's mouth.

"I had an idea," Pete says.

"No," says Dub. "Not even sure I'm going, but if I am it's a missing persons thing."

Pete says, "Like, all the time you spend staking out these hubbies whipping out their cocks to stick it in the Mexican maid? You should bring a video camera and sell it as porn."

"Brilliant," says Kid. "The problem being nobody wants to pleasure himself watching a fat bald jackass plugging his fat sweaty mistress."

Pete shrugs and blows potsmoke into his dreads. "There's people who'll beat off to anything."

After a while they get up and walk under the bridge, looking down on a couple of bickering canoeists, looking askance at pretty joggers. The trail ends at a flat outcropping of rock, and a fence. Through the fence they can see Barton Springs Pool, lifeguarded, algae-free, teeming with kids whose moms paid admission. Up here, though, with the hippies and the dogs, this is the Free Side. A dozen folks are sitting around smoking cigarettes, soaking their feet, tossing tennis balls into the water, and also kissing plus maybe a little more than kissing. Dub sees one hippie gal with pale skin and a purple tattoo, she's wearing a bikini and she has the biggest, roundest ass Dub has ever seen, and she keeps lowering the bikini bottom for some reason, meaning Dub and everyone else can surreptitiously scope her goods.

Pete strides over to a leathery older guy and slaps intricate five with him. Kid and Dub take off their shirts and sit in a few inches of the freezing cold water. Dub doesn't doff his ancient UT ballcap, though. He'd be embarrassed to admit it, but he's got a thing about people seeing his bald spot, and when his hair gets wet it looks even more pronounced. From the front you can't see anything. Facially he looks young for 42, often passes for 30. But whenever someone gets a good look at Dub from the back or, worse, from the top, well, it about drives him crazy thinking that they notice the sand-dollar-sized patch of hair that's gone so thin his white scalp shines. Much of Dub's mental energy, if he's honest about it, goes into triangulating his physical geography so as few people as possible can sneak up from behind and notice The Spot. He thinks back to his time with the platoon, all the public showering and sleeping curled up heedless of location, the cramped quarters inside a Hook where guys might be stacked so tight behind you you couldn't turn around…it would all be intolerable to him now mostly because of The Spot.

"So what the hell happened to you?" they hear Pete saying to the older man, who's out here with a black lab that's going crazy playing with a floating plastic duck.

"Broke my goldurned neck is what," says the gray little guy, as he tries to bend over and get his dog's toy. "I was in the rodeo for 20 years, man. Broke both my wrists, got a titanium rod in my leg, fractured my ribs a bunch of times, got these scars on my forehead. But the thing that took me down was riding my goldurned bike with flipflops, swim trunks and nothing else, saying goodbye to my girlfriend so I could cruise over to free swim at the Pool over there. I wasn't digging the blues they were playing up at Zilker and it was dark and I just rode my bike into a ditch and broke my goldurned neck."

Dub calls over and says, "I notice the Ranger tattoo you got there."

"75th Airborne," he says in his southern surfer patois. "Even an old fart like me gets jazzed up when they start bombing like this. Got glued to the neighbor's television last night, couldn't stop watching. How about you, my man?"

"Oh, not me. Just thanking you for your service."

"Don't believe him," says Kid. "Our boy here knows 1,001 ways to kill a man. Back in the day, he was Special Forces. You should see him in the field. Instincts take over, pulse slows way down. Cold-blooded killing machine."

"I do believe you boys is high," says the old Ranger.

"He ain't so tough," shouts Pete. "I could take Dub in a fight. I could take you, Dub!"

"Hey," Dub says, "I think your duck is floating away." Sure enough, the dog's toy is drifting upriver and the broken-necked rodeo dude watches it go, pleading with the lab to swim after it. He staggers toward the end of this rock shelf without bending, and has to beg some fat kid in the water to go after it and toss it back to him. "Come to Hippie Hour at the Continental Club," he calls back to them. "Tuesday 7 to 10. You never know who'll show up and play."

"Will do!" says Pete. "You know I'll be there!"

Meanwhile Kid puts his feet deeper in the water and reclines straight back, so the sun is on his chest. He was always the handsome one. His pupils are two black discs and he says, "Where we watching the game, Dub? UNC-Asheville the first fucking sacrificial lamb."

"Oh, shit. What time is it? I gotta go."

"That thing in New Braunfels is tonight? Man, that is seriously uncool."

"It's not a thing yet. I'm out to Westlake. You'll find a ride wherever you're going next, right?"

Kid closes his eyes. "All I wanted was a smoke, some sun, and the game with your worthless ass. Now you get all arteriosclerotic on me." Dub gets up to go, and his bathing suit drips on Kid, but the Kid doesn't flinch. "Man," he says, "you act like you think this shit lasts forever. Next time we come back here, they'll probably have it all blocked off."

"Let me borrow your shirt," says Dub.

*

The Easleys live on a million-dollar avenue in Austin's most recherché dominion, but the Friday rush-hour traffic

Dub crosses to get there is awful. He thinks someone should rewrite "The Yellow Rose of Texas" to "The Orange Cones of Westlake." He arrives at 5:15. It's a mustard-brick mansion with two-story brick columns in front; they begin at the ground two bricks across, then get thicker as they climb and by the time they hit the roof they're 20 yellow-painted bricks across. It looks like the house has fangs. Fangs with dental plaque.

There are no black-and-whites out front, no cops lingering anywhere. Angela invites him inside, bites her gone fingernails, installs him in a baroque study. She opens her mouth to speak, but nothing comes out, and instead she frowns and disappears behind sliding wood doors. Dub has a view of a Mayan-blue swimming pool and beyond that a branch of Lake Austin, which isn't actually a lake at all. He sits in a stripe of sunlight, and off to the side a wall-sized mirror returns his image: cabana shirt and the camo bathing suit, topsiders and sunglasses, the entire ensemble chewed up by time. The rest of the study is getting dark by increments.

Heather Easley enters from an unexpected direction, via a false door.

He'd know her anywhere, even a couple decades since high school, even in a decidedly adult black suit/skirt combo that looks like it cost more than the combined contents of Dub's entire wardrobe. She's blonde as ever, cleft chin, face pale and thoroughly unmarked. She says, "You're Mr. Storm?"

This is a bit of an ego crusher, but Dub rolls with it. "She was a woman who could make a freight train take a dirt road."

She blinks. "Do what now?"

"I'm him," he says. "He's me. We know each other. You went to Westlake. I went to Travis."

She shows pearly whites whose canines look particularly sharp. "Well, I think I remember you. Mason, isn't it?"

"Call me Dub."

Heather doesn't exactly seem happy for the recollection. She crosses her arms—fingernails unpainted, no wedding ring—and says, "You went into the army or something wild like that."

"I did."

"If I'd known it was you I was coming to see," she says, "I'd have thrown on the old cheerleading sweater." She sits behind the desk, but Dub can still see her close-together knees straining white through black stockings. The place between his neck and left shoulder blade zings with covetous pain.

"When did you get out?" she says.

"Oh, it was…end of '98? So maybe four years."

"Which means you're missing all the fun that started over there yesterday."

"Never been to Iraq. But there was other fun then."

"And now you do this. And it turns out we're bosom buddies from way back. Did you ever meet Angie back then?"

"Don't think I ever made it as far as your family homestead," says Dub. "And come to think of it, was she even born yet?"

"Well, that's right. She's the love child. Married and divorced quicker than you can say prenup. Never really left her daddy's sweet embrace. I'll just tell you this up front: she spent last year in the long-term ward at Timberlawn, up in Dallas. She's had…problems."

"…"

"She and Wyatt. They still have a twisted thing going on. I think she's sleeping with him again. And a little bird told me they got into another fight at a show Saturday night. Now she swears Wyatt called her, and Hunter's been kidnapped. I don't know what to believe."

"You talked with the police."

"I did."

"What do they say?"

"Mr. Storm. Mason. I'm pleased to see you again. It's a funny coincidence, though I guess if you stay in a small town long enough eventually you meet everybody twice. But you can probably tell Angie's in no condition to be hiring out subcontractors."

"She's upset," says Dub. "But she's right about one thing. If the boy really is missing, you're wasting time. Kids who don't get found the same day they disappear, it doesn't usually end well."

"So we should hire you," says Heather. "What can you do for us that the police aren't already doing?" He watches her unreadable smile, but feels he understands some subtext between them.

"Mm. Calm your sister down?"

She swivels to look at the pool. "I'm sorry I didn't recognize you, Mason. It's not like me. Usually I remember every shark I meet."

"I could drive down to New Braunfels, just take a…whaddayacallit. Look-see."

"Well, I guess you have to be a salesman."

"Free of charge," says Dub. "If it's a car ride to just confirm what the boys in blue think, and it helps a mother in distress feel better? Well, how could I charge a bosom buddy for that?"

Heather stands, offering no thanks. She looks at her watch. "I know you're eavesdropping, Angie."

The younger sister pads back into the study, occupying her tangle of roles: gudgeon, supplicant, scamp. Dub can't help making comparisons that Heather wins convincingly.

"Have you heard anything from Detective Berkshire?" Heather says.

"Don't you think I'd tell you?" says Angela. "Don't you think I'd come in here running?"

"Well, I'll bring Mr. Storm to Dad. Why don't you show him outside while I grab my things, and then please try and get some rest. And leave your car keys out where I can see them."

They all shuffle out, leaving behind the gilded room to deflate and go black without them, and passing close to Heather, smelling violets, Dub says, "Do you know what they called you back in high school?"

Before departing, she gives him the full magnitude of her beauty, square in the kisser, and says, "I'd imagine they called me a lot of things."

Mostly late at night, Dub thinks. Mostly with a tissue close at hand.

So he and Angela stand in the driveway's upper half, squinting back up at the house, into the sun's windowed offspring. "He's got this way," she says, "like he's older. He likes to look at bugs in the grass. He doesn't talk much. They were worried something was wrong, but I knew better. He talks when he's got something to say."

"Do you remember exactly what your ex told you on the phone?"

"He said he woke up and Hunter wasn't there. He said before he found the note he figured Hunter was out back playing. It's a big yard. But deep down he knew something was wrong, because Hunter doesn't ever let him sleep late."

"But for some reason he didn't actually tell you what was in the note?"

She gives him an elfin cross-eyed little look. "I don't like the way you said that. You *don't* believe me."

"I'm sorry, ma'am. I didn't mean anything by it. Sometimes I forget my manners."

She chews the inside of her cheek, biting her own expression. "Don't tell me you're a phony, too," she says.

Dub is letting himself stare at an upstairs hallway window, letting the sun's doppelganger burn holes in his retinas. It hurts a little but also feels good, waking him up after a day of varied toking, and also focusing his mind by clearing away all past associations. "Guilty as charged. But since we're being honest, let me say: I don't feel a whole lot of urgency from your family."

Angela gazes at the emerald lawn seeing ghosts. "Maybe I made mistakes before, and that's why they don't take me seriously. But that doesn't mean Wyatt didn't call. You saw my phone: he called. I'm not making anything up. But oh no, this is a *big* time for Easley Partners. The company is making a *big* announcement Monday. Blah blah. So they don't *want* to take me seriously. They don't want unnecessary…whatever, publicity. I wouldn't be surprised if they told the police to back off, Mr. Storm. They want to hide the crazy daughter and all her fake problems."

Somewhere a screen door claps loudly shut. Dub turns and the world is blotched purple and gray. He can see legs—Those Legs—parading this way. Dub has dismissed attachments, has made a big internal production of living simply in the years since his discharge. He'd take pride in his drama-free life if taking pride wasn't its own form of drama. He won't allow himself skirt-chasing, or moneymaking schemes, or deep entanglements of any kind…and all right, maybe he's a little proud. He knows for instance that David Umber, who was in Dub's SFAS class in glorious Southern Pines way back when, left the platoon and jumped with great fanfare to Wall Street, lost when the tech bubble popped, then disappeared into the Lord Our Righteousness Church in New Mexico. Dub understands. It's not just the lack of a mission once you're out, or of an overt brotherhood. It's also that the goals in that other life—take that hill, burn that IED, kill that target—are transient and fast to arrive. By comparison, a life of cumulative striving requires one kind of patience Dub doesn't have anymore.

"Oh," says Angela, after a fine comedic pause. "I get it. You want to fuck my sister."

Rubbing his eyes, Dub remembers something an old bunkmate used to say. "Your tongue's quicker than a knife fight in a phone booth," he stage-whispers, and here's Heather after a wardrobe change, wearing a green halter dress: for him, apparently, drama personified.

*

She doesn't want to talk about it. He takes MoPac south to William Cannon, and she deflects inquiries. Her thighs shine in each passing streetlight.

"Did you notice if your sister was drinking at that party last night?" Dub says, but Heather merely turns a silver phone over and over in her fingers. "Do you know who Wyatt socializes with?"

She directs him up Brodie Lane and into a fenced-in lot. It's nearly dark. Silhouettes of construction equipment impend, and over there is a security guy with a shiny rifle. Dub doesn't get nervous in moments like this. It's when you don't see the firearms. The bare earth here is as yet untouched, and electric light burns in a foreman's shack.

"Come on in," Heather says.

Dub remembers Thomas Easley. A barrel-chested dad in a red convertible, giving his daughter a lift and any surrounding males the stink-eye. Except Heather was a cheerleader and football players were exempt; she took up with the Travis High quarterback, an okay kid, and Dub would see them around Town Lake, the three of them, rigging a little skiff to take out under the Lamar Bridge. Heather looks squarely at Dub now, and he sees her nipples jabbing the green dress.

"Dad," she says. "Mason Storm."

Thomas has raccoon pouches under his eyes, a couple gray streaks in his hair, but otherwise looks the same. Alarmingly so. He gets up from the small desk and smaller television and strides over, so the plywood floor takes notice. Thomas is big and trim, his hands are like waffle irons, his necktie and shirt strain as he moves. "Thank y'all for coming out," he says.

"Dad, Mason knows us from high school." On the TV, the president is saying something and looking pained. "You've met him before."

"Well, hell," says Thomas, and they all step back down into the near-dark where the air feels good.

"Obviously I spoke to Angela, sir," Dub says. "Feels like I'm stepping in the middle of something."

"That girl has bad timing. Always did. A man tries to build something to leave for his family. We can't do with her spells right now, can we, Piper?"

Heather says, "No, sir."

"I don't believe for one minute my grandson has gone missing. Y'all need to understand. I try to have patience. But when a girl-child lies about stealing, when she lies about where she spends the night, when she lies about…. Well, when she lies about getting raped." He starts a cigarette and stands in a cone of electric light. "Now, I know Piper doesn't think I'm being fair, calling 'em lies. But whatever they were, they never proved out to be truths."

"Because I was going to say," Dub thinks it wise to mention, "she seems sure what the ex-husband said."

"You probably heard what's going on here in Sunset Valley," says Thomas. "Big-box store trying to build on that lot just over there, and I'm putting up a grocery right here. Pretty big mess, lots of squealing from the tree-huggers. Looks like the permits finally come through Monday." He takes a long drag, smiles at Heather. "Three days, fingers crossed."

"We don't need any more attention," Heather says.

"I've never been surer about anything in my goddamn life but that little boy will be back home with his momma Sunday night, just like he's supposed to be, just like he always is. Y'all can take it to the bank. We been burned too many times. But Piper loves her baby sister, and if she thinks it's all right to spend a little money and keep her happy."

"That's one thing," says Heather. "We haven't settled on a price."

"I wonder what gets a man into y'alls line of work," Thomas says. "It's very interesting."

"I guess I enjoy figuring things out," Dub says, bringing forward a little twang of his own.

Thomas nods wisely, folds his arms. His cuffs are unbuttoned and flop a little in the gloaming. "Tell me what y'all think about nostalgia, Mr. Storm."

"Nostalgia. Hm."

"Y'all seem like a good Austinite. A solid citizen of the world."

"Now that you mention it," Dub says, "I guess nostalgia is maybe Austin's leading export. Someone always seems to be telling me how much better the city used to be."

Thomas laughs loudly, which makes Heather grin.

"Then again," says Dub, "nostalgia is hope for recovery of the lost thing, right? And recovery of the lost thing is why I ever get hired. So maybe it ain't all bad."

They shake hands again, and this time Thomas doesn't try to crush Dub's smaller mitt. "The world is full of complainers," he says. "Down here in Texas, in the end you're on your own."

Heather says, "Your rate?"

"Three hundred a day."

"'Plus expenses,'" Thomas says. "I read all those old gumshoe classics."

"But assuming I go down there and find the boy tonight, there's no charge."

"No, we'll gladly pay y'all for today." Thomas kisses his daughter on the cheek. "It's good business to *seem* old-fashioned and whatnot, Mr. Storm. But we live in the real world, too." He pulls out his wallet and counts three bills onto Dub's palm. "Now if y'all will excuse me," chuckling, "I've got to go back in there and keep figuring out ways to ruin the town's natural resources."

"Well," says Dub, back over by the Accord. "I believe I'm your ride."

"No," Heather says, "I'll call the service."

"I have to go back north to pick up my associate anyway."

"Your associate."

"I have a whole team of one."

"What makes you think I live north?"

They're leaning against the car, with Dub looking down a few inches at her lovely, affectionate mask, gilded by, what, decades? He knows enough to retreat into untouchable cool. "North is just where I figured an ice queen would hail from."

She blinks, then laughs. "Fuck you," she says amiably.

*

Dub and Kid drive an hour on I-35 to go see the boy's father, jockeying with homicidal truckers. This is the way to San Antonio and then Mexico, a deceptively long run that angries up the blood. Even before San Marcos, Kid has counted aloud what looked like three dead cows by the side of the road, corpse-shaped heaps fallen not far from strip malls and medical clinics, and Kid says, "Schizophrenic fucking place we live in." But truthfully Kid is just peeved because he miscalculated the tipoff of the Longhorns' NCAA tournament game, which was over by early afternoon, with Texas winning by 21. Now they chase Indiana versus Alabama up and down the radio dial, but neither of them really gives a crap.

"So," says Dub. "Wyatt Parsons."

"What do you wanna bet he's got round tortoiseshell glasses?" Kid says. "Everyone I ever met named Wyatt had round tortoiseshell glasses and a floppy brown haircut."

"I knew a Wyatt who didn't."

"You're so contrary," says Kid. "Let me guess. He had a high-and-tight. Which doesn't count, because before he got it shaved I bet anything it was a floppy brown haircut."

"We'll get to the bottom of this in five minutes and turn right around. And you're driving back." Dub looks meaningfully at the Accord's glove compartment, where Kid's nightly stash resides. It's truly the main reason Dub asked him along.

"Oh. Hey, Guitar George is having a rager this weekend, man."

"Forty hours in a drum circle singing 'Kum-ba-yah,'" says Dub.

"You're anti-hippie," Kid says.

"I'm not anti-anything. Peace and love."

"You like it whenever ravening hounds are released on innocent protestors. You live for tanks popping the heads of the girls who put daisies in cannon muzzles. Your red-white-and-blue underpants are showing, man."

"Dude. I only said I don't like Guitar George's parties."

"I dunno. They got high-quality women, even if they're a little grimy. Hell, I'm a *lot* grimy. And you gotta know someone to get in. None of that there hoi polloi scrounging booze or jive. A good, honest crowd of fuckups."

"They have a washer/dryer?" Dub says. "Damn, I need a new one."

"Yeah, bring your laundry. Always the first step toward getting laid."

Getting laid is what Kid does, has always done. His oatmeal-colored smile notwithstanding, he's still wildly good-looking, but of course it's more than that: he's droll and uninhibited, derisive and kind in appropriate measures. Nearly every room into which Dub has stepped with Kid has contained at least one woman ready to be seduced by him. They light up like bloodstains under infrared. It wouldn't be fair to say Dub has always envied Kid, because envy implies that only chance separates the envier from his object of envy, that the envier believes—with the universe's blessing—he can attain what the object of envy already has. Instead, Dub looks on his oldest friend almost with pleasant despair, at his easiness, his near-infinite network of friends, his decidedly bald-spot-free curly black hair. But of course, Dub doesn't really want Kid's life: its byzantine romantic entanglements and drug dealing. It does occur to him now, though, to keep the Kid far, far away from Heather Easley.

They arrive at the prescribed New Braunfels address, a one-story house on Cedar Elm Street. Dub parks a couple blocks away facing the lunar-looking limestone quarry into which Cedar Elm feeds. Wyatt's place has an above-ground pool, and a tin-roofed dog run in back. Through the desiccated yard, they can see a gun shop a block away, beside a Jehovah's Witness center. There's also an empty APD black-and-white parked in Wyatt's dirt driveway.

Dub says, "This is not the fun part."

Kid gets out of the passenger's seat and clicks his door closed quietly. He sneaks out into the night. Dub gives him a few minutes, then climbs out himself, and slams loudly. Two cops come clambering out of the house in the universal badass posture, batons rattling, flashlights whirling.

"Halt," Dub says, "who goes there?"

"Wyatt Parsons?" says the first officer. "Step away from the car, sir."

Dub clenches his teeth and says, "Who the fuck's asking?"

"Police, sir! Step away from the car!" A gun is out, and it flashes in the March moonlight.

"Hey," Dub says, "aren't you the guy from the Village People?"

They're close now, all lambent chrome and plastic, and then hands are on him, he holds his ground for a moment, they push and spin him around and he loses contact with the planet, lands hard against the Accord, his chin bounces off the hood and he spread-eagles, they frisk him convincingly and come out only with his billfold.

"I know what you boys want," says Dub. "Go on through my wallet there, Mr. Abraham Lincoln will change your mind."

"Shut it, burnout," the first cop says.

"'Mason Storm.' Who the fuck are you?" says the second.

"Where's Parsons, dickwipe?"

"Where's the little boy?"

"Listen, asshole, you're looking at felony kidnapping."

"Fucking stoner burnout."

"You don't wanna be in the pokey for hurting a little boy."

"Fucking kiffy hophead fuck."

"You'll start singing soprano so fast."

"All right," Dub says to a rust spot. "I'm sure sorry officers. You got me mistaken for somebody else. The family hired me. The Easleys. I'm a private eye, men. They hired me to find that boy."

The policemen stop talking.

"I mean, I've got business cards," says Dub. They let him up. He makes a production of straightening the collar on Kid's cabana shirt. "Pretty long night down here for a couple Austin po-lice. Haven't cracked the case just yet?"

"Shut it."

"Way you boys drew down, I'm lucky there's no extra ventilation in me."

"Nobody drew nothing. Shut it."

They keep him snug against the Accord, and one of them takes Dub's license over to the squad car and makes a call. He returns a few minutes later and gives back the billfold.

"*Fuck*," mutters the other cop.

"If we see you again," says the first one.

"You'll what? Make me talk to Jesus? C'mon boys, we're fighting for the same side. Why don't we pool our resources, get cozy, maybe get a bottle of wine...." Just now, though, Dub realizes how lucky he is these cops didn't rifle through the glove compartment, and he shuts up, lets them retreat back inside the house.

He gets back in the Accord. A couple minutes later, Kid has returned.

"Checked every room," he says. "They tossed the place, from the look of it they didn't find jack. They're up in there playing gin rummy and watching hoops. Speaking of which," and he turns on the radio.

Dub brings back a bag of candy corn from his trunk. He shakes a few like loaded dice, pops them in his mouth one-by-one, ruminatively. "Let's think," he says. "If Wyatt's tormenting Angela, that's one thing. Guess he could've taken the little guy camping."

"Could've brought the little guy to a new girlfriend's for, like, a sleepover."

"Some other kin. His own parents maybe."

Kid breaks the filter off a regular cigarette and lights up. "He could've given up the joke and brought the little guy back to mama already. Except then your girl would've called, right?"

"You didn't spend the evening with this family," says Dub. "I wouldn't say they put other people's feelings high on the priority list."

"Heather Easley," Kid says.

"Yup."

"Hot as shit, if I recall. I may or may not have tapped that."

"Yup."

They listen to Alabama rack up an 11-point halftime lead, then gag it away in the second stanza, interrupted every ten minutes or so by a news update about the Iraq invasion. With a minute left, the Crimson Tide drains a three-pointer, then gets the ball back down three. The radio announcers are beside themselves with the delicious possibilities. "*This is a*

Hoosiers team that played for the national title last year! And now they're taken to the brink!"

"Hundred bucks they tie it," says Kid.

"I don't want money."

"Then we'll play for what's in there," and he points at the glove compartment.

Dub grins, but weirdly is starting to get a little bit of a bad feeling. He says, "Why would I make a bet for something I'll be enjoying for free in a matter of minutes?" The sound of one particular auto engine has separated itself from the distant traffic baseline, and gets louder.

"Williams...! Up the left side....! For three...!"

"Here we go," Kid says.

Dub sees a pickup flip off its headlights and caper this way, at near ramming speed. Its wheels chirp in protest, are quiet for half-an-instant, then shriek as brakes are savagely applied. Dub steps out of the Accord and sets his feet wide.

"It's no good...!"

"What the fuck y'all doing here?" shouts the driver. It's hard to see him in the ghostly gray light.

"Just here to make sure the little boy's okay," says Dub.

"The fuck y'all are! Bodean! Get 'em, boy!"

Dub sees a blackened gray shape bound over the pickup's roof before he hears the skittering claws, and the moonlight now feels more like hindrance than help. The dog clambers down the pickup's hood and Dub says, "Get in there and close the door!" He hears Kid click the Accord passenger door shut. He can't see anything, so he slams his foot hard against the pavement. If the dog doesn't pause to regroup, Dub has problems.

But Bodean keeps a safe distance and begins barking savagely, a sign he's no cold-blooded killer. Dub can see the dog's mouth now, bright white in this monochrome-gray world. Big fellow, a shepherd mutt, fangs and spittle in full effect and hysterical woofs rebounding off a neighborhood that right now couldn't feel more countrified. Dub thinks: I wouldn't mind a little help from law enforcement about now.

"All right," he tries to say in all this racket. "If we could just talk…."

"Bodean! Get 'em!"

And Bodean does leap, aiming at Dub's right arm and not his neck, once again signaling his status as amateur enforcer. Dub whips the arm away and the dog snaps into nothing but air, and in mid-leap finds itself shoved by the hindquarters so it lands pelvis-first against Cedar Elm Street. Bodean rears around and takes a sideways lunge at Dub's ankles—another minor-wound-seeking gambit that earns Dub's sympathy—so when Dub kicks the dog's face it's not at full speed, and nothing breaks. The dog, still growling, whirls around and finally makes his big play: a frontal assault with front legs up, a leap that exposes his chest. Dub can actually *see* very little of this, but he feels it, trusts the dog's mid-air weight pressing against him, knows he could kill Bodean by capturing his neck and wrenching him around. But there's no need. Given the appropriate incentive the dog will stop. He removes his face from Bodean's attack path while using his thumbs to gouge canine eyes that (Dub could swear) give back the moon's light with a slightly red refraction. The dog screams.

"Bodean!"

Kid punches the Accord's headlights and Dub is fine here off to the side, but having stepped out of his truck Bodean's daddy is squarely in the beams, so master and dog both squirm around blind. Dub walks over and stomps on the guy's foot, plus grabs his left ear. He's a big handsome Latino with half-a-mustache. His dog sulks away blinking out of the light.

"Why would you do that?" says Dub.

"Awwwwww!" says the guy.

"Wallet," Dub says, forcing the boy down face-first against his own truck, and discovers through a Pier 1 Imports card and then a driver's license that this, in fact, is Wyatt

Parsons.

"You asshole!" says Kid rolling down a window. "The fuck you doing? What if we just wanted directions!"

"My name's Storm," Dub says. "I'm a detective. Your father-in-law hired me."

"Fuck you!" says this big buck. "Why'n you get a real job—awwwwwb!" Dub bends his arm back behind him, and finally there's commotion up by the house, and the APD strolls out.

Quickly, lowly, Dub says, "Slow your roll, partner. I'm one of the good guys, right? I'm here to find out about your boy."

"Lemme go! Lemme go!"

"If I let you go, you gonna talk to me, man?"

"Awwwww!"

Here come the cops, swaggering in, Dub lets go of Wyatt and they separate, Dub puts up his hands, the cops are shouting for everyone to shut up. Dub sees Kid slump in the passenger's seat with a smirk on his face.

"Somebody got him!" Wyatt shouts. "Somebody took him!"

"Sir!" says a cop. "Sir!"

"If you hurt my dog!"

"The dog's fine," Dub says, hands raised to the sky. "We're here to help. We're going to find your boy. Talk to me, and I'll find your little boy."

Wyatt Parsons begins to cry. He's tan and really young and sporting a "Keep Austin Weird" t-shirt, and he lets slip the cord of control that separates man from beast.

"All right," says Dub, knowing adrenaline's metal tang by its fading aftertaste. "All right." It's comforting, in a way, to have people he stumbles across on the job fall into clear categories. It helps him pull the thread until the truth gives way. Wyatt will be the boy who views himself as self-reliant, and will take the news that he's not—or that self-reliance isn't enough—very hard. While the police frisk Wyatt, Dub says,

"I think this is the part where you're supposed to say, 'What's all this about, anyway?' and then I say, 'Shut up, I'll ask the questions here.'"

Wyatt shields his eyes against the headlights, bending over the hood of his pickup, and a twist of snot links nose to sheet metal. "Please. Please, she'll kill me! She'll fuckin' kill me I don't find him!"

The officers restore order. They sit Wyatt on the curb and give him a cup of water. They talk to him gently, asking what he knows. One of them nods at Dub, kind of a tacit agreement that if he'll wait right over here, they'll figure out just what the hell is going on. Dub tries to approach Bodean on the front lawn, but the dog growls and whimpers, a veteran's admonition. Life in all its stupid confluences streams around them like a Texas sirocco. Kid is still in the car, chewing, staring down into the bag of candy corn.

"Says he was out looking for the boy," one of the cops softly tells Dub, out in the street.

"Just driving around looking," Dub says. "For a three-year-old."

"No accounting for people. You think he did something with his little boy?"

"I don't know the man. Never met him before."

"You'll, ah, tell Detective Berkshire we got this guy on our own?"

Dub says, "Whatever you need."

The cop nods and puts out his hand. Dub thinks it's for some fraternal shake, but there's a piece of paper extended his way. He takes it, unfolds it, and reads magazine cut-out letters:

to GeT HIm Back StOp KiLling JusTIN

*

After interrogating Wyatt, they trail the police back north from New Braunfels. When they arrive in Westlake, Angela is asleep. An inconsolable Wyatt lies down for a rest, too.

Thomas Easley grits his teeth and says, "Don't make sense. If it's the tree-huggers' last try before we break ground for the supermarket? Don't make sense. What's the end game? Y'all take my grandson and seriously think I'll just shut the Brodie Lane development down? And even if I do, then y'all give him back and believe I won't just start it on up again?"

The detective—a light-eyed guy with colorless hair named Berkshire—has no outward opinion. He sits in the same chair Dub occupied earlier today and furiously writes notes in a small book as everyone speaks.

"Mr. Storm here," says Thomas, "he told Piper: we don't find that boy in the first 24 hours, we ain't gonna find him. Is that true?"

"Just hold on," Berkshire says.

"Parsons said the little boy is his alarm clock," one of the uniforms tells the detective, "so when he woke up at noon he knew something was wrong. He found the note. No sign of a break-in, but he keeps the front door unlocked. He called the mother. Then he says he drove around looking, just hoping he'd see something."

"No ransom," says Thomas. "Goddammit, why didn't

they ask for money?"

A car pulls up outside, and everyone waits. It's Heather, in a sweatshirt and shorts. Dub feels air leave the room as she walks in fraught and scowling. She hugs her father and looks at all the men.

"It was dark when he came back and ambushed us with the dog," Dub says. "Dark for an hour. You don't find that suspicious? What was he out looking for?"

Berkshire makes more notes. Without raising his head, he says, "We've got a couple too many cooks."

So they write down Dub's number and he gets up to go. Thomas shakes his hand vigorously, mournfully. Heather mouths the words *thank you* through a freshly-woken pout. The uniform goes upstairs to roust Wyatt, and Dub steps outside, feeling for his phone. Angela is standing beside the Accord, in a nightgown.

"You heard."

"Every minute," she says.

"…"

"Every minute of your time, I'm paying for it. I promise I'll find the money."

"You're in shock," says Dub.

"You know my sister will pay. Please." She clutches fabric around her neck, beyond tears. "He's just a little boy."

"The police believe you now. They'll find him."

"It won't hurt to have you looking, too. You found Wyatt. Say you'll do it. Say you'll take my money."

*

An hour later, music and chatter from Guitar George's float across West Lynn Street, but Dub and Kid Collins haven't gone in yet. They've cleverly positioned themselves in the dark between streetlights, but it's chilly, and Dub can see gray puffs whenever he breathes out.

"You know you got a problem with the sticky," says Kid, "when your dream girl's family needs your help and you're out here getting mellow with me."

"It's just a job," Dub says, then inhales hard. "Punch in punch out. And who says she needs me?"

"Don't get me wrong, bro. I love being the sidekick. I'm just saying her nephew gets kidnapped, maybe she's giving out blowjobs to the one that finds him. Maybe she wants to remedy old wrongs, suck you off listening to the Sex Pistols the way she should've in high school."

This is good shit. It takes something for Dub to feel it this strongly. It tastes like oak and strawberries, that peaty overture, that soft sweet finish. It's damn good. Dub just feels all right, and is aware that he really *likes* to feel all right: it's a pleasure, this out-of-time awareness. It's why booze will truthfully never do, because it soaks you in itself, you get saturated in how you feel and you lose the doubleness of commenting upon your own state. That multiplicity, that revealing of worlds and selves. It's *on*. They're sitting here on the false springtime grass which will die out before the real stuff grows in May. Really, Dub has anchored them both here because he doesn't want to go into the party.

"I mean, Austin PD is squarely on it," Dub says. "And they never screw up."

What can he do? He's got a blank check from the Easleys and no place to cash it. He lies back with his hands behind his head and watches a sky that's fancy with stars. Whoa. His equilibrium is gone and his lungs feel golden. He imagines his soul contained in a single molecule.

After a while, Kid says, "Let's go spend a shitload at the Driskill, man. It's on the family." He smacks his lips. "Is it sad the best fantasy I could come up with to blow a rich dude's money is brioche-crusted Bristol Bay cod or whatever?"

"You're a bobo," Dub thinks he hears himself say.

"Yeah and the Driskill's, like, totally not open this late anyway."

Why *wouldn't* the kidnappers ask for money? Pretty serious gambit for some conservationist just to make a point. And what was Wyatt doing driving around for hours? Why'd he attack them?

"I think I like the father," says Dub. "Wyatt."

"Easy there, slick. Don't solve anything until the first couple checks clear."

"He had an accident. Something happened to the son. He panicked, made up this whole note thing."

Kid says, "Maybe. But he's a pretty good actor, then. Not like I saw a bunch of cut-up magazines in his house."

"…"

"Man, I dunno. Maybe little tots were always disappearing or whatever. But I don't remember bad shit like that when we were coming up."

"My God," says Dub. "Is someone really playing 'Stairway to Heaven' in there?"

He can see Kid's chest shake with laughter. Thirty years ago they were drinking behind a church with four or five other boys, absolutely bombed (12-year-old Mason Storm weighed eighty pounds) and smashing empty bottles against a rectory wall. He was furious then. Nobody knew it. He played baseball, poorly, and he tooted the clarinet in jazz band. He was fogged off from his parents, and in the new public library on Guadalupe he'd read this novel called *Americana* where everyone had all the trappings of being happy and successful but instead were just bored and did stupid, self-destructive things. The book didn't glorify these things, but Mason thought he'd do them anyway. Being good. Being good was rooted in fear of the alternative. When Mason hurled empty beer bottles, he wasn't just desecrating religion. It was everything. Other kids laughed and admired the spray pattern of broken glass.

Young Mason noticed a light go on and didn't say

anything. Soon someone from the church—not dressed in a robe or a collar, some workman maybe—ran outside shouting, and one boy got away but the rest of them wound up face-first against that same brick wall. Mason panted in the evening air. A couple boys were crying, and he knew they weren't his brothers. He was so angry. A cop asked him questions, pressing against him from behind and breathing in his face, but Mason wouldn't answer. They would've had to kill him to get him to talk. Most of the others gave their names and addresses, pleaded for clemency. But young Danny Collins—they didn't start calling him Kid until high school—also seemed ready to die. It happily broke Mason's heart to know this. Still kissing bricks, they silently looked at one another and really *saw*. Not talking to a poor beat cop who probably just wanted to let everyone off with a warning, it didn't mean anything. In fact, it got them both introduced to the juvenile courts. But just then Mason felt this unnecessary, over-the-top loyalty toward Danny, and felt its absence in just about everyone else in his life. Seven years later, Dub joined the army without understanding he was still trying to find more of it.

"You really want to go in?" he asks Kid now.

"There's probably food."

"I'll go. I'm flexible, man. I can ask George a question or two, maybe."

"You ride a tall horse, Mr. Storm."

They get up and walk (Dub staggers) across West Lynn. The house is white clapboard behind a tall fence. Party chatter swirls. Here's a couple of chubby young ladies stumbling out as Dub and Kid stumble in; one of them smiles at Kid and the other vomits into the street. Before he crosses onto Guitar George's lawn, Dub surveys the downtown skyline above these trees and sees that unfinished new bank building with its weird lighted crown that looks like bat ears or maybe an owl. He has no opinion on its artistic merit, but it's amazing how it looms.

Young folks stand and sit in a front yard brightened by Christmas lights; like true Texans they're wrapped and mufflered against the night's "chill." (It's a humid maybe fifty degrees.) One older man is flopped on a sheet of plastic and what looks like his grown daughter is trying to drag him down a tiny little hill in the side yard, some homage to sledding on the slick grass. No, there's no snow, and in fact there are still bugs out, popping and sizzling in a zapper. Kid sees a pretty girl he knows and is lost: she takes his arm and shows dazzling teeth. Dub presses forward alone into the ramshackle house.

Guitar George has been waging a battle against the city for years, fighting an eminent domain claim that he's always reportedly on the verge of losing. By now Dub is unclear exactly what the plans are for this land, because there are condominiums a block away that aren't going anywhere and a ritzy single-family home right across the street. But this neighborhood—Clarksville—is just a few blocks west of downtown, so its sporadic dumpiness is forgiven in the eyes of open-minded urban planners. George's shindigs are usually going-away parties.

"Man, don't pull rank on me, man. I've surfed Teahupoo in Tahiti, Ghost Trees in San Francisco, Waimea Bay in Oahu, so like just 'cuz I live *here*, man." It's Guitar George shirtless and cross-legged on his blood-red couch, giving the what-for to some poor miscreant unlucky enough to open his mouth in the living room vicinity. Dub runs his finger in some horseradish hummus that's sitting out here on a side table. "That's just some total mess you're talking, but it's okay. For as long as my house is still here, the only surf sounds we have is just the traffic on MoPac, man, but don't sweat it. Namaste, dude. Om shanti shanti shanti om."

There's a mosquito on Dub's arm and he fights the urge to slap it, instead tries to brush it off. But he miscalculates and smears it bloodily across his skin. He winces and regrets this, but also internally praises himself for giving enough of a damn not to kill creatures indiscriminately.

"You see that guy over there?" George asks his several conversational attendants. Dub thinks George must mean him, but he's pointing to a thin Indian dude stepping out of the kitchen. "We call him the Intel Skeleton. Yo, Skelly!" The guy waves noncommittally.

"Are you really getting a fig tree planted in the back yard?" says the woman beside George on the couch.

"It's a symbol," George answers. "You know. Siddhartha and all that. But it'd be cool if we could all sit under it, right? Suffering ends when craving ends, yo."

Everyone assents vigorously. George is ugly in a handsome way, is *striking*. He's leonine with a finely trimmed beard, spiked brown forelocks, sun-damaged skin, bulb nose and thick-framed glasses; he's a light-sucking egoist with a deity catch-and-release program. Right now apparently it's Buddhism, but Dub has been here for get-togethers where the crowd was intensely Hindu, or intensely Christian, or intensely Muslim.

"What up!" George says. "It's Dub! The Dubber! Yo, Dub, c'mon in here and join up with the coalition of the chilling."

Dub waves and sits in a rattan chair. Someone hands George an acoustic guitar, and he wails away with his tongue casually out, his jaw loose, looking at the guitar neck and his flashing fingers but also carefully looking around at his audience digging the riffs. The blonde beside him scooches closer to George, touches his tan shoulders and closes her eyes. Dub has sat here like this a dozen times the past few years, looking around at the hippie chicks, testing his power to deny desire. George is around Dub's age and speaks with a slightly lispy Jersey City accent, is full of facts and agendas and a stream of hyperactive talk. His coterie changes regularly because eventually they realize he's a smart-sounding empty lecher with no visible means of support. For the time he has them, though, George is kind of a religion unto himself, spawning mini-Georges with hipster 'tudes and the trappings, if not actual symptoms, of self-loathing. Gumshoes in the movies get wall-eyed informants or bombshells with mixed loyalties. Dub, it now occurs to him, gets this asshole.

"There's bombs over Baghdad," George says. "The French are pussies because they didn't want to invade. Our own retired generals say Iraq is like the sixth or seventh most important place to fight this glorious War on Terror. We butcher UN Resolution 678 to do whatever the fuck we want. And the worst part of all is smart-thinking people in our country are forced to sound like we're defending a scumbag dictator who kills his own people just because we don't think it's a good idea to throw over foreign governments. Wake up, boys and girls," and his current admirers really *are* barely more than boys and girls, "because it'll take a century to fix what we're fucking up right now. And this from a shitbag who wasn't really even elected."

Dub has earned the soldier's disdain for politics, and yawns. He thinks: I should've made myself come in earlier, before the Sermon on the Recount.

"I can't get a rise out of you, Dub?" George says. "I can't get you railing against us pinkos with the temerity to protest this fucking invasion?"

"Probably not," says Dub. "I'm pretty baked, man." This gets a laugh from George's congregation, and the man himself nods and offers a *touché* smile. "Hey," Dub finally says, "you know Wyatt Parsons by any chance?"

"Names," George says. "I don't keep a lot of names up here. That's not me being evasive. Really, do I know a single one of your names?" pointing at the six or seven children gawking up at him. "I'm not sure of your name, sweetheart," he says to the blonde beside him, "but I think I'll call you gggahgggahggahggaww," miming a cylindrical object going down his throat.

"Just an off chance," says Dub. "Guy who married into the Easley family. It only just occurred to me you might know him, considering how tied in you are."

"Flattery," George says, and shoos Dub away. But later Dub is in the backyard feeling a small campfire on his face and wondering where Kid is with that killer stuff, and George skulks over, now alone. He says, "I must really piss you off."

"Nothing pisses me off anymore, man."

"Enlightened, you're so enlightened. But I just wanted you to know, we're good."

"Okay," says Dub.

"No, it's like. I mean, I know what you did, man. I know who you were. But you came to my party, what, working a case? Groping around for leads? That's kind of fucked."

"I really didn't. It was on my mind. It just popped into my mind to ask about this guy. His little son's missing."

"But I think you know what it looks like to my friends if I even acknowledge I've heard of the dude," George says. "Suddenly I'm a narc or whatever. I mean, I like children. I don't like to see children get hurt."

"Okay."

"I wanted to tell you next time I saw you. You and me, we have a mutual friend, Dub. Except neither of us are friends with him. Believe it or not, I recently found out he's like first cousins with my old man, who I wouldn't say I ever exactly got along with. But my old man died a couple weeks ago and there was a funeral and this guy showed up. And somehow he knew I know you. Pretty fucked up stuff, right?"

Dub gets a glimpse of Kid walking around the back yard with two empty plastic cups, looking for the keg. Kid looks pointlessly sullen and vanishes into darkness beyond the fire. Dub realizes he hasn't eaten dinner.

"Partridge," says George. "This guy from my dad's funeral's name is Partridge."

"Oh, shit," Dub says despite himself, and touches his own face.

"Yeah. He told me some things about you, man. Some wild fucking things."

Major John Partridge. Major Partridge knows where Dub lives—it's the only Stateside address he's ever had—but the sober quadrant of Dub's mind lets a paranoid thought occur. That Partridge would red-light George's father for the sole purpose of justifying a casual approach of Guitar George at a funeral.

"Crazy old Uncle John," says Dub, "likes to exaggerate."

George nods. "Mm, and what an eye for detail. He got real quiet and told me this one bit about Somalia, way after all the shit in that Black Hawk movie. Like, you worked with this one warlord we supposedly hated, and helped him shoot the president. As in, the president of Somalia. No, that's not really what he said, you didn't *help* shoot the president. You *did it yourself.* So we could install the president's son, who also happened to be an ex-marine."

"Don't know what you're talking about," Dub says. He frowns at George. "Dude. Sorry I asked about a suspect at your party, okay? Jeez."

"I don't know what kind of crazy-ass bullshit you're into these days, Dub. I just can't afford any, like…extralegal shit. I mean, the city wants this land really bad."

"Trust me, George. I don't have anything to do with Partridge anymore. This is a real case. A real father, a real missing son. Three years old."

They watch the campfire crackle. A Jehovah's Witness pings finger cymbals and dances for drunk, goggling college students. Bodies fringe George's fence, live scarecrows kissing and pawing one another at his property's edge. Everything beyond the fence is just black. George isn't stupid. It dawns on Dub that George doesn't believe for one second his father was related to Major Partridge. And maybe George even got a messenger's fee, for off-handedly mentioning his run-in with Dub's old commander, adding to the illusion that even now, years later, the old platoon is everywhere.

If it's an illusion.

"So you do know the name?" Dub ventures anyway. "Wyatt Parsons?"

George looks old. He says, "What I know you could fit on the head of…something really small. I'd say my penis, but that would be vulgar."

"Anything you've got on him," Dub says.

"I don't ever remember meeting the guy. But yeah, you hear stuff about the Easleys. Wyatt Parsons was a construction worker, and the youngest daughter used him to get attention. Listen to me. I'm fucking Deep Throat."

"You know anyone else who knows him?"

"Well, now, see. He also dipped his toe on the other side. Which always seems fucking stupid to me, I mean, you're making a few shekels hammering nails in some new office park then you turn around and protest against the developer? But it was a smoldering little scandal a few years ago, the heiress and the lefty wetback carpenter. And you know: she couldn't have him, she couldn't have him, then she got him and didn't want him. Or something. Anyway, you ever met Jebidiah Sparks? He's got rallies scheduled this weekend against the shitty chain stores that wanna open down south. He has to know more about Wyatt Parsons than me, Dub."

"All right."

"I mean if I knew you were such a badass…. But it's too bad you were working for the wrong guys, y'know?"

"Hm. Did Partridge seem like a wrong guy to you?"

"The wrongest, Dub. The absolute wrongest."

*

Sure enough, there's a message waiting on the answering machine back on Johanna Street. Dub has a cell phone and thinks he shouldn't keep a landline, too, with money perpetually so tight. But it's still the same phone number his parents had, and apparently he's a sentimental fool.

He's sober but practically out on his feet. One at a time, he discards articles of clothing on his way to the back bedroom, savoring a day's and also four-plus years' worth of pot residue on his teeth and tongue, wondering what Heather Easley would taste if she kissed him. Another day wrung successfully dry, another day of just being.

He pushes the blinking red light, dreadfully.

"Lieutenant, I believe you know who this is. But for the moment, shall we say that I am the embodiment of your country, placing a call in a time of great need. The events of the last few days are not a surprise to you, lieutenant, because you are trained to know when these things are coming, as a dog smells the rain before it falls. There are urgent missions in a new locale that need our old platoon, and I would rather not resort to coercion to get you to heed that urgency. We both know there are events in our past that, if made public, would render your life difficult. Once again I truly hope you will decide to call me back."

SATURDAY

It must still be nighttime. It's dark in here and it feels like the central heating has kicked on, plus there are crickets singing outside the back window. A robust sleeper from his earliest days, Dub rolls on his side feeling slumber ready to crash back down. But something tells him the crickets are wrong, and the heating is wrong, and he understands the darkness is only because his eyes are closed. In fact, light fills this back bedroom. He sits up, finds himself tightly wrapped in a too-heavy blanket. And the chirping is Pete Bellingham throwing rotten pecan shells against his window.

"Dub! Dubber! Dubbermeister!"

He stays in bed and lights a cigarette. His eardrums give off radio static and his thumbnails feel too long. The mattress beneath him is oddly slippery and he realizes that nighttime thrashing pulled loose the bottom sheet, but he remembers no dreams. Across the bedroom is a closet whose door has been coming off its track for thirty years. The only trophy he ever won—Pinewood Derby, age nine—is on the desk over there. Yes, the room is light, but it's also dark in places. His dresser is immersed in gloom; in its furthermost recess is his M9 pistol.

Dub phones the Westlake police and asks for Detective

Berkshire.

"He's off today," says a man's voice.

"I'm pretty sure he's not."

"Smart guy. I'm looking at the duty roster."

"He's working a case," says Dub. "I saw him last night."

"Pal, I'd tell you to blow it out your ass, but my dick's in the way."

Dub has to admit this is a pretty good line. He leaves a message.

He doesn't want to get up. Or, rather, he wants to get up, find Kid, and get high. This straight cig burns, its curtain of smoke drifting out into the sunlit room and assuming an odd translucent shape, like a topographic map of Somalia or maybe Iraq. It took him a year in this old bedroom before he could get used to four walls and a ceiling again, rather than some tent somewhere, or the open sky. Even on the occasional leave over those many years, when others flew to the beachfront hotels in Muscat, Dub usually camped in a national park down in Kenya and slept eighteen hours a day. Like the best snipers, he'd been blessed with blackness in dreams. The highest-profile thing he ever did—a single shot from 630 meters that struck the Somali president's chest— never caused him a moment's pause. Of course, his final mission for Major Partridge was a different story: Abdi and al Qaeda in Kismayo. When he dreams unanesthetized these days, those are the scenes he sees.

Dub stubs out the butt and rolls groaning from the bed. Out in the backyard on the sand-and-pebble driveway, Pete wings shells at a grackle. Dub gets a burst of sunshine square in the face but passes into the shade, sitting at an old wrought-iron table.

Pete says, "You got a cigarette?"

"I don't smoke."

"I've seen you smoke."

"I don't smoke cigarettes. You kill my pet bird and I'll make it rain hellfire."

"Put some shoes on, Dub. I'm hungry."

"Kid's your gravy train. Don't look at me for sustenance."

"You're the one with any money. Come on. The café's right there. You ever had their tofu scramble, man?"

"A million times," Dub says. "I told you to try it."

"They know you there, dude. Help a brother out."

"Seen the Kid today?"

"Naw. He was at Guitar George's last night. Fucker froze me out, man, he was getting nicely baked out back, like, I think he saves the good shit for himself," Pete smiles, and despite his desert-rat deportment somehow has the world's cleanest ivory choppers, "and meanwhile he sells me wobbly tea."

"Sells, huh?"

"I was just stoked to meet his buddies, but he gives me this look, like, 'get away.' So whatever, man, I just split. You should let me drive with you down to those investigation things, Dubber. Those stakeouts." He coughs up something liquid and spits it into the fenced-in portion of this backyard, where rotten pecans and limitless amounts of bird waste cover ground Dub partly imagines sacred.

He never walks in there anymore; phone and air conditioning repair guys are urged to clomp around the front and squeeze past the kitchen window, rather than take this direct route to the circuit boxes. It's like a very small part of Dub (the sober part) imagines his parents are buried right here, beneath the withered grass.

He inherited this house indirectly, via his Uncle Jesse. In the months after Dub's parents' disappearance, Jesse moved into the place, disbelieving that his sister was really gone. He lost his job and wound up on food stamps, making phone calls all day, hitching rides all over the place, looking for clues; this went on for years and Dub—still overseas, still incommunicado—didn't know anything about it. Jesse wrote Dub long handwritten letters where he tried to work everything out, what would make a husband and wife just leave. After a while Dub stopped opening them, they were so crazy, and after that he was buried pretty deep in situations where soldiers don't exactly get mail. But the bodies had never been found, and Jesse started to think they were alive somewhere; maybe he moved into this house so he'd be here when they came back.

So the front bedroom was Jesse's, too, after it had been Dub's parents'. A lot of Jesse's clothes still hang in that front closet, next to theirs. Those years, Jesse walked around the neighborhood talking to himself, and according to the journals Dub found, he had dark days where he believed they were dead. But he always came around. He always found some newspaper article at the library that set him off, a dozen more phone calls to make, more leads to follow up when someone in a photograph taken in California or Brazil looked a little like one of Dub's parents. Jesse made friends with a police sketch artist and gave her pictures, so he could see what they'd look like aged five years, ten years. Eventually Jesse contracted leukemia and didn't take care of himself, and by the time Dub came back to the States for good, his uncle had been dead for a couple years, and the house was empty once again.

But Dub doesn't let himself think too much about this stuff.

"I'm good company," says Pete, "and unlike that pussy Kid? I can fight." He springs around the driveway, pirouetting manically, shadowboxing, and accidentally punches the Accord's sideview mirror. "Ow."

Dub says, "What do you know about the Easley family?"

"Nothing, man. Easley does it."

"There's a daughter about your age. Angela Easley."

"How can I concentrate with no food, dude! Yumma yumma. I don't get paid to be the sidekick, yo. You want me to start paying attention to like, *life* and shit, them checks gotta come correct."

Dub leans back and puts his bare feet on this chipped-white table, this totem from another time, thinking the cascade of departed years is everywhere if you let it be. But Dub is loosed from time, inhabiting a weekend like any other weekend, tickled by a case like any other case, the sash of his uncle's ancient blue terrycloth robe just dipping and dragging in the dirty grass as he breathes the morning and wonders where his sunglasses might've gotten to.

"Man," says Pete, "your trees is weird, man. Like, I can see the sky up there, but I can barely see my hand?"

Dub wants to see Heather again today and he wants to find that boy. He likes it when things make sense, and knows this about himself. There's that protest George mentioned, certainly a target-rich environment considering the ransom note: *Stop Killing Austin.* There's whatever the police are doing to get info out of Wyatt Parsons. There's Angela, and whatever she's not telling. (There's always something.) These are all puzzle pieces, but not the kind most people mean. Sure, maybe they add up to answers. Probably they do. But there will be other cases. Austin is growing so fast there's more cheating and double-crossing than the Wild West. No, these puzzle pieces exist to prove that the puzzle exists, that there can still be cause and effect like there's always been, that there can be retribution and comeuppance. Dub tongues the grit on his teeth and nods to himself. *There's* your reason to get up in the morning.

He takes Pete a few blocks over to Bouldin Creek Café. They pass several little emblems etched in tile around every sewer grate, little frogs reminding the world that this spot "Drains Into The Creek." When Dub was growing up here, his neighborhood was sketchy and often drug-infested, and the only warning signs anyone posted were "Security Camera On Premises" and "Register Contains Max $100." They also pass a nicely manicured lawn that for some reason has seven or eight shopping carts on it. A hand-cut "No War" sign hangs from a tree.

He loves the café, but knows the waitresses consider him something of a crank. When the place opened, the clientele was hippies and hopheads but now it skews toward yuppies, and Dub feels like a relic among the baby strollers and laptop-toting students. He's a regular and they treat him well, but once one of the waitresses asked him, "How long have you lived in the neighborhood" and Dub made the mistake of saying, "42 years, off and on," and the young lady said, "Oh, I never met anyone who's been here more than six months." So now someone in the café is always trying to show him how appreciative they are of local traditions like junk art and display cases with Virgin Marys inside and half-off for kids from the deaf school up the street, plus someone always seems to be handing him a Keep Austin Weird sticker.

The food, though, is a panic. He and Pete both order the tofu scramble and look one another in the eyes, finding lust and starvation.

Pete disappears to the bathroom and Dub sags on this bench. The table to his left has a boy and a girl talking about the war, and the boy is so loud it's actually rather an incredible panegyric to complete self-unawareness, and he's very cheery and chipper and laughing at everything, so it's hard for Dub to be annoyed by him. The table to his right has three women, one younger than the other two: a blonde with sharp brown eyes relating stories of a recent ex-boyfriend with whom she'll be having a meal soon, and she's also talking about her band and she has a large feather tattoo on the semiopaque inside of her right forearm. Dub finds it lovely and fascinating, but the woman notices him staring and turns away, putting her left thumb over the tattoo and rubbing.

"You just watch!" the boy shouts happily. "The first sign of an Iraq civilian getting killed and the media will go crazy! One bomb accidentally hits a school with some, whatever, janitors in it? They'll write folk songs about the Arab sanitation workers of '03!"

Dub stares at his hands and laughs.

"Oh, let me guess!" says this blissful boy, turning to Dub. "You lived through Vietnam! I couldn't possibly understand!"

"Naw, man," Dub says. "Just thought it was a funny joke."

"C'mon, it's okay! Let me have it! You expect students like us to protest! If we're not wide-eyed idealists, we're missing the flower of youth!"

"Truly," says Dub. "I couldn't care less, my man."

"Sorry," says his girlfriend. "I'm trying to get him to switch to decaf."

"I didn't vote for Bush!" the boy says. "I don't like what he stands for! I'm embarrassed he comes from Texas! But when it's war, y'know? When it's war, there's no choice! He's your president!"

Pete comes back reeking of Dutch Passion Blueberry. His sunburned brow glistens, and he takes an extra moment to steady his chair before sitting. Quietly he says, "Dude just told me something in the crapper, man. Said we're putting up the first skyscraper since 9/11, right here in town. That really just fucks up my shit, Dub. What if they take it as a dare, man?"

"Who?"

"The terrorists, Dub."

"I never knew you had it in you, Pete. You're an appeaser."

Pete rolls from frightened to glassy-eyed in a heartbeat. He says, "*Dude*. Did you play Kirby's Dreamland on Gameboy? Peezer was that fuckin' little one-eyed crab, right?"

The food doesn't disappoint. Dub smiles helplessly at their waitress and eats even faster than Pete. He doesn't work out much anymore, but can't put on weight. He's still a hard 180, via some trick of genetics or muscle memory. The feather-tattoo girl is still here, but the angry patriot tosses folded money with disdain and gets up to go; only then does Dub realize that he's been seething for minutes, and that in another life he'd have taken pleasure in breaking the boy's orbital bone. On principle, even if he might kind of agree with the lad. This is a hard thing to wake up to with your gaze on a folded crust of toast and your fork scraping tofu, this instinct. The anchor points in Dub's mind—the current state of his self-regard, perhaps—are apparently atop some nonstick surface, and when he takes stock he's always surprised how far the whole mess has slid off course.

They walk back down South 1st listening to a guy in a leather jacket and tie talking about Philip Morris losing millions for misappropriating the term "light."

*

Austin is still in a post-coital daze a week after South By Southwest. It's 9 a.m., and Dub's is about the only car out on Riverside. Clouds now quilt the sky and Town Lake seems covered in gold dust Dub only identifies as fog after pulling over at Auditorium Shores. A couple people are out walking dogs—who snuffle past downed cyclone fences to root through concert garbage now seven days old—but this huge park is mostly abandoned. Dub sees a thickly-muscled silhouette grappling with a chin-up bar, and hears the long-tailed birds—Quaker parrots and Monk parakeets—that have populated the trees down here for a decade. A natural gas truck is pulled diagonally across two parking spaces, and the technician therein furtively smokes a skinny cigarette wrapped in brown paper. Dub fuzzes out for a few moments, sees a blasted, sun-drenched landscape in place of this verdant one, then snaps himself awake and drives to the Westlake police station.

"Are you holding Wyatt Parsons?" he says to a middle-aged lady just inside the door. "I'm his lawyer."

"If you're a lawyer," says this silver fox, "I'm Britney Spears."

"What gave me away?"

"You're working on a Saturday, ain'tcha? Plus you smell like patchouli."

"Little quieter around these parts than last week, I'd imagine."

"Yessir," says this lady-cop, "the last of the drunken trust-fund bunnies cleared out middle of the week. They do carry on at night, I'll say. So y'all are a private dick, I take it."

"Your radar is amazing, ma'am."

"That, and I was told to be on the lookout. You ticked off Detective Berkshire."

"I ticked him off? I barely said two words to him."

"I only know what I'm told. Which isn't a lot, if y'all want to know the truth. We surely have that in common. Not too many favored children of the APD wind up on the Saturday morning desk. Nobody's back in the pens. Y'all are welcome to take a look yourself."

"Who was answering the phone before?" says Dub.

"Berkshire's the only other soul that's been in here."

Great, Dub thinks. "You wouldn't happen to have a cell number I can apologize into."

"I do."

"But I can't have it."

"You can't."

"Well, gee, you've been a big help."

"I aim to serve."

Dub contemplates another drive down to New Braunfels, but he figures the Parsons house is cordoned off by now. But hell, maybe they found the toddler overnight. Maybe it's over before things ever really got going. He drives back over to Michaels Cove.

Three black-and-whites are in the Easley driveway. Three news vans are parked across the street. Dub pulls up to a neighbor's house and sits, the Accord ticking like a movie bomb. He has a headache and searches the glove compartment, but there's nothing left from last night. In many ways he's still a planner, but not when it comes to weed. He pats himself down but his cigs are back in the bedroom.

He cribbed the Easleys' house phone number yesterday, but it's busy. This isn't staking out a cheating spouse or tracking down a stripper's birth parents. It's his first missing child. It leaves him cold until he really thinks about it, imagines some mossy closet or icebox warehouse. In the movies they hire someone to make nice with the child during his captivity, keep him healthy and quiet within a well-lit oasis. Play board games. Dub's instinct tells him real life isn't so kind. He gets up out of his car and strolls around this neighbor's house with the connecting backyard, hands-in-pockets, making like he belongs. The plan is sneak around back and maybe poke through some unpoliced point of entry, but when he loops behind this expensive grilling equipment and luxury pool accommodations and peeks through the fence, Dub sees a dozen people in the Easley back yard.

It's a press conference. Thomas Easley rears up over several reporters and cameramen, with Detective Berkshire beside him on the deck. Neither of the daughters is here. Ragtag reporters write in notebooks and extend recording devices, and the scene looks archetypal: the grandfather imploring, the media happy to be fed. "So again, please," says Thomas. "Please. Here's his picture. We're not angry. We're just looking for y'alls' help. I know I'm controversial, I do. I'm sorry there's people out there who think I hurt 'em. But this isn't the way. This is not the way." Easley's eyes are wet and his voice holds back tears. "I can't believe this is happening. I can't believe I'm standing here."

Dub walks through a door in the fence and past maybe the coolest topiary he's ever seen: three consecutive bushes shaped to look like a half-submerged sea serpent, with one bush as its head, one as its poking-above-the-surface midsection, and one as its tail. Nobody pays Dub any mind. Berkshire has stepped forward to answer a question. He pats his forehead with a gold paisley handkerchief; Dub wants to find fault, but the bland fortysomething dude is doing his best: answering what he can, leaving the specifics vague, deflecting inquiries about the kidnappers and focusing on Hunter's return. But if Berkshire is hell-bent on treating Dub like an interloper in this case, it's time to interlope.

He just walks in the front door. The main hallway is a tunnel of sheen, dark except for the blinding illumination coming from a faraway back door. As Dub steps forward someone taps his arm, and it's a uniform sitting on an antique bench, making no pretense at work.

"There a bathroom I can use?" Dub says. "I'm with the *Statesman.*"

"C'mon, pal," says the cop. "People are grieving."

"They'll be grieving more I don't find a bathroom. Berkshire doing a bang-up job on this one? Loving the spotlight?"

"Aw, he'd fuck a woodpile if he thought it might have a snake in it."

Dub takes a right turn and finds a staircase up. He can't see his hand in front of his face, but climbs. Things open into a billiard room, and after that comes a bedroom suite. A muted TV shows a mustached reporter trotting alongside a tank, holding his camo helmet down over his head and shouting into his microphone. Heather and Angela are here. Sunlight slices through Venetian blinds.

"What do you know?" says Heather. Her hair is pinned and she's without makeup; she wears a form-fitting white sweater and the determination of a blacksmith. Angela is even thinner than Dub remembers, spread out on this bed and now eager with her rubbed-raw eyes.

"There's a protest starting in an hour, at the site in Sunset Valley. If whoever did this is ticked off about the development…."

"Is that all you've got for God's sake?" says Heather.

Dub says, "What do you know about the detective down there?"

Heather looks at her sister. "What's that supposed to mean?"

"I'm trying to get my head around he's doing this thing with local news, but how is he not sitting with Wyatt every second of every hour sweating him until he drowns? He's the only lead in this case, ladies. Nothing's coming from anybody but Wyatt."

"Someone could see Hunter's picture on TV!" says Angela. "Someone could call in!"

"Okay. You're right. I guess they could."

Heather says, "You think Detective Berkshire is more concerned with getting his picture in the paper."

"I just think it's a little fishy I'm the guy who found his lead suspect, and Berkshire won't take my calls."

"What are you doing here!" says Angela. "Get out of here and find him! You don't know anything and you're stealing my money! You didn't even shave!"

Dub slants his jaw.

"Don't be a brat," says Heather.

Angela says, "I can just hear the grand old man now! 'All hands on deck. All it takes is a little elbow grease. The engine of America is stick-to-itiveness.' Fuck! Why! Is! This! Happening!" She thrusts her face into a pillow for a long time, and Dub watches Heather fail to react. She's pale, the older sibling, as though enameled and then encased in the hothouse of Westlake, a garrison with no moat but alien to Dub just the same. Whenever he leaves these million-dollar manses for Austin proper, he still feels the road behind him like something his car is excreting. "He didn't do it," Angela finally lifts her face and says. "He couldn't. Say what you want about Wyatt."

"Can I ask you a couple questions?"

"Don't treat me like a mental patient."

"You *are* a mental patient," says Dub. There's a pause and Angela grins despite herself. "I asked you about it yesterday. Heather told me you had a fight at a concert last weekend."

"No we didn't."

Heather says, "Angie. You called me in tears."

"What show was it?" says Dub.

"Joe Jackson. I never really heard of him."

"Any good?"

"Don't," Angela sits up, "don't do that. I like you better when you're mean. Wyatt was drunk and he was hugging me from behind and we were listening to the music and it was really nice. But this is the kind of stupid thing Wyatt does, I mean, he does it on purpose. He was watching this hippie chick dancing on the grass in front of us. He couldn't really even see if she was hot, but between songs he goes, 'Let's ask her to have sex.' I mean, this girl was *dirty*. She had dreads."

"Because if she was clean," says Heather, "you'd have strongly considered it."

"You've been back together with Wyatt since when?"

"We're not back together."

Dub says, "You've been sleeping with him again since when?"

"He didn't do it. He didn't do anything. You should *see* him with Hunter."

"A month," says Heather. "About a month, right, genius?"

"Leave me alone! I just want Hunter back! Give me Hunter!"

Heather strides across the room and slaps her baby sister's face so hard that Angela flips backward in the bed, banging her skull on the headboard. She cradles her ears and weeps anew.

Heather takes Dub out of the room, back to the pool table. The overhead lights are out, but the billiard balls pick up ambient sparks like a distant triangle of smokers in the dark. She half-sits on the green felt edge looking—there's no other way for Dub to think it—sheathed and dangerous.

"It was quite a courtship," she says. "He was just some cute worker at one of our sites. I don't even know how she met him. One day she was dating some Brad or Chad, next day she was with the lummox. All she wanted to do was hurt daddy, and she did. My father forbade the whole thing, which cornered her and she did the thing she always does when she gets cornered. She upped the crazy, and got pregnant."

"So it's a month since Wyatt's back in her life."

"I mean, he never left. He moved to New Braunfels but he still sees Hunter every weekend. What Angie says is true: he loves that boy. But you're saying you find the timing…funny."

"Miss Easley, I do believe you could do my job."

"I couldn't stand your job, Mr. Storm."

"But so Wyatt gets your sister's guard down, makes it easier for him to hide the little boy. He'd be working with someone, which gives me hope Hunter's okay. The note doesn't mention money. But maybe it doesn't stay that way. Maybe another note is coming."

"My father didn't want this getting out. If we don't start building on Monday…."

"Where do the police have him?" says Dub. "Where's Wyatt? He's not in the Westlake station. Has Berkshire said anything?"

"Detective Berkshire told us he believes Wyatt's innocent. But he said it in front of Angie, so I don't know what he really thinks. What I'm saying is it's a delicate time. The city council finally shut down debate, and is letting the national chains come in. We're on the ground floor."

Dub feels himself smile. "But the main focus is finding the little boy." He can see her silhouette running a finger along the pool table.

"I'm the best aunt you ever saw," Heather says. "Don't

you worry about that."

"The most important thing you can do is grab Berkshire and make him call me. Hell, lie to him. Tell him I've cracked the case wide open."

"Maybe I could tell him you think he's a shitty cop who just wants to be on TV."

"I love the police," says Dub. "Johnny Law is my friend."

"I knew things were happening too fast. I knew there would be consequences. It's the kind of thing you just feel coming down on you."

Dub takes a step toward the stairs then a step much closer to Heather. The nearer he gets to her, the more static fills his brain. "I'll fix this."

She sighs, "There's what you want, and there's what's good for you."

*

No sooner is Dub merging onto Capital of Texas Highway than his phone rings. His first thought isn't that it's Berkshire. His first thought is that it's Heather. But the number is unlisted, and in his momentarily exalted state, he decides to finally deal with this.

"Hello."

"This is a pleasant surprise. To speak with the man directly after so many missed connections."

"Who is this?" says Dub, but he knows who it is.

"A friend from the Horn of Africa. Ras Kamboni and Mogadishu. Galkayo and Bosaso and the unfortunate days in Kismayo. You've been avoiding me, my boy."

"I misplaced my old contract, major. But I don't believe there's a reserve clause in there. I'm a free man."

"Of course you are. Of course. But you're a soldier, and

there's a mission, and I've been asked. I don't do this lightly. I don't threaten my men lightly. You know that about me, lieutenant. You learned that about me. I've left you alone for four years because that's the way you wanted it, son. I've made due."

"Keep making due."

"I see that Richards is back in. Do I know these names? Odom, yes of course, Odom. Let's see. Umber, Bruno, Nelson...."

"Bruno's dead, major."

"My mistake. I read that wrong. So he is. Of course, many of your old friends never left. They've been toiling away without you. Scurrying over hill and dale. Fixing what needs to be fixed."

"Breaking what needs to be broken."

"That's not charitable of you, my boy. Anyway, it's all fixing these days, I assure you."

"I find it impossible to believe the whole thing falls apart without little ol' me."

"Well. No single man is bigger than the platoon. But that's not really the point, is it?"

"The point being you get what you want when you want it."

Partridge snickers. "I was going to say something about service and duty, but I like yours better. It's time to come back in the fold, Storm. You're wasting your life with stoners and petty hustlers. You're frittering away at the fringes. And of course, I know all my jabbering is having absolutely no effect on you, but it was important to keep you preoccupied while a couple friends of mine get in place for a Readiness Protocol."

Dub whips around, nearly loses control of the Accord, checking rearview and sideview in a flash, measuring these cars around him, recognizing what a sitting duck he is between these flashing walls of limestone on either side of the highway. He hits the brakes hard, eliciting a couple honks, ditching into the right lane to see who might follow. The Accord careens onto the shoulder and fishtails in sand, and Dub has a finger on his seatbelt and his left foot stomping the brake pedal, the showering sand underneath him momentarily drowning out everything. The stack of paper on his driver's seat—Hunter Parsons' little face reproduced a dozenfold—slides onto the floor.

"I'm kidding, of course," says the voice in his ear. "Would that budgets were so tolerant."

At rest, Dub wheezes like an overheated Chihuahua and keeps scanning for attackers. Partridge's Readiness Protocols were legendary and usually resulted in black eyes or broken bones, but Dub was never caught out. They tried to get him again and again in Somalia, but never once did. Now he thinks it's bullshit about the budgets. But he can't find anyone outside the car tracking him.

"Though I do understand you're working for a powerful real estate man," Partridge says, and it makes Dub's scalp prickle. "I don't have the name right here. But so let me tell you something about my life these days, Storm. I've reached a point in my life where my deepest sense of well-being comes from actions that give me a sense of permanence. But there's no joy in it. I repeat and I repeat—say, taking the same walk every evening, swallowing the same old man's pills before bed—and each time I feel a vague wonder that I'm still repeating, and I touch a deep illusion of immortality. But that's far from the same thing as happiness."

Dub touches his sweaty forehead. "That's deep, man."

"Ah, so in your silly little detective's life, you know nothing of waking death?"

"All this research you've done about me," Dub says, gathering the Accord back up and clicking his left-turn signal to merge back into Austin's arteries. "Am I supposed to find it creepy? Because you're coming across creepy, major."

"We have an opportunity in Iraq," says Partridge. "We're being given this chance."

Dub hangs up.

*

The Easley site on Brodie Lane is abuzz. Lowe's has plans to build a 162,000-square-foot store just north of here, and Thomas Easley is placing a bet that the home-improvement giant will win its battle with the city council. This area looks like a nondescript pasture abutting a not-particularly-lovely forest, but is actually in the Barton Springs Zone of the Edwards Aquifer, which provides drinking water to three million people. The council tried to block Lowe's from developing the land, but the Texas state legislature intervened, and now there's a standoff. Easley Partners' site is technically outside the disputed land, but permits anywhere around here have been difficult to come by. According to Heather, the council is due to rule specifically on the Easley supermarket in two days.

And that's why the Aquifer Assurance Association people are here. They know sitting around the Lowe's site up the street all day won't draw much attention, since no construction is happening over there yet. But Easley's people are prepping equipment and taking final measurements this weekend, and that gives the protesters someone to shout at. Brodie and William Cannon are choked with hundreds of illegally parked cars; Dub has to drive way south to the lot at Covington Middle School and walk back half-a-mile. The AAA is out in its fullest force, having drawn in families with promise of a cookout, and there's a whiff of carnival around the fence that protects the Easley site.

Also, Dub doesn't know if so many TV crews would be here without the news of Hunter's kidnapping. But that press conference in Westlake is probably over about now, and here they all are.

Dub asks a guy in a "Fuck The G8!" t-shirt where Jebidiah Sparks might be, and gets directed around the corner to a service road. Sparks has three reporters grilling him on the Parsons boy.

"Of course we don't know anything," he says. "Our good name is getting dragged through the mud! We're here because wood beams treated with arsenic are about to go into the ground a hundred feet from where your drinking water comes from." He's a skinny, intensely bearded guy with a blue bandana stretched over hummocks of hair. "It's time people who love Austin stand up. We don't want to be Los Angeles." Dub blends in with a few chanting hippies ("Hell no, we won't grow!") and waits while Sparks goes through his objections with the media, who don't seem interested. When a reporter again asks whether the police have interviewed him about the kidnapping, he says, "Come on guys! We didn't have anything to do with that!"

Sparks eventually extricates himself to take a sip of bottled water, and Dub steps forward and says, "The thing I don't understand is what's your next move?"

"I know," says Sparks. "It can seem overwhelming, but patience, right? Every little brick is something when you're making change."

"No, I mean: you don't want to kill a little boy, but how do you give him back?"

"Hey, you can't say shit like that!" says Sparks, looking around. The reporters have moved on, and people are elbowing forward to hear someone speak through a bullhorn. "That's a bunch of bullshit! I want your badge number."

Dub plants a finger hard in Sparks' chest. "My number is F-U-C-K-Y-O-U. How about I beat the shit out of you 'til you tell me where that little boy is?"

"Whoa. Easy. I—" But Dub has taken Jeb Sparks' lower lip between his thumb and forefinger and yanks up, hard, until Sparks groans and falls back across the street and against a baby evergreen someone recently planted in a left-turn island. Dub reaches into his own shirt pocket and pulls out one of the folded copies of Hunter's face.

"I saw the ransom note myself, and there's two choices," he says evenly. "Either you did this, or you know who did. 'To get him back, stop killing Austin.' That's kind of a familiar refrain for you and your buddies, right? His mother hasn't seen him in more than a day. Can you imagine what that's like?"

Sparks rubs his mouth. "Hey! Help!"

"You don't want any more attention from me, Sparks. Say something useful."

"I didn't do shit. The cops came through here a couple hours ago, is how any of us even heard."

Dub reaches down and flicks this man's nose. "Try again."

"We're not so organized. My God, we're a web site and a monthly meeting. I never thought we'd get a turnout like this."

"You've really got your finger on the pulse."

Now that he's being talked to instead of shoved around, this hairy lollipop tries to stand up but gets caught in sapling branches, so he squats and steadies himself on the spongy ground. In the meantime, someone else crosses the street, coming to Sparks' assistance: a short guy with blond streaks in his hair, thick funky glasses and a soul patch. Dub sees him coming and holds out a forefinger, which stops the new man's approach.

"If you're not organized," Dub says, "you can't know who might've done what."

Sparks says, "That's true. I admit it."

"What's going on, Jeb?" says the blond-streaked man. "You all right?"

"Everyone's fine," Dub says, finger still extended. "Go light a draft card on fire. Go play the banjo or something."

The new guy thinks for a second, and says, "What's a draft card?"

"They *lie*," says Sparks. "They hire lawyers who come in and talk about 'engineered water quality controls,' which is basically just sprinklers that are supposed to spray polluted runoff but they don't work. You know what it looks like when all that runoff sucks the oxygen out of groundwater? You ever seen an algae bloom choke the life out of a water lily? There's no coming back from that, man."

"So give me names. Give me suspects. Somebody who believes what you believe, somebody who talks like you talk…they kidnapped a three-year-old boy. Every minute that goes by…."

"Are you gonna let me get up?"

Dub hasn't decided yet. He's acting, of course. But also his temper feels sharp.

"Fine, kick the crap out of me," Sparks says. He tries to get up again, and Dub looms, keeps him down. "Shoot me then. Shoot me in the face."

"Dude," says the blond guy. "Jeb."

"It's okay, Tarasco. I mean, what better publicity. Take a bullet for the team."

"Jesus," Tarasco says.

"Names," says Dub. "I want a list of your members, Sparks."

"If I wouldn't give it to the police without a warrant, I'm not giving it to you."

"What about you?" Dub says to this Tarasco. "You the resident peacemaker? Second-in-command at the eagle-freak convention?"

"Man, who the fuck are you," says Tarasco. "Kicking the shit out of a guy who weighs, what, a buck-ten?" Now a few other protesters are shouting across the street, and walking this way.

"There are skinny kidnappers in the world, too," says Dub.

"Come on," Sparks says, "finish the job."

"A little boy," Dub says. "Anyone check you guys for a

heartbeat recently?"

Both these young men pause, as this seems to land. Three other people also cross to check what the shouting is about. The sheer numbers are starting to stack against Dub, but Sparks says, "I mean, everybody knows that family. Nobody wants to see a little boy get hurt."

"The Easleys," says Tarasco. "That's what this is about? You work for them?"

Dub says, "All I can think is people with nothing to hide would be a lot more forthcoming."

They all look at one another, and Dub feels mist falling from the sky.

"Who is this guy, Jeb?" says a new short bucktoothed kid.

Sneakers scuff pavement sand. "Yeah, who the fuck."

"Or else we just don't *know* anything," says Sparks. "The Easleys are in another stratosphere, man. I never met them for one second. I'd like to. I admit it, I'd love to talk to them face to face about what they're doing to the watershed."

Tarasco, the one closest to Dub, is wearing a tie-dye t-shirt with the word "WEIRD" emblazoned in the Technicolor eye. He has scabs on his elbows and soot in the creases of his face, and an ancient nylon piece of measuring tape tied around his left wrist. He says, "We heard people talking. What, the older Easley daughter has a kid now?"

"Younger," Dub says.

He nods. "I just never heard anybody say they were gonna do anything like this either. I swear."

"Look at you guys," says Dub. "All of you can barely contain your glee this is happening to them."

"Of course not," says Sparks. He pulls off his bandana and rubs the sweat off his cheek and neck. "If I hear anything, man. But pretty fucked up they send, what, a hatchet man down here."

"Back off, asshole!" says someone new.

"This guy works for Easley!"

Dub says, "You take a powerful guy's grandson, everybody will want a piece of you. The cops, the judges. And for kidnappers in jail there's a special level of hell."

"Is that rain?" says Sparks, still down near the ground. "Is it raining? Aw, man, that figures."

Dub takes a breath. There *is* a hierarchy of evil deeds at hand here. Turning all these protestors to dust to make the next step and find the missing boy. Dub can feel his arms tense in anticipation. It's rare these days when he isn't reserved by first instinct; having to bridle his temper makes him feel like a different person, a person he used to be. And should he bridle it? He's *frustrated*, and wants the erasing pleasure of physical release. He says, "I don't have time for this," and doesn't actually know what he means, whether he's about to step off and mosey around the fence to look for other likely suspects, or whether he's about to make these advertisements for unfocused liberal dissension swallow their own teeth.

And then a splice occurs.

Strolling by himself across William Cannon as the rain begins is Wyatt Parsons: hands-in-pockets, following other stragglers toward the rally. Dub blinks. His hands spread-eagle into a posture of surprise. "Wyatt? Hey, Wyatt Parsons?"

"The fuck?" grumbles Sparks from below.

Wyatt's head turns and indeed there's his big handsome half-mustached face with a half-frown of inquiry, his sweaty hair disheveled, still wearing the Keep Austin Weird t-shirt from last night. Dub feels the magnetism of coincidence, the tingling in his face, that the world can unfold itself thus. They're stopped, like this. They are gunslingers, and neither will ever draw. Dub has the chills but also knows what's about to happen.

Wyatt takes off running. A nebula of thought opens across Dub's mind—why did Berkshire let his only suspect go?—but this takes half-an-instant as Dub releases these branches, lets them pop down into Jebidiah Sparks' face, and begins chasing.

They run down one of the city's choked east/west boulevards, two lanes back to MoPac, two lanes across to I-35, and by now capitalism has sent every sire and spawn out into the world at once on this first Saturday of the rest of the nation's life, presumably to vote with their wallets. So cars are just everywhere. And horns bleat, everyone is cranky, Dub is half-a-block behind Wyatt and gaining. They pass a strip mall, a bus stop, an open field, much faster than anyone behind a wheel, probably giving rise to identical thoughts among dozens of motorists: it *would* be faster if I just ran. Wyatt can move for a big dude, but of course Dub still has this body, the one they made for him in all those years of training and deprivation. It's not a fair contest. It'll be another couple blocks and he'll be on Wyatt's heels, will trip him, will send him splatting to this concrete sidewalk. But then Wyatt takes a right turn down a side street, cutting the corner close, and Dub loses sight. He accelerates, wet with the light rain but not breathing hard, feeling nothing in his lungs despite his long-term concerted effort to lay waste to his whole cardiopulmonary apparatus. He sees Wyatt go right again, an alley or something in this residential neighborhood whose locale is far less tony, but which frankly could be Dub's own: squat stone houses, unnecessarily wide streets, low-hanging trees to mess up the light. All of Austin seems to be this sort of biggest little place, these sprawling live-oak districts with slate roofs and crushed-stone yards. Wyatt has dashed down a narrow passage that it turns out enters into another construction site.

It's a new apartment complex, about one-third assembled. Four buildings have their foundations poured, but another two are already framed-out and dressed in Tyvek wrapping. There's a trench for the swimming pool. Dub can hear Wyatt's rapid footsteps and he follows around the furthest building, sees a dumpster and checks to make sure his quarry isn't hiding inside, steps around loose nails and sawdust piles, kicks an abandoned hardhat as he slows down. There's a fence around this property, and only one way in or out. His phone rings and he clicks it silent. There's a blue plastic tarp folded up back here, the kind used to protect a power saw or generator, and Dub slips it under his arm. He steps to the corner of this lot, puts his butt against the fence and gives himself a view of the alleyway in.

He waits. Wyatt is obviously inside one of the Tyvek-covered buildings, huffing and scheming.

"Did you hurt him?" Dub shouts. "You didn't do it on purpose! You didn't mean to! Tell me where he is, Wyatt! It's the only way things can get better!"

Yes, there's thumping around upstairs in this closest building.

"You're not a bad guy! You love your little boy!"

The rain increases. Dub can see through the bushes behind this fence; there's a bowling alley across the way, and its neon sign reflects off the blacktop like broken candy.

"Doesn't matter what the cops told you! You'll burn for this, you don't make it right!"

Dub looks at his hands: wet, steady, remorseless.

"Don't make me come up there, Wyatt!"

His pulse is down to near nothing, and sadness descends on him. Dub has never really wanted to be a father, though in younger days people told him he'd make a good one. His military career made the question moot. Since he's been back he's bought extra Girl Scout cookies and taught a neighbor child how to fend off bigger kids, but the biological imperative has apparently been curbed. Yes, this is merely a twist on a standard case: missing persons. But instead of standing here and playing it smart, Dub walks around to the building's front and steps in what will eventually be a lovely entrance, though its lavish-looking parquet is only half-installed. He wonders why he's doing this, and also why the place isn't padlocked.

It's really just so dumb to climb up in here after Wyatt. The big lug could be around any corner, ready to swing a lead pipe at Dub's face. The moldings here are precious, the staircase affected. Why has this trickle of sadness tipped into anger? Is this a Picasso print already cemented into the hallway wall? He still has the blue tarp under his arm, and looks among the paint cans and rolled-up fabric for a weapon. He feels a naked little shiver go up his spine at the notion of his thumbs popping Wyatt's windpipe.

There's a pneumatic nail gun charging over here in an atrium and he picks it up.

Dub can sometimes see things before they happen and right now he sees his own blood smeared on this white wall. Stepping heavily past all these open apartment doors, he knows Wyatt is motionless, tensed, ready to swing. Dub will take the blow to fire a nail into his prey's heart.

Give him anything, any weapon, and he's maybe still a genius. A savant. These memories never return to him, never, but now he remembers. He worked himself out of some tight spots back in the day. There was a time with nothing but a length of chain. There was a time with an aerosol can and a nickel lighter. That's not him anymore, but his trigger finger presses down until he feels the gun tense. He steps forward, the interior decorations abate and soon so does the sheetrock, it's bare studs and pressboard and now there's only this last apartment-to-be, no doubt a desirable one, a corner view on an elevated floor but Dub sees it's nothing but frame, this is Wyatt's final retreat, nowhere to hide so he'll be stretched to his full height behind this last stack of wood beams, Dub will accept the punch, will take whatever the big man can do with his one shot, his cool is gone, he strides ahead, whips around, fires a preemptive nail, hears it find purchase with a thunk....

And Wyatt isn't there.

Dub sees out this rain-soaked rectangular hole where a living room window will be: Wyatt is already downstairs and sprinting away, back down the alley, lumbering big-hipped into the street and the unseen beyond. Dub drops the nail gun.

He walks back west, clear-eyed, rain dripping from his hair. He thinks about his bald spot, then he hears the AAA demonstration before he can see it: a big echoey voice encouraging civil disobedience—maybe Sparks' voice—followed by the crowd's cheers. Dub looks in the eyes of the drivers crawling along William Cannon and finds the begrudging acceptance of farm animals.

A few of the protesting families have fired up hibachis, and packs of prepubescent boys tangle with one another up Brodie Lane. There are a thousand people here. Dub sees young couples waving their arms in assent and grandparents squatting on lawn chairs, smokers coolly listening in a row, a weeping twentysomething woman overcome by visions of a future someone is painting. Everyone is wet, some are muddy. It dawns on Dub this gathering is now as much about the war—though nobody seems to be speaking about the war—as it is about developing on the Edwards Aquifer.

He walks past, and follows this row of illegal parkers toward MoPac. This is the direction Wyatt came from, and sure enough, among the Honda Insights and Toyota Priuses Dub finds a gas-guzzling red pickup that transported an attack dog as recently as last night, down in New Braunfels. Yes, Wyatt is still out there running around taking evasive action, and here's his empty truck.

Dub climbs in the bed, lies down on his stomach, and spreads the blue tarp he boosted from the apartment site over himself. He's warm and dry and he waits.

He hears voices of many passers-by over the course of perhaps half an hour:

"…makes y'all think anyone with any power is telling the truth? That's too naïve. Listen to what y'all's own brain says when y'all…."

"…a hermaphrodite, but you don't know she's a he for a really long time. But that's not the point, I mean, it's really about the immigrant experience of these...."

"...you ever *driven* in Houston? A more miserable experience I'll never hope to have. It's like farmhouse, skyscraper, farmhouse. If Austin goes that way you can...."

"Why don't we just go get us some Taco Cabana, babe?"

"You think we fight about oil, just wait until we fight about water!"

"Hans Blix. I mean, Hans *Blix*. What kind of name is that? It's part Swedish and part James Bond villain and how can...."

"Love Plants! People Be Damned! Love Plants! People Be Damned!"

"You were looking at her! I saw you looking at her! Don't...."

"If they really stop Lowe's from building this thing, I'll eat y'all's hat. I'll eat y'all's car and house and the busy boulevard y'all live on. Never gonna...."

"...got Jager and what's that other thing? Rumple Minze. Dude, I got so fucked up like I was puking candy canes...."

"No Blood For Oil! Don't Kill Our Soil! No Blood For Oil!"

"I'm Not A Moyle!"

"Old Fruit Is Spoiled!"

"...me seven bucks, and I ain't playing. Seven goddamn dollars or I'll shoot him in his gall bladder."

There's no limit on how long Dub can wait like this, at least none he's ever found. He can see his own ludicrous patience, can watch himself refuse to shake loose cramping muscles or circulate blood to sleeping limbs, can even wonder at it. It isn't only necessity that makes a man this way. Why, a couple months ago, a comically stoned version of himself sat Indian-style on the grounds of that restaurant in a white Victorian mansion three blocks away from his house, watching a wedding reception unfold over several hours, trying to get a good enough view of the bride to decode what felt like mystic insights implied by her white dress. It was unbearably peaceful; if he moved before dusk someone would see him, but he wouldn't, so they wouldn't, and he could simply puzzle over the young woman's brown shoulders and diaphanous veil, wait and see if the sweetness quotient in this scene could reach a level that might punch a hole through reality and offer revelations. Well, he was *stoned*. But nobody saw him, and the bride herself came tantalizingly close after sundown, stepping out under the grand live oaks and the starlight, covering her eyes and weeping alone.

Be a cipher and be a vessel. Solve.

Dub feels a screwdriver or some other tool jabbing his ribs. He could sleep like this, and it would be pleasurable no matter what the physical discomforts because when life is boiled down to the next elemental moment, it's how things are supposed to be. Elaborate complications are manmade and needless. Now he hears a forward clicking, a wrenching sound, a slam. He can even hear Wyatt breathing hard in the pickup's cab. Then the ignition fires, and they're moving.

Dub keeps his head down. The road chatters. Any swing left or right sends loose material in the bed sliding like objects in a doomed seaplane. They drive for twenty minutes, first on a highway—Dub has to hold down his tarp—then on slower streets. The pickup squeaks to a halt a few times, presumably at traffic signals. Each time Dub holds his breath, seeing his own hairy forearm tinged by blue-filtered light, and each time the truck continues forward. They haven't driven to New Braunfels. They weren't on the highway long enough.

The pickup stops again, but this time there's that wrenching sound in reverse and another bang shut. Dub waits ten minutes and hoists himself up. Kneeling, he peers over the cab.

He's in the driveway of another of these sprawling single-level Austin houses. A fat ancient pecan tree curlicues overhead. The house is brown and pink. Five other homes are on this cul-de-sac—one is under construction—but no neighbors are evident, only empty yellow lawns. Dub climbs silently out of the truck.

He walks behind the garage, opens a gate, and steps into the backyard. The rain has stopped, but the daylight is still gray. There's a cracked cement fountain back here, some homage to cherubs, overgrown in its disrepair. The ground is soft and wet, and Dub's feet leave behind impressions. But better that than flagstone footprints. He ducks below a kitchen window, creeps into a garden hose's concentric coils. There's a stone patio and a dingy hammock and a back door. Dub hears voices from inside. Sure enough, the door is propped open. Dub turns and examines the fence; it goes all the way around the yard and ends in another gate, a perfect enclosure to contain a toddler at play.

The voice is Wyatt's. At first it's even, it drones, but then there's a thinning, a sharpening, Dub can't pull apart individual words but surely he's relating his close call to an accomplice. Dub is invisible. He has full confidence he could creep through this door and slink around inside the house, but decides to ascertain which room is Hunter's first. He presses his back against a brick chimney, looks at the ground and sees the exact landing spot where each of his footfalls must go on his way around the house, as though each step is illuminated. He moves and isn't even particularly tense. There's foreknowledge here, that this path means safety.

He glides past a living room window and there's nobody inside. He arrives at the house's back corner, presumably a bedroom. The casement window here is shuttered, so Dub can't see in. He opens the fence's second gate and there's no sound. He checks for nosy neighbors, sees none. His fingers touch the house's scratchy ledgestone corner, he peeks into the narrow side yard, sees only fallen leaves on dead grass. He steps to this back bedroom's other window, whose shutters and blinds are open.

He has a moment of pride over how good at this he still is.

With glacial slowness, he brings his head around.

There's no boy here.

Wyatt is on a bed, naked, on hands-and-knees. Another man squats above him, pounding his cock into Wyatt's anus.

Dub holds still. The top man is turned away and Wyatt's face is rapturous: eyes closed, brow lifted, the expression of one enjoying a concerto. Dub doesn't have his camera. He urges the top man to reposition or lose his balance, reveal himself. The man is hunched over but seems large and athletic. Wyatt's fingers are splayed against the headboard. Dub hears nothing. Their rhythm is unbroken. Wyatt could be bathing in perfectly pleasant water. He could be tasting filet mignon.

Dub walks on, past a window revealing an empty bathroom, and then to the front bedroom which oddly has no furniture in it at all. He continues around to the front yard, sees a picture window and a sparsely decorated living room, devoid of occupants. Unless he's locked in a closet, Hunter isn't here.

Lacking better ideas, Dub paces back to the lovers.

They're still going at it, perhaps more furiously now. The unknown man is half-standing, making use of his size to drop himself onto Wyatt's equally large ass, creating reverberations of flesh that slop and echo against each other. It goes on for an impressive length of time, and then the man lifts his elbows to his eyes and stops, spasming. Then he collapses atop Wyatt, still facing away from the window. Dub silently curses. The mystery man is paler and trimmer than Wyatt, but just as broad, just as tall. His hair is either sandy brunette or dirty blond. No birthmarks Dub can see, no ring on his left hand. The man scratches between his own shoulder blades, spooning Wyatt. His biceps are big. Yes, Dub assembles these clues per usual with only minimal regard for bad luck. Squirrels streak gibbering overhead, gray silk bodies up against the gray sky. Dub assumes the lovers will sleep now, and weighs his options, which include busting in through that open back door or waiting until someone needs to go to the bathroom. And just then, the man rolls over to rest on his left side, and Dub sees it's Detective Berkshire.

*

One thing at a time. Dub checks the street sign to note where he is, then crosses the cul-de-sac and stands against a tree, hidden from the pink-and-brown house. He phones the Westlake Hills station again and asks for Berkshire. A male cop offers to take a message.

"I'm Frank Boggs with Austin Home Security, and we're getting a signal from his house over on Greenbriar."

"I can connect y'all with dispatch."

"Ain't that kind of signal. More like, a connection's gone bad. Well, I mean, that's what I'm supposed to check on."

"Check away, son. He ain't here."

"I'll be honest, from one working man to another, I'm trying to save a trip and he ain't answering his phone."

"From one workin' man to another," the cop says, "why don't y'all do y'all's damn job?"

"Yessir, I will. You know how it is. Figured if I could catch him at work I'd save him the hundred bucks to go out there with a van. I'm down in Bluff Springs so that's gotta be, what, twenty miles. Where the heck is Greenbriar Court, anyway? Pretty far north, right?"

The cop pauses and says, "Well, now, wait a minute. Berkshire lives out in Lakeway, doesn't he?"

Dub hangs up. Next he phones Kid, who answers on the first ring.

"Can you get a ride? You still have spare keys: I need you to pick up my car."

"I can do better than that, daddy-o," Kid says. "I got wheels. Hey, what happened to you last night?"

"Guitar George delivered a message and it bummed me

out," says Dub. "What wheels do you have?"

"You know. A friend's."

"How do you feel about some recon work?"

"I'm pretty baked, dude."

"Two cars are better than one. See if you can't find someone to pick up mine, too, at the middle school on Brodie. I'm at 45th and Greenbriar now, hiding out front."

One more call. Dub flips through his "recents" and finds the number he ignored while chasing Wyatt. He dials it and gets a woman's voice.

"I couldn't get her to sleep without promising I'd ring you up. I'm sorry she's such a spoiled little bitch. Did anything happen at the rally? It's a little bitty thing, right?"

"Heather," Dub says. "You didn't ask Detective Berkshire to call me?"

"I guess he zoomed out of here. I didn't even see him."

Dub thinks about this. "All right." He can picture her—a window's cross-hatch shadows dividing up her body—doing some antediluvian task: darning socks or cleaning a typewriter. Here in the new millennium anything goes. Suddenly Heather Easley can be on the line, lousing up detachment. Dub says, "I know that boy hasn't done one wrong thing in his life."

"But it'll be okay."

"Yes."

"I remember you now, Mason. I'm sorry I didn't recognize you at first."

Dub hears himself say, "What do you remember?"

"Not a jock, not a punk, but always there hanging around. We went to that big Fourth of July thing in Dallas, the hottest day of the decade, they had a black tarp on the field and all the kids were passing out. Ted Nugent was playing and I talked to you. I was drunk but you weren't."

Dub says, "I remember that. I probably was pretty drunk." He peeks to make sure nobody is leaving the Greenbriar house. He needs Kid to get here first.

"You were shy. I don't know any of those people anymore. It kills me to think I was some high school princess who peaked at sixteen."

"You can't tell me you don't still know Willow Liles. Your best friend in the world?"

She says, "Last time I saw Willow was twentysome years ago after a UT football game and she was riding on a big guy's shoulders facing the wrong way." She catches herself laughing, clears her throat. "Angie was a baby then. My mother was still alive."

"..."

"I liked you, though. I wanted to tell you that. You were quiet, but you were one of the good guys."

He remembers her in Social Studies class, front row, nearest the window, canted in her seat so she could look at the teacher and back at the students. Nothing so droll as a corona around her face, but she was archetypal, the sweet approachable blonde ready to laugh at anything that smacked of cleverness. He kissed her once when they were in the first grade; for some reason his parents had dressed him in a suit and late in the day he wore the necktie like a headband, and this is a stab of history, the embarrassment of a patchwork self. He says, "Somehow I found a way to make all that pretty blurry. Do you have Wyatt's cell number?"

She gives it to him. "Call with any news."

A half-hour masquerades as a year. Nobody makes a move anywhere on this abbreviated street. Then he hears a car pull in from 45th, and it's Kid driving a cherry-red Miata with the top down. Dub signals to pull it into this other driveway.

He says, "I love your car, ma'am."

"Look at that sourpuss. Who died, you douche?"

"My car's on the way?"

"Pete was right behind me."

"You never ran into a cop named Berkshire, right? He's in charge of the Hunter Parsons case, and he's in that house over there, having sex with Wyatt."

Kid's jaw literally drops. "Holy shit."

"Yeah."

"He's drilling for oil on the moon?"

"Yeah."

"He's bogeying hole number two?"

"The question is what now?" says Dub. "It can't be a coincidence this guy's on the investigation."

"Yeah, no. Prolly not."

"The cops tried shaking down that protest, Easley's Sunset Valley thing, but they didn't shake hard. Far as I can know, the kidnappers haven't contacted anyone today. 'Stop Killing Austin.' Doesn't have to be these particular protesters. Could be anybody."

"But why leave the note with the fuckup dad, fifty miles away?" says Kid.

"And now there's this cop in charge, maybe he's bad. So maybe he's pulling Wyatt's strings, maybe they both know where that little boy is…."

Kid says, "You think maybe the whole thing's an inside job."

"If it is, the mother's not in on it. She's a legit mess."

"What about the father?"

"…"

"Or the beauty queen?"

Dub looks across the street. The driveway is curved concrete, and Wyatt's pickup is insolent. "I almost barged in there," he says. "Could've gotten myself shot."

"Not you," says Kid. "You'd dodge the bullets, Matrix-style. I remember one dirty badge, while you were off being all you can be. Redheaded fucker. Tried muscling in on a delivery route, holding up trucks for bullshit traffic stops, trucks carrying out-of-state grifa. People several levels up the drug chain were pretty displeased with this dude. He wound up hanging from a streetlight with his balls in his mouth." They're leaning against the little red car. "Where the fuck *is*

Pete?"

"I want to sweep that house once they're gone," says Dub. "I mean, what is this place?" He and Kid look at one another seriously, then laugh a little, at the absurd tension.

Kid reaches into his pocket and comes out with a plastic bag. "Spliff?" he says. "You look a little ragged."

"Come on."

"It's like one-tenth herb, man." He lights a first, done in cellulose paper. "Mostly just a cig."

Dub has a headache that feels a little like nicotine withdrawal, and a little like the world making him sick. It's three-thirty. He nods.

So they smoke, waiting, Dub thinking that among bad influences in his life, surely there've been much worse. He scratches his forehead and feels better. Anxieties lose their bounce, things feel clearer: Berkshire convinces Wyatt to hide the boy somewhere until they can engineer a ransom. Berkshire orchestrates the whole thing from in close. Bilk the Easley family, the family that did Wyatt wrong. Except why hasn't anyone asked for money yet?

"Crazy runaround shit like this must remind you of the service," says Kid. "Maybe minus the giggle weed. Hey, man, people invading countries, blowing up bad guys over there. You getting an itch to jump back into some camouflage and crush it again? It'd be more than understandable."

Dub grins. "What, and let chaos descend on my defenseless hometown?"

"Oh, chaos comin'," Kid says, doing an old man's voice. "Chaos comin' faster than a priest at a strip club."

And on cue, here comes Dub's Accord, blasting reggae. Pete's dirty dreads bob behind the wheel. Dub looks at the sky and Kid gives a throat-slash gesture. The radio clicks off.

"The fuck kept you?" Kid says.

"Pussy, dude. Dunno what the shit was goin' on in Sunset Valley, but I had to talk to this one little beehive. You gotta keep some spontinuity in life, right?"

"Get out," says Dub.

"Naw, man. I'll drive. Where you headed?"

"Get *out*. And Kid, get your phone. Call this number. It'll be Wyatt so disguise your voice. You're his neighbor in New Braunfels. Tell him somebody's poking around down at his house. You don't know who it is, but they busted in and they're making a racket."

Streetwise Kid does a bang-up job. He does a West Texas drawl the key to which, he explains afterward, is imagining a lozenge sitting on your tongue. Just a minute or two later, Wyatt Parsons rushes out the front door by himself.

"Pete, get *down*." Dub squashes the dreads, which feel like greased candles. Wyatt starts up his truck, and pulls gingerly down the serpentine driveway.

"Yup he's alone," Kid says. "Which do you want, cop or daddy?"

"I'd better take the cop," says Dub. "Go."

Kid fires up the Miata, pauses a few beats while Wyatt waits to make his left turn onto 45th, then pulls around. He says, "Texas Longhorns, Purdue Boilermakers, tomorrow, 3 p.m. Lock it down, Dub. This case is solved by 3 p.m. latest." He salutes. "Wait. What were we talking about?" He guffaws and zips away.

"Where to, chief?" Pete says.

Dub feels tight and alert. "Whose little red number is he driving?"

"Dude, who gives a shit? It's a vagina with wheels."

"Pete, it's time for you to go."

"Like I'm s'posed to know? Like I'm s'posed to keep track of the billion chicks he scores? It's not natural how much he gets. You guys are, like, *old*."

The garage door across the cul-de-sac begins a mechanical ascent. Dub opens the Accord's passenger door and yanks Pete out, shoves him so they're both kneeling on this driveway. Berkshire reverses in a silver Altima with police plates, and Dub regrets not having the Accord parked a block or two over. He'll have to give Berkshire a long leash; he's presumably also headed to New Braunfels. Little calculation wheels spin behind Dub's eyes. He gives Pete a twenty and leaves him crouching behind a tree. "Just stay here. Find a phone and call me if anyone goes in or out of that house."

"Wow," says Pete. "I can retire."

Sure enough, Berkshire heads east on 45th. Traffic is thick, so Dub can hang back one lane over and let the masses conduct him. Everyone seems to have on the same radio station, which gives news updates about the invasion. Dub is starving; they cross Burnet and at the stoplight there's that bakery he likes, he can smell the damn cinnamon rolls. It's funny you can stand at a hundred different places in this town and it feels low-tech and sleepy and provisional, like thirty years ago. A lady waddles on the sidewalk carrying a carpet bag with cat scenes embroidered on it. A gas station that someone's converted into a used-car lot has two items out front: a beaten-up copper Porsche and a vintage Ford F-100 Ranger, the latter of which has a suggestion scrawled in soap across its windshield: DRIVE DOWN MEMORY LANE.

Austin's east/west travel is just as maddening when you're up north, but finally Berkshire bangs a right and climbs onto the upper deck of I-35. Dub rolls down his window and is just very cool. He's three cars back steering clear of hurtling tractor-trailers. The two highway decks merge and here's the ridiculous beige flan in which the UT hoops team plays its home games. (This has been an amazing season for T.J. Ford and the 'Horns—Texas has a legit shot at its first Final Four since '47—and Kid took Dub to probably six or seven games this year, all wins, which explains why the Kid thinks Dub has a horseshoe lodged in his posterior, basketball-wise.) They go over the lake and under Oltorf, and Dub assumes he's repeating this same drive from last night, until Berkshire's Altima veers hard right, taking an exit ramp east onto 71. So much for New Braunfels. This is the way to the snazzy new airport, but the Altima exits again down onto Ben White, turns left and then again. They pass public storage units and anonymous office parks, and Berkshire spins off into some twisty neighborhood Dub never knew was here. The street names belong to other places—Santa Monica, Laguna, Grenada—and there are no other cars. The thought is: if Berkshire has a place on Greenbriar Court, why not one around here, and wouldn't this be a perfectly nowhere place to hide Hunter?

But Dub has to let Berkshire lose him. He pulls over and waits ten minutes, then canvasses the streets, looking for the Altima. He has a pulse-pounding moment seeing a little boy playing with a white dog, but the boy's too old. Finally he finds the cop's empty car parked in a dead end. He pulls alongside and kills the Accord's engine. This lane ends in a stand of maples, and there's an asphalt path that hooks out of view. There's no choice but to follow. He gets out of the car and hears a distant highway hum, but also birds squeaking from inside this forest or park. There's plenty of daylight left, but as he steps down the path this colonnade of trees drips rainwater on Dub's face and blocks the sky. He moves silently, and sees a large open field beyond the maples. He looks for footprints. He listens for a child's voice.

Then there's something against his temple.

"Mr. Storm," says Detective Berkshire. "You don't have much respect for my ability to spot a tail." Dub understands there's a gun pointed at his head.

"Thank goodness," he says. "The police."

"Why don't you just show me your pockets one at a time." Berkshire pats him down, finds no weapons. "Tell me what you think you're doing."

"You've got that pistol on me pretty good, man. I'm having a hard time concentrating."

"Give it the old college try."

"Well," Dub says, "just struggling along so badly, looking for clues. I guess I was just hoping you were onto something.

Kidnapping-wise."

Berkshire's pale face wrinkles. He's got a colorless mole on his cheek, and a pointless handsomeness. "I'm not telling you anything, asshole."

"Then that's settled. I'll just be scooting on back to my car."

"You gave it to him good," says Berkshire, not lowering the gun. "I mean, he sicced his dog on you. But you roughed up the father last night."

"Did I?"

"Yeah."

"Like you said, there was a dog."

"And you brought him on back. Bagged a prime suspect. What a hero."

Dub says, "I think maybe I'd feel a little more comfortable if we got out from under these trees, man."

"I did some checking. I called around about you last night. What I hear is you're a fuckup nobody takes seriously."

"That hurts, Detective Berkshire. For a second I thought I was some kind of solid citizen or something."

"But you got your hooks in the Easley family, right? Got the mother asking you to go rogue, shoot from the hip, fuck the police *you'll* get it right and find the little boy."

"The way you said 'prime suspect' makes me think you don't believe it."

Berkshire keeps aiming.

"Because," Dub says, "I mean, you let Wyatt go. Who else you got? Angela? She'll snap in half if you look at her funny. If nobody's asking for a ransom, what's any of it for?"

"Maybe it's some go-getter who knows Austin inside and out," says Berkshire, "someone with a past connection to the family and some street smarts. A couple friends in the press, a couple more on the force. Just waiting for the right time to pop the money question."

"Me?" Dub grins. "Yup. That's probably it."

"I'm glad to review the mountains of evidence you've

got on Wyatt Parsons. Hand it over, I'll do it right now."

"That was a pretty great press conference you put together. Really tugged the heartstrings."

"You might as well tell me where you were yesterday morning," Berkshire says.

"At my house. Alone. I do wonder how Wyatt got out of jail so fast. It's almost like he had a pal on the inside."

"Well, aren't you a piece of shit."

"So where do you have the little boy, detective?" Dub shifts his weight, sets his feet. "And why haven't you asked the family for money yet?"

"Jesus Christ, are you a fucking moron? I have a gun pointed at you."

"Well, that's…true."

"Wouldn't be the first time a private dick jumped the fence," says Berkshire.

"We've got a real difference of—" but Dub has seen Berkshire's gun hand get lazy and he's close enough to drop to the asphalt and execute the sloppy cousin of a Muay Thai leg sweep, making excellent contact with the cop's ankles and sending him ass over teakettle. The gun clatters on the ground, and Dub picks it up. He makes a rather loud production of releasing the safety.

"Aw, fuck," Berkshire groans.

"I think maybe stay down there, man," says Dub. "And seriously, why don't you tell me where Hunter is."

The cop blinks, taking stock of his injuries. Then he laughs. Dub fires a round, which rips up a perforation in this sidewalk, directly between Berkshire's high-gloss Bates Lites. The laughter stops short.

"Now you're thinking the sound of a gunshot could be to your advantage," says Dub. "I got the drop on you, but maybe help comes running. Well, let 'em. I'd be glad to bring in a dirty cop. I'd get a medal."

"Dirty cop, hell."

"You think it's a coincidence you just picked up my tail

now? I was watching you. Over at the house on Greenbriar? Some aerobics with our friend Mr. Parsons?"

Dub sees Berkshire's chin drop.

"Hey he's a divorced dude. I dunno, maybe you're a single dude. I'm not here to judge the beauty of love. But I'm gonna go ahead and guess today isn't the first time you boys hooked up."

"Fuck. You."

"Oh, me next?" Dub twiddles a little with the gun, kind of doing a little Wild West thing with the trigger. It's actually been a long time since he handled a firearm. "You know that family is freaking out, man. You're really gonna put them through another night of hell before you give 'em their boy back?"

"Die shithead."

"Seems to me you've pretty much spent all day calling me names. First on the phone, now this. C'mon. Get up. Let's go."

Berkshire stands with his hands half-raised.

Dub says, "How long you been with him?"

"Don't know what you mean."

"Hey, man, that piece of equipment you got dangling there? I've seen it in action. Be a shame to get it shot off."

Berkshire says nothing.

"Fake-kidnap your boyfriend's son for blackmail. Get assigned to the case to make sure nobody comes close. I mean, I get it." Dub marches them back out to the cars. Nobody is here waiting for them; nobody has reported gunfire. "I guess you're driving," Dub says. "Let's go downtown, give your fellow cops a story." His phone rings.

It's Kid. "Well, we've arrived," he says. "Wyatt's out front of his house looking confused. I'm guessing it's a pretty goddamn common facial expression for him." Dub can hear a dog barking in the background.

"And he hasn't seen you?"

"C'mon, man. What am I, some useless stoner?"

"So that means neither one of these jokers jetted straight to wherever Hunter is."

"Oh," Kid says, "you got your eyes on little boy blue?"

"More than my eyes. His gun." Dub winks; Berkshire blankly stands against his car.

"Make sure you frisk him for another piece," says Kid. "Don't they always carry, like, multiple? Hey, I was listening on the way down. Marquette took out Missouri in overtime. Another Big 12 team gone, but we crushed Mizzou, so whatever."

"Dude."

"Dunno what to tell you, Dub. He's at his front door, looking in, looking around, yelling at his dog. You want I should go brace him, I'll go brace him."

"Except he outweighs you by fifty pounds and you can't fight. Just sit there and watch. See where he leads you." Dub puts his gun hand over the phone. "Anything you want me to relay to Wyatt?" he says to Berkshire. "No?" The cop rolls his eyes.

"It's a pretty good fucking plan they hatched," Kid says.

"Bodean sounds like he's going apeshit," says Dub.

"Not the brightest example of the species."

"Right, so I'm taking in Roscoe P. Coltrane. Call me back if anyth—" but Dub hears something over the line, a burst of static, and then another. Kid isn't talking, Bodean is still barking, but louder, closer, more angrily. "Kid? Hey, Kid?"

"What the shit?" the Kid says.

"That, ah, didn't sound good," says Dub.

But now this call's other side yawns silent toward infinity. Dub looks at Berkshire, squints to listen. Suddenly there's more barking, more static, then the barking stops. The line acquires the universal rustling sound of a dropped phone, and very far away Dub hears Kid stage-whisper, "…fucking shotgun."

"Kid? Dude?"

"He shot the dog," Kid says. "He shot Bodean in the face."

"Who did? Wyatt?"

"He just killed the dog. He's looking over here. Shit. Shit."

Dub grits his teeth.

"Come on," says Kid. "Come on. I lost the fucking keys, they're on the.... No! No!"

Dub paces away, curling in on himself, listening.

"Big black dude!" Kid suddenly shouts. "Big scar! Big gun!" Glass smashes. Then the phone is dropped again and in the background Dub can hear his friend say, "C'mon, man! I got a mountain of weed here! Take it!" and then there's another burst of static, much louder.

Dub says Kid's name over and over, but there's no reply. His neck prickles. His throat closes, and his face is stiff with fear. He hates himself.

He opens his jaw to say something to Berkshire, some way to understand a horror that's apparently unfolded out of absolutely nothing…but a shape blots his vision, a rushing dark shape as the detective charges and Dub accepts an elbow to the side of his head. Phone and gun disappear from his hands and the world reduces to a bright twinkle that promptly switches off.

*

The light was hard enough to leave bruises. Three soldiers stood over a crouching, unfamiliar boy, who frantically tried to reassemble the wrench kit he'd just stolen and dropped. The men cast long shadows across Highway 1, which on another deployment would've been their MSR— main supply route—but here was simply a road to nowhere. Or worse than nowhere, given recent history. Their weapons were lowered. The boy was shouting at the ground in a mishmash of English and Maay, so the only thing the soldiers definitively understood was, "I not take! I not take!"

"Hear that, Corporal Nelson?" said one of the men. "Fucking thing just fell out of his nightgown there, scattered all over the place. But he didn't take it."

"I heard," said Nelson. "That's why these fuckers is known as the most dishonest people in the world. Just lie to your face."

The wrenches flashed in the sun as the boy scrambled on hands and knees, a kind of glittering that could signal an unseen conspirator to attack. So the soldiers stayed alert.

The first soldier said, "'Not take!' 'Not take!'"

"You think he really believes it?" said Nelson. "I swear to Jesus H. Christ, Odom, these people got a breakup from reality."

"Yeah," said Odom. "Like: it ain't *really* a hundred ten degrees out here."

"Like: I ain't *really* sweating my balls off in my fucking DCUs."

"We ain't *really* eating shit-ass bullshit for supper tonight."

"I ain't *really* hornier than a four-balled tomcat."

The kid had about finished reassembling the kit, but was one wrench short. He scanned the parched earth, shouting nonsense, fretting with his hands. The third soldier kicked the ground and there was a rolling, thumping sound, and the missing wrench thudded against the boy's dirty macawis. Nelson and Odom looked at this third man: First-Lieutenant Storm, the platoon's laconic security officer.

Storm said, "And we're not *really* in Somalia."

The sky was a blue and swallowing force. Under so vast a roof one felt utterly contained. Twenty-eight men—not quite Green Berets, not exactly *de oppresso liber*, most definitely off the U.S. government books—kept each other alive in this bizarre place, with its lush forests bounded on one side by desert and the other by beautiful white beaches. This was weirder than Mogadishu. Everyone from Major Partridge down did sentry duty as the locals feigned acceptance but schemed. The dialects this far south were confusing; the Americans were all trained in Northern Somali and could mostly understand Benaadir, but down here was this Maay gobbledy-gook. Twenty-six of these roughneck Army bastards thought they were here for humanitarian reasons, to build a water treatment facility, that kind of thing. Only Major Partridge and Lieutenant Storm knew the truth.

The cold fact was: the locals could slaughter them at any time. Kismayo was a city of 150,000-plus, filled to its impoverished brim with gun-wielding lunatics; if attacked, the platoon would take a sizable chunk of the locals down with them, but eventually they'd run out of M249 nutsacks and get overrun. This posting nominally started as a request by the Red Cross/Red Crescent because life in southern Somalia was turning into one big bout with cholera, and whenever the RCRC tried placing its own people in Kismayo to help make cleaner water and effective clinics, they'd get vandalized and terrorized by the local qabils. So the RCRC and the Somali Patriotic Movement—which passed for a government here in the south—cut a deal with someone up the Army or CIA food chain and *voilà*: here was Partridge's platoon.

For most of the men it was a plum gig, if you overlooked the whole 150,000-people-want-to-kill-you thing. They were under orders to stay out of the city proper, but got to swim in the Indian Ocean (with snipers up on a hill watching for sharks) and mostly sleep regular hours, plus there was the fringe benefit of directly helping mankind. Between a rudimentary water treatment plant, a medical clinic, a power station and now some Habitat-For-Humanity-style barracks built to withstand monsoon season, a hearty little American-built subdevelopment was cropping up outside the Farjano district. After a few weeks of high tension among the locals, things were calmer now. People brought them lunches of camel meat and rice, and also this sweet coconut thing called gashaato, plus the kids had gotten bolder, striking friendships with the soldiers, asking for mementos, offering to find them alcohol in the form of fermented goat's milk. It was easy to take their presence in Kismayo at face value.

Any visit to Partridge's tent disabused Lieutenant Storm of that notion.

Once inside, Storm would sweep for listening devices, while Partridge silently opened a spare footlocker's false bottom, and retrieved their dossiers. They spoke in near-whispers, discussing what they'd found. On today's visit, Major Partridge seemed especially reserved, which meant he had something.

"A confirmed sighting this morning of our Comorian," Partridge said. "Farid Mohammed."

"*Fazul* Mohammed," from Storm. "Yes sir, I saw him last week."

Partridge pulled a wise expression, some complicated facial minuet conveying a lesson about double-sourcing. "Now we've both personally seen Fazul and the other one, the Kenyan."

"Saleh Ali. Which means Al-Sudani can't be far behind."

"Here is what I have to say about that, Lieutenant Storm. Anyone who believes these three men have let their guard down doesn't understand their particular movement. I believe we'll eventually see this al-Sudani in the flesh. But the idea that all three men lounge around together, waiting to be killed in one fell swoop...."

"Yes sir."

"And of course, killing one will send the other two scurrying."

"At least it would be something, sir."

"Yes," said Partridge. "I'm sure there's an aphorism about a tiny chunk of revenge still tasting sweet. My memory isn't good enough to have it at my fingertips, I'm afraid."

"And so the question is...."

"I don't know the answer to that question."

"Yes sir," said Storm.

"I don't think you'd say he was well-guarded this morning. Fazul. Many men around him, and I'm assuming lots of guns. But not what you'd call on high alert. Pretty goddamn ballsy, too, knowing we're poking around here."

"Maybe as far as they know this really is building low rises and soup kitchens."

Partridge allowed this to pass. "It's possible I didn't see his real protection. It's possible they're overconfident because they know we're a humanitarian smudge they could erase in a heartbeat." Seated fastidiously on his cot's edge, he absently rubbed his knees. "You still believe this forthcoming event is our zero hour."

"At least it's something, sir," said Storm. "It's worth pursuing until it isn't."

Partridge nodded. "Get out there and help build something before supper, would you? Let your boy Abdi play with his friends. Contribute your hard work to the great progress at hand."

"Yes sir."

*

Abdi waited outside Partridge's tent. The boy didn't indulge in peace-sign pandering or other emblems of America. He'd spent his first years in Hargeisa, a westernized Somali city way north; the reason for his family's presence in this hellhole Kismayo was unclear. Abdi was probably eleven or twelve, spoke good English and showed Storm around without saying much. The other Somali kids around the platoon pretended to be soccer-playing dopes while unsubtly burrowing their way into soldiers' confidence. Abdi was smart, hovered at the perimeter, had the green-tinged teeth of a khat-chewing wiseguy. Storm didn't trust anyone outside his twenty-seven American brothers, and given his real mission here, maybe he even had a developing problem with them. But Abdi presented the reasonable facsimile of a reliable kid.

Storm ignored the major's order to join in the afternoon's construction. He said to Abdi, "Two destinations. First: you know where Major Partridge was earlier today? Where he spotted a particular man he was looking for?"

Abdi nodded.

"I can't go there dressed like this."

Abdi shook his head.

So off came his desert fatigues, and Storm donned his white jellabiya and a turban. His beard was thick-black and convincing, and Abdi had found him leather jaangeri sandals with walnut half-shells decorating the straps. Abdi himself wore jeans, sneakers and a clean red t-shirt that read "San Juan Islands." They walked in the shade of fever trees, then across a dirt lane into a marketplace. Gaunt men with walking sticks and soldiers in camouflage unis spoke respectfully over beds of roots and vegetables; women in jilbabs and head scarves nodded at passers-by. Storm kept his dirty face down, assumed a hooked posture, made little eye contact. He did all this by second nature. Among other things, he was a professional blender.

Abdi walked him across half the town, hands in his pockets, never nodding to a friend, never interacting with another soul. They passed several "technicals"—flatbed Toyota trucks mounted with fifty-cal machine guns— alongside huts decorated by dried palm leaves. They moved through a neighborhood of brick and concrete buildings painted tropical colors, past the Haji Jama mosque, near a loafing congregation of young soldiers planning mayhem. Abdi stopped in a palm grove and Storm halted behind him. Abdi said a few words to an old man in a taqiyah cap, meanwhile pointing across the grove. Storm had caught *his* glimpse of Fazul Abdullah Mohammed outside a Farjano mosque. Apparently Partridge saw Fazul today at those picnic tables right there, outside a stone building adorned by a hand-lettered "Pharmacy" sign. Several men in baggy western shirts and short pants were lounging over there now, but none were Fazul. Storm surveyed the scene, envisioned sniper sightlines, and understood why Fazul wasn't overly concerned with security around here: no feasible approach, too many innocents around, too many escape possibilities. He nodded at Abdi.

"Now take me where the trivia thing will be."

Abdi—four-foot-six, mature-featured and smile-free—didn't hesitate for an instant. He didn't roll his eyes over the inconvenience of doubling back, or demand payment before services were fully rendered. He nodded and walked the way they'd come. Storm wondered about the boy's self-control, tried to place him within a familial unit, tried to imagine him goofing off with friends. Then he fantasized about deploying three expert marksmen and simultaneously shooting three targets between the eyes. But no, impossible. He and Partridge had almost no recon, no sense of the targets' daily movements. This wasn't shooting the president. They didn't have inside help. And as good as Umber and Barzini were, Storm didn't trust them to trail quarry of this magnitude in this scorpion's den unseen.

It was December of 1998. Four months earlier, American embassies in Kenya and Tanzania had been attacked by suicide bombers; according to Partridge's file, the attack was planned down the coast in Ras Kamboni and three of the masterminds—Saleh Ali Saleh Nabhan, Abu Taha al-Sudani and Fazul Abdullah Mohammed—subsequently slinked north blending in with a couple thousand Somali fighters. Now these high-level operatives were in Kismayo, plotting who-knew-what. What Storm wanted to know more than anything, and the question Partridge couldn't yet answer, was if they could only kill one of their targets, which should it be? For now, he'd have to content himself guessing possible locales where all three men might convene, and even in that unlikely occurrence it was entirely doubtful they'd be able to call down a missile strike in time.

As they hoofed it back to Farjano, Storm said, "You know the guy Partridge was watching today?"

"No sah," said Abdi.

"If I showed you a picture, I'm betting you could find him. Follow him."

"Yes sah."

"But that's not a position I want to put you in, kid. This is a dangerous man."

They found a crowd in a square, peacefully standing behind a banner with unfamiliar quasi-Arabic writing. Men strapped with bandoliers stood expectantly on second-floor balconies. Others stood military file wearing black masks decorated with decipherable Arabic: "There is no god but God, and Muhammad is the messenger of God." Young men milled angrily, an older guy in a beret shouted in Maay and waved his M16. Dozens of citizens went about their business in this wild scene. Boys Abdi's age rolled in the dust. Storm never broke stride.

They passed a burned-out Hummer U.S. soldiers left behind in '93. A bullet-riddled building with a corrugated-tin roof, in front of which goats milled. Perhaps a hundred watermelons rotting in the sun.

"Do you sleep in the street, Abdi?"

"No sah."

"You still don't want to tell me where you sleep."

"No sah."

"The other children never stop talking."

"Yes sah."

"I can give you more money. I have more to give. You deserve it."

"I will not take advantage," said Abdi. "When you find your three men, sah."

Storm half-grinned at the blight around them. "I haven't

said anything to you about three men, have I?"

Abdi didn't answer.

"Where I come from, someone like you, we call him a go-getter. Pay attention to get ahead."

They continued to an empty square perhaps a half-mile from the platoon's subdev. The colors in this city were so saturated Storm felt as though a layer of unreality was peeled away here, some gauze that had prevented him from truly seeing while he was in other parts of the world. At the peak of this afternoon heat the African sun did magic unknown in the west. All surfaces belonged to the same Technicolor surface, making of Kismayo a begrimed peacock feather. Abdi halted again and said, "Here sah."

It was an improvised shelter strewn with old chairs and benches, bordered on two sides by brick buildings. Abdi had told Storm about a popular contest regularly held here: groups of young men competed to answer questions about the Koran and Somali geography, and the winners were given assault rifles, hand grenades and landmines. The next gathering of this perverse game-show would happen in two weeks.

"The only time I saw Saleh Ali was a just couple blocks away," said Storm. "He might've been coming from right here."

Abdi nodded noncommittally.

"Or who knows if these guys would even come to an event like this."

"Yes sah. But many of the big men do come. It is a good way to make the young people interested. Many new boys start this way."

Storm looked around, feeling eyes on him. "How do I know you weren't recruited just like that, Abdi? How do I know you aren't a living, breathing double-cross?"

Abdi thought for a moment, and said, "You don't sah."

Storm bit a grin. "Two weeks, then," he said.

"I take you back to your camp, sah."

"That's all right. Here." He handed Abdi several American dollars; any larger bills would lead to questions wherever he tried to spend them. "I can make it back. Come by tomorrow morning and we'll take another lap."

Abdi looked at Storm fondly, parentally. His face was defined by well-proportioned ridges around his lips and absolute smoothness below his eyes, a wise and true reflection of his survivor's canniness. He had an old scar on his forehead and new abrasions on the side of his neck. He said, "Yes sah."

But as he walked back out toward Highway 1 and left behind the denser part of town, Storm saw the kind of buzzing, vibrating crowd that marked daily torment in southern Somalia. Dozens of squawking men fretted and fussed, several women wept from within burqas, many children looked legitimately shellshocked. Storm ventured in close to see what was wrong, and Abdi strode with him.

At the scene's center was a block of wood, a trembling boy and a knife-wielding man. An old cleric read from the Koran, and then Storm recognized the kid. It was the same boy who'd lifted the wrench kit just a few hours before.

"No no," Storm heard himself say. "No, it's all right. We got them back! We got the wrenches back!"

But nobody heard or understood over the crowd's clucking madness. Storm stepped ahead to intervene. Someone pulled the boy's arm from his side, extended his hand onto the block. Everyone yelled.

"No wait!" Storm said, and Abdi yanked the sleeve of his jellabiya, it was impossible to get directly through this circle of men and the boy wailed. Storm prepared to do his worst, to bash through these people and separate this maniac from his knife. He would explain the misunderstanding over the wrenches. He would incapacitate anyone who tried to stop him. The knife-man shouted to the crowd: "There is no god but God! There is no god but God!" Abdi tried to tell Storm something, but it was too late, Storm had a strong bodyguard-type around the neck, was pulling him down, kneeing his gut. He broke the bodyguard's wrist. Someone else touched his shoulder and Storm swung hard, dislocating another man's finger. The knife-man was still chanting. A woman was shrieking. The tussle around Storm grew, other men protesting this form of justice pressed ahead, pulling at the hair and clothes of those closest forward. Storm swam into this mix. He saw the boy's terror-stricken eyes. He felt someone pull around his midsection and prepared a savage kick, but it was little Abdi trying to wrestle him away.

"Please!" Abdi cried. "Please!"

"No!" said Storm.

"Please! You will die!"

And now Storm knew there was no stopping this; the fighting echoed into mere jostling, the mob's will was clear, perhaps these other men had simply been clamoring for a better view. The knife scraped the impossibly blue sky and came down with no sound Storm could hear, not over these madmen. The boy's severed hand leapt into the air and fell lifelessly into the dust.

Abdi pulled Storm away. The men he'd injured didn't follow.

"Jabir is a bad boy," Abdi said. "He steals many things from many people. He is given many warnings, sah."

Storm was hunched over and felt himself whisked past the fever trees. Abdi propelled him. The mob's noises faded. Here were palms swaying in ocean breezes. Storm hated purely, clinically. He pictured the punished boy growing older and bigger, but his hand staying the same size. What had they just made of this person? Who would this Jabir be from now on? Storm's rage blinded him. His sandals were moving. Abdi was saving him.

"I sleep," said Abdi.

Storm discovered that his filthy white hand was wrapped inside Abdi's chestnut one.

"I sleep in the house of my baba. My daddy. But he is

not as good a man as you, sah."

An hour later, Storm picked a fight with LaCapra, the platoon's biggest, toughest kid, and broke his jaw.

*

"It wasn't always like this," said Major Partridge. "For instance, Mogadishu used to be a fine town. Kind people, top fabrics, kicked out the Communists and welcomed us in. I know that bastard who used to be in charge was a horrible guy and did bad things. I know the people had to rise up. But this…."

He and Storm stood behind barbed wire, surveying the outskirts of Kismayo from within the subdev. Time had passed, and the trivia contest was now only a few days away. Storm hadn't learned anything new about whether the embassy bombers might attend, but nobody with authority had yet stepped in to say the preparation of a cruise missile attack was impossible.

"And listen," said Partridge. "It's not Islam. For God's sake, who's the tall one we've got, the Muslim?"

"Sergeant Aziz, sir."

"I've spent more hours of my life under Allah's watchful eye than anyone else's. There's a reason they keep calling on me for these gigs, Storm, and it's not my winning personality. It's not any religion makes a place go this bad. It's not Islam's fault here any more than it was Christianity's fault in Nazi Germany. I don't know what the fuck it is."

Storm was soaked through from eight hours of hammering a frame into an honest-to-goodness structure: a third barracks in this growing compound. Foundations had been poured for three more. Maybe they were getting carried away, but they'd been sent down with a rather overwhelming supply of building materials and were going at it hard. The momentum to make something permanent was palpable; this platoon full of covert operatives and trained killers had morphed into a force for progress. The men joked about meeting up Stateside and starting a construction company. Partridge in particular seemed possessed, kept walking local dignitaries through the subdev, emphasizing over and over that soon he'd be handing over the keys to the people of Kismayo. The RCRC flag flapped above them.

"That one young man's problem," said Partridge.

"Corporal Bruno. Yes sir."

"You're efforting."

"Yes sir."

"I don't mean to micromanage. Nobody is more capable then you, lieutenant."

"I've asked her to be here shortly."

"Abdi is bringing her?" Partridge nodded, and watched sand swirl. The very fact of his inquiry—and subsequent silence—made clear his dissatisfaction. Storm knew this by breathing, had a talent for ingenious subservience. "I understand," said Partridge, "our latest R.P. failed to catch you off guard."

Storm smiled.

"You know at this point it's simply become a matter of pride," Partridge said.

"Odom made that clear, yes, sir."

"He's greatly invested. You derive entirely too much satisfaction in being the only man not to cry uncle during a Readiness Protocol, Storm. At some point, one might think you'd accept the implied order to submit, if only for morale."

"Is an explicit order to submit forthcoming, sir?" said Storm, cradling the knuckles he scraped last night, avoiding Odom and Barnett's sneak attack just outside his tent. They hadn't gotten in a single punch; only a broken bear hug and some harsh words, followed by a quick and measured beating from Storm.

Partridge walked away, sing-songing, "You know it's

not.”

Abdi approached the subdev with a tall ebony woman in tow. Long-necked, high-cheeked, muscular and svelte, she wore a multicolored, multipatterned guntiino like a supermodel Girl Scout. On seeing Storm, she grinned and it was powerful stuff. He sent Abdi to fetch Corporal Bruno.

“Speak any English?” he said to the woman.

“Little English,” she said.

“You’re friends with Marcus. You know Marcus?”

She beamed noncommittally. She was perhaps eighteen years old. Perhaps.

“Have you been here before?” said Storm. Then, in Northern Somali, he said, “Has Marcus brought you to this place before?”

That smile. It wasn’t innocent, but it wasn’t guilty. She appeared kind, indulgent, wise. Storm understood Bruno’s attraction: not merely beauty, but also a self-contained quality. No mere cipher onto which one could project a colonizer’s fantasies. But then, Storm could get carried away when it came to women.

Here came Marcus Bruno in his DCUs, a camo baseball cap, sunglasses and work gloves and boots. Like Storm, he was soaked by the sweltering day’s exertions. He was olive-skinned and handsome, with facial stubble he manicured regularly. But on approach, Storm could see his expression turn from neutral to concerned.

“There’s no point in denying anything,” Storm told him, “so I’ll cut to the chase. Corporal Bruno, we both know our official policy on compromising romantic entanglements, and we both know it hasn’t always been strictly adhered to in the past. But I think you understand this isn’t a traditional deployment. Our lives are in great peril here. You and I know we’re doing good, but as far as a great percentage of this city’s population is concerned, we’re a Great White Satan imposing our will without permission. And that’s why when we arrived five weeks ago, I made a speech to the platoon. I don’t like giving speeches, Corporal Bruno. Do you remember the content of that one?"

"Yes sir, lieutenant."

"Then you'll understand my surprise on meeting Nadifa."

Bruno looked crestfallen. "Yes sir."

Storm maintained his polite tone, looked at the woman peacefully. "She seems like a smart one, Mr. Bruno, so I'll guess she understands what's going on right now. She may understand it better than you. I say that because she hasn't disobeyed a direct order, while you have. In lieu of me stomping around spitting and losing my shit, I want you to explain yourself as best as possible."

"Sir, is love a good enough excuse?"

"You're, what, thirty, Mr. Bruno? Do we know how old Nadifa is? She's a child. Has she been sneaking out to meet you? What do we think might happen if this is discovered?"

Bruno swallowed.

"You know what my job is," said Storm. "I'm here for the sole purpose of keeping every single one of us alive. I think you'll agree that you're making my job harder."

"May I...speak, sir?"

"Am I going to like it?"

"What about him?" Bruno said, pointing a gloved hand at Abdi. "He's in and out all the time. And there are other kids. Every day there's kids in here getting guys water, selling them cigarettes and the stuff that makes your teeth green. I don't think this was so different, sir."

Storm felt his temper flare. "Except it *is* different, Bruno. It's completely fucking different, unless you're accusing me of taking this little boy into my tent and sticking my three-point-five inches of manhood into his rectum."

"Of course not, sir."

"Seriously, if I have to explain this.... What happens when someone checks to see if she's still a virgin? They'll kill her and come after you. All of us." Storm was exercised, but part of his volume was dedicated to snuffing out the sudden jealousy he felt because Nadifa was so lovely. He hated this. "This isn't the fucking movies, man! Nobody's letting you take her back to New Jersey on your lap! She can't be in here, and you sure as fuck can't be out there!"

"We met down on the beach, sir."

Storm looked at the woman, as she adjusted her pink-purple-and-white shoulder sash while holding back tears. "It's over," he said, quieter. "I'm sure there was a time this could've worked out. We're way too far along now."

Bruno's straight-line mouth trembled and he saluted—this wasn't a group of soldiers who did a lot of saluting—and refused to look at Nadifa before striding away. Storm shook the woman's hand and touched her smooth bare arm, as now her tears did fall. She smiled, weeping, and raced from the subdev, the way she'd come.

Storm imagined himself as a person who'd chase after her. Certainly the tongue-lashing he'd just given Bruno was the most he'd said to anyone in a long time; perhaps it gave him a glimpse of himself as more human. Because he typically *was* a machine. They called him the android. He hadn't had traditional leave in three years. It was easier to hold himself above—without religion, without a fanatic's regard for country—because the high standard had its own life. A demanding existence removed options, and Storm was fine with that. He was smart and agile and funny, and his heart ached on occasion. But in all, belief was very, very good to him.

Abdi was still here, watching Storm, then there was hissing behind them, "Hssst! Hssst!" and Abdi said something in Maay. Storm turned and saw a middle-aged man crouching within this compound, wearing a threadbare corduroy jacket and chino pants. He answered the boy back. He was asking for an audience.

"It is my baba, sah," said Abdi.

"Yes, your father," Storm said.

"You are very busy, sah."

"It's fine."

Abdi looked at his father. "He talks very much, sah."

"Don't be ashamed," said Storm. "Never be ashamed of your people."

"Yes sah."

So Abdi signaled and his father stepped forward to shake Storm's hand. He was a big man, darker than his son, with pink eyes and scars on his jaw. "It is a pleasure to make your acquaintance," he said in English. "I am Gaal Ameer Suleman. You have been very good to my boy. Thank you, thank you."

Abdi squirmed in the manner of an American teen.

"You're welcome, Mr. Suleman. He's an exceptional boy."

"Thank you, thank you."

Storm said, "I believe 'Gaal' is a nickname that indicates you've lived abroad?"

"Yes, yes, I have lived in Yemen and Djibouti and Eretria. I have many children in each place, it is a very big family. This place cannot contain me!"

Storm nodded.

"It is a very good thing you are doing. I am very impressed," and Mr. Suleman gestured at the subdev: the exposed pipes of the crude treatment station, the sun-scorched aluminum roofs. "Not everybody in Somalia is a violent devil. We many people want to raise our families and live good lives, but it becomes impossible. Anyone who would look at what you are doing and call you evil, they are bad men."

"Thank you."

"I am a simple farmer, sir. But I will be glad to send you food. Please allow me to do this for you."

"If it won't cause you any trouble," said Storm, "yes, thank you."

"No no no, no trouble. My honor. Please. Thank you."

When his father had gone, Abdi sourly said, "He never was in Yemen."

Storm laughed and gave the boy seven dollar bills.

*

He dreamed about her. Heaven help him, he dreamed a domestic situation back in Texas, Nadifa and several cocoa-colored children, teasing play in the front yard beneath the magnolia trees, walking around the neighborhood, Christmas lights tacked to the houses year round, lawns not of grass but multicolored crushed glass, wind chimes that don't chime but rather clank like bamboo in the breeze, past the brick castle-house at Mary and 3rd, dogs fenced in almost every yard so when you walk down the street it creates an echo chamber of barking. And Nadifa wanting him, giving him sly smiles even with the children around, kissing him lightly but suggestively, so the children became marginalized in the dream, Storm forgot about them, instead now it was Nadifa taking his lily-white hand in hers and pulling him into the front bedroom (the one that had been his parents'), pulling him down on top of her, bringing her ankles up around her ears and guiding him home, Storm's hands pressed the back of her knees and his own legs squeezed Nadifa's narrow hips and he thrust directly down, down, the way to pleasure and damnation. She moaned. This was all he ever wanted. I'm wound so tight. Release like this.

When he woke, he'd ejaculated into his briefs.

Now it had been nearly two weeks since Storm or Partridge had seen any of the embassy bombers. The trivia contest was tomorrow. Partridge delivered the news: no missiles would be forthcoming on such flimsy surveillance. There was no guarantee the three men were even still in Kismayo.

"I'm sending you out there today with a rifle, and without Abdi," said Partridge. "I want you to prove you can get in and out of the city hiding a weapon, and that you can get an elevated sightline toward that trivia shelter."

"What if more than one of them shows up tomorrow?" Storm said. "Shouldn't we get three guns up there? Hasn't that been the whole point, to get all three at once?"

"First off we still don't know what the fuck that Sudanese one, what he even looks like."

"Al-Sudani. Yes, sir."

"So there's that. And I'm sorry, lieutenant, but I'm weighing the costs and benefits here. Now it's *three* men shoving an M24 where the sun don't shine, getting in and out of what, if it isn't already enemy territory, certainly will be when the bullets start flying? And there's every chance once the three of you get up there, you won't have a single target?"

"Yes sir," Storm said, "better to lose just one man."

"The *point*, lieutenant, is you're the one I trust *not* to get himself killed doing crazy shit like this."

"Yes sir."

"I've never much cared for the idea of having a political officer around, but this wouldn't be a bad time. Because if you're right, and if one of these terrorist fucks shows up and you plug him—hell, if you plug more than one—I don't think we have a real sense of how bad the blowback is. We bug out. But do we bug out shooting?"

"There are plenty of Somalis who'll be happy," said Storm.

"You're out there today with a rifle *and* a radio. Prove to me it all works. A boat can be out in the port to pick us up with three hours' notice. Never thought we'd even be here this long. I mean, we're building a fucking city by now. And now we're betting on…trivia night."

"It's a major recruiting effort of theirs, sir."

"I hope they're there," Partridge said. "Good goddamn, I'm ready as anyone to stop being a do-gooder. Prove to me you can make that shot and wipe someone off the planet."

So Storm ventured alone out into Kismayo proper. He strapped an M24 sniper rifle to his back, and hid the scope, the stand and a radio in an improvised interior pocket he'd sewn into his jellabiya. He walked slowly, head down but otherwise upright, the picture of a devout Muslim contemplating eternity. And really, it was all in the pace: a gliding, leisurely stroll amped up just slightly, indicating the fear that comes from continual violence, but also impatience and exhaustion with that fear.

The shelter abutted by the two brick buildings was exactly as Storm had last seen it: empty chairs, tables and benches, with only the occasional passer-by. Across this dirt lane was a pair of two-story residences bisected by an alley; each roof provided a brilliant view of this gathering place. Storm hiked his rifle up between his shoulder blades and kneeled facing east, praying for the purpose of scanning every window and doorway, every shadow and crevice. Of course, he couldn't lean fully forward and prostrate himself toward Mecca, but he rocked piously, squinting, mouthing babble, seeing the footsteps he'd take into the alley, knowing which footholds he'd use to climb, already seeing this scene from above. A caravan of trucks thundered nearby and Storm stood, briskly moved out of the sunlight, found a ladder already in place…there was no guarantee tomorrow would go so smoothly if organizers arrived early, but today finding his assassin's perch was simple. He assembled his equipment without conscious thought, dropped to his belly, looked through the scope. The shelter was perhaps a hundred meters away. It would be an easy shot.

Lying here, scanning, totally immersed…an alarm went off in Storm's head. It was fast. He was fast. There was no pause between thought and action. He heard something. Or felt it. He was never wrong. He was aiming the rifle and then he was pointing the M9 pistol from his ankle holster at a figure behind him, also on this roof.

Abdi's eyes grew gigantic, but somehow he avoided crying out.

Storm put a finger to his own lips, and saw that Abdi was hurt. He had scrapes and blood on his cheeks, his lip was split, his eyes were swollen half-shut. Worst was his right ear: the lobe had been pulled hard, so now it dangled too far down, and there was a black, glistening wound where the ear attached to his head. Storm knew what horseplay looked like, and this wasn't that. He'd taken a beating.

They climbed back down the ladder. In the dark alley, Storm said, "You were following me? You were stalking me, Abdi?"

"Yes sah," the boy said.

"What happened to you? Who did this to you?"

"I found your third man, sah. Abu Taha al-Sudani."

Storm's mind reeled. How did Abdi even know who al-Sudani was? "Tell me how," he said. "Tell me everything."

"The boys are talking about him. He is Mr. Boom-Boom."

"Mr. Boom-Boom." According to Partridge, Al-Sudani was the munitions mastermind behind the embassies. "And you saw him?"

"Yes sah."

"Talk to me, Abdi."

"My friends say they will go see Mr. Boom-Boom, and I followed. But once we arrived, the men do not let us in. I know who this man is. I know what he has done. I go inside when nobody is looking and I see him and I hear him. He told the people he will come to this show tomorrow."

Storm pointed out into the square, to the shelter.

"Yes sah. It is important for al-Qaeda to find the bad boys when they are very young."

"You know that name."

"But the men who do not let us in, they found me and...." He pushed out his chin.

Storm bit his lips while the boy looked up at him eagerly.

This smelled bad. Abdi's wounds were genuine, but it wasn't beyond a mass murderer to beat up a child for subterfuge. This felt like too much coincidence, like the mother of all setups. The kid just happens upon one of America's most-wanted criminals, and that criminal just happens to already be planning a visit to the trivia contest? Abdi smiled faintly and Storm could see one of his front teeth had been knocked out.

"You'll come with me?" he said. "You'll be able to point him out to me?"

"Yes sah."

"Tomorrow morning, then. Come to the subdev. I'll be waiting."

Things had gone too far. When the platoon had taken out Aidid a couple years before—and had even assured safe passage for his son who subsequently became president of the country—the men all understood the mission to one degree or another. That was the way it worked, the way the brotherhood stayed strong. Now the boys were having a grand old time with their construction and their dips in the ocean, and meanwhile Storm was off on his own. That night he tried mingling in the mess, laughed at pranks, sang along when Jefferson and Nelson brought out a guitar and did some passable James Taylor, but he was a specter, he wasn't here, he couldn't really even see these young American faces sitting around in their heartsick patriotism. He couldn't eat, and he couldn't talk. There seemed no way back.

He said nothing to Partridge, and he turned in early.

He dreamed he was back in high school. Some classroom, probably math, something he hated. That lighting: fluorescent gray. Major Partridge was the teacher, drawing on a chalkboard. Kid Collins was here, with his hand hiked all the way up a girl's skirt and grinning at Storm, who for some reason was wearing his dress uniform. He sat quietly sweating, knowing his name would be called. There was a tree growing inside the classroom, and someone was throwing nuts down onto the students. Storm had a series of magnets on his desk and was trying to get them to line up while still listening to his teacher, but the polarity was mixed up and the magnets kept repelling each other. A window was open and a rainbow elbowed into the classroom, but it had no color, just different shades of silver, iron, granite. Partridge called his name (called him "Mason"), and asked for the answer.

And then Storm was standing in his tent, his arm around a man's throat from behind, one-quarter awake. Coming to himself, he knew this was another R.P. and they hadn't caught him out…but the man he was choking was smaller than Odom and an expensive wristwatch thrashed in his line of sight. It was Major Partridge.

"God," the major said. "Goddamn. There's a…there's been an episode."

"…"

"Storm. Storm, snap out of it. Get some clothes on. We're going into town."

The two of them left the subdev wearing shorts and t-shirts. It was 4 a.m. and windy, but still tropically hot. Partridge met a tall boy and handed him several dollars, and the boy led them deep into Calanleey, the city's oldest district. Even in disguise, Storm hadn't dared venture in this direction. The African night sky was overfed with stars; the buildings here seemed taller and older, though it was difficult to see much detail. The roads were still dirt, and there were dozens of people sleeping outdoors. The boy pushed on, down what felt like an endless tangle of paths and passages. Storm was trying to clear his head and believe this reckless dash was actually happening, presumably Partridge trusted they'd go unharmed by sheer dint of late-night brazenness. They speed-walked for perhaps fifteen minutes, then a stone corridor opened into a mosque's exterior plaza and electric light blazed, focused on one spot like a highway crew doing night work. As they approached, several men and women in various stages of undress turned to examine them: hollow-cheeked, expressionless, silent. The mood was détente.

Storm and Partridge stepped toward the light and saw carnage.

Destroyed bodies had fallen here. The first impression was blood: an estuary of blood that covered the bare toes of three boys who blithely passed through this crime scene. Hacked-off fingers and ears and noses were discarded all around. Fabric from torn clothing sat in mashed piles. One headless body supplicated near a bush. An eyeball stared up at Storm. Onlookers shook their heads and tut-tutted. Partridge stepped into the blood, leaned forward, pulled one torso up, let it fall back down. He paced around the plaza, trying not to splash in these dark puddles, examining bodies. There were six or seven dead. Storm stepped toward the mosque, where a couple very small children had begun weeping. He stood over them until they noticed him and dispersed, leaving behind a human head. It was face-down. He looked around for something to move it with, but found nothing. So he gritted his teeth and toed the head, nudging it so it rolled into a cobblestoned groove.

It was Nadifa. Blood stained the upper lip and it looked as though her tongue had been cut out, but it was obviously Nadifa.

"Oh, no," Storm said aloud.

"Get over here! Get over here now!" This was Partridge. Storm stepped through the massacre and found his c.o. holding a scrap of bloody clothing. It was U.S. camouflage: the sleeve of a desert combat uniform. They looked around frantically.

Storm saw something. Two kids were playing catch. He rushed over, leaving bloody footprints. The smaller child saw him coming, and flung his toy away. It slapped wetly to the ground. It was a Caucasian penis.

*

They found what they could of Corporal Bruno's body, wrapped the pieces in a blanket, and somberly marched back to the subdev. They hailed the sentries who saw them returning, and Partridge had presence of mind enough to say, "Lamb tonight, boys. Gift from the locals." They took Bruno to the major's tent, left him there, changed their blood-soaked clothes.

Storm's face burned. Bruno stood before him just a few days ago. He'd been a good-natured guy and a brave sonofabitch. They'd pushed him into venturing out; what harm would there have been if the girl kept coming here? Storm's stomach went through convulsions. Dawn had broken and Partridge said, "Not a word, not even to Abdi," then retreated to the mess tent. Storm sweated, furious, wanting revenge.

He saw Odom, Whitecliff and Aziz smoking near the treatment building. They faux-saluted him and it was so casual, so kind, something to let him know they saw him, they knew him. But of course, they didn't know him, not anymore. He'd veered off: his schemes and his secret mission. God, he knew when and where a platoon member had been butchered and was keeping it secret? The point of this group was to live together *above* frittering bullshit and get close to life's marrow. But now he and Partridge were using their brothers as cover, allowing them to devote weeks of sweat and emotion to a well-financed decoy that might as well be some banking job, some graphic design job, some extraneous cog that gives off light and noise while the real power brokers divvy up the world. Storm felt twisted. He was helping construct a maze.

But he had to finish. It was his duty to finish.

He donned his costume. He and Abdi stepped out of the subdev, probably for the last time. The boy's face was dark with bruises and scabs, and a crude bandage covered his entire right ear. His eyelids were deep purple now. They reached the alley overlooking the shelter, but Storm eschewed the building they'd climbed yesterday, chose the second one.

It was eight o'clock and already the day's heat was rising as though summoned by a wallop. There was no shade on this roof. It would be ten hours up here. Storm had brought several small pears, and he tossed one to Abdi. The boy dug in with his remaining front tooth.

"You heard about our man," said Storm.

"Yes sah. Corporal Bruno."

"What do you know about it?"

"He comes into a bad part to see his friend. But her brother is bad."

"Nadifa's brother killed him. Killed them all."

"Yes sah."

They were silent a long while. They heard Kismayo rouse itself to full consciousness, all its engine revs and random firearm discharges, a smattering of Bollywood music, kids chattering in what sounded like some variant of Swahili, mothers laughing and horns honking and dogs barking. "We shouldn't be here," Storm said.

"No sah. You will get the bad men."

But Storm was exhausted and overheated, too angry to eat or drink, his face was itchy under its beard, he wanted to leave. He checked in with Partridge via the radio, but the major didn't communicate back for fear his synthesized voice would be heard below. Storm reminded himself that there was still some purity here. The men he was after were evil. But he saw Bruno's face everywhere.

"You think you have such a good inventory of yourself," he said aloud. "You're convinced you know yourself well. Then one day you take stock, and it feels like a piece has gone missing. Where did it go? Is it really gone? Now there's just…less of you."

The boy didn't respond.

"I've never had to lie like this, not to these men."

"Yes sah."

"You can't get it back. And the worst thing is having to imagine the rest of your life. I mean, the days will just keep coming. And you'll remember what you were and wish you could filter everything through that. But now you're this new thing. How does this new thing react? What does this new thing believe in?" Storm withdrew his rifle's scope and stand, as well as his handgun. "I might just as well have cut off his cock myself."

Abdi put down his swollen head to rest in the lurid sunshine. When he believed the boy was asleep, Storm said, "Are they coming to kill me, too?"

Perhaps he, too, fell asleep. It didn't feel like it. When in the future he looked back on that long, tormented wait, Storm chose to believe he never lost consciousness, and that the resulting attenuated sense of time was a gift. Minutes passed like days. And the universe was whittled down to a twenty-by-ten concrete slab roof with a brick lip. Lying on his back, with his skull propped against brick, he could only see slab-lip-sky. And he could make it all rock to and fro as though at sea, or give it the turbulence of air travel, or the rat-a-tat of an M1 battle tank. He could make it hot or cold. He could feel other shoes on his feet, other clothes wrapped around him. He was swimming. He was falling. But none of this was true, and he knew it. He spent hours hallucinating and stricken by the fear that there was no way of organizing all this sensation, no way to tell what he really felt or whether that feeling might change over time. He was terrified, but also in a way deliriously happy. His consciousness over-broadened. Some part of him wanted to be given an order.

By five o'clock he was weak and shaky, and Abdi forced him to drink some water, which by now was scalding hot. It sounded like many kids had gathered below. Someone tested a portable public address box, first saying "test test test" in English and then singing "yah nabi salaam alaika" over and over. The susurrus was good for Storm. He stretched his neck, his shoulders, his back. He looked suspiciously at Abdi, but the fact remained: they'd been up here all day and nobody had arrested them or shot them.

"So this is it," Storm said.

"Yes sah."

"I'll give you the scope. You look around until you see al-Sudani. Tell me what he's wearing."

"Yes sah."

"And also, if you happen to see Fazul or Saleh Ali…."

"I do not know what they look like, sah."

"Right."

They peeked up their heads and watched. It was quite a show. Many masked, black-clad swordsmen mingled in a crowd of children, showing them their glinting steel. Parents clucked and laughed and prayed. Water and tea were passed out in abundance. The prizes—guns, grenades, rifles—were lined up on a table and heartbreakingly small kids were squeezing past each other to gawk and run their hands over the weapons. A turbaned man stood and held the microphone but didn't say anything for a long while. He felt many children bobbing against him, absently touched their heads and shoulders, smiled at parents. Finally, he signaled and the masked men began clanging together their swords, a slow rhythm that the audience matched with claps. People sat. There was a rumbling approval of male voices.

"Here he is, sah. He is coming to sit at the big table."

"Which one?"

"Light-skin man. He is wearing a macawis and over it is a white shirt with brown squares."

"I see him. He's sitting down right now?"

"Yes sah."

"The one who just scratched his head?"

"Yes sah."

Abdi handed him the scope, and Storm attached it to his rifle. He looked through, and the man was of young middle age, had light eyes, smiled as the microphone man began speaking. He was in a row of dignitaries, all of whose postures were relaxed and philanthropic. Neither of the other two embassy terrorists was here, not yet. The scope told

Storm his target was about ninety meters away. He stood his rifle on the roof's lip, checked around the target to see if any children were likely to rush the improvised stage. He breathed deeply and quietly. He put his finger on the trigger.

Then he pulled his head away from the scope and turned to Abdi.

"Who is it?" he said.

"…"

"Who is this man?"

"Abu Taha al-Sudani, sah."

Storm kept his expression neutral.

"He is al-Qaeda, sah."

"…"

Abdi put both hands on his face, to feel his many wounds. The tip of his left index finger was newly missing; in its place was a cauterized black stump.

They faced one another for a long time, as the microphone man below began asking trivia questions about the Koran. Abdi was used to his silences earning him a free pass; Storm recognized he'd been falling into this trap for weeks. Now he just stared, waiting.

"He *is* al-Sudani," Abdi said.

"…"

"This is what the bad boys tell me."

"…"

Abdi's adult mask fell away. He began to cry.

"That's not going to work," said Storm. "Tell me."

"No."

"Tell me, Abdi."

"No, sah."

"…"

The boy put his palms together and brought them to his lips. "He is my baba."

"…"

"He is my daddy."

"Then who…was the man you introduced me to?"

Sobbing, Abdi said, "I give him money to say he is my baba."

Storm looked through the scope, saw the man smiling and nodding. Neither Fazul nor Saleh Ali was present. "Jesus, kid."

"I am sorry, sah."

"Tell me why you would do this."

"No sah."

Storm took a step toward the boy. "Tell me."

That microphone voice echoed in excitement, it was a county fair anywhere. Now that they were standing, they could see a blond landscape under all that blue, and palm trees lurching, and a shanty mosque's blue-painted roof, and a single line of black smoke rising to the stratosphere, and Storm told himself that the smoke was actually rage and humiliation coming off him. He knew the answer. Of course he did. But he wanted to hurt the kid, to make him say these things aloud.

"He hit me, sah. He cuts me. He knows al-Qaeda, he tells them many things. He paid for the prizes, he wants to train bad boys to kill many Americans."

"He did all this to you?" indicating Abdi's ear, his face, his hand.

Abdi wept. This little stoic Boy Friday.

"You've been lying to me, Abdi. I trusted you."

"Yes sah."

Storm thought he could see the fire that was sending the smoke skyward. It flickered in the distance, way inland, in what looked like an inaccessible shantytown: a couple teardrop trailers, some pickups, maybe an ancient motorcycle. That was where his embassy bombers were. He just knew it. They were careful, they knew no American could touch them. They mocked him for all his preparation, for the futility of this whole thing. He'd been his organized self. Where had it gotten him?

He said, "You've been playing me."

"I shoot him," said Abdi. "I will borrow the rifle and shoot him, please?" His purple-lidded eyes stung Storm for their legibility.

"I don't think so, kid."

The boy whispered: "He is…more than three-point-five inches, sah."

"…"

"Let me do it, sah. Please."

"…"

Abdi stepped to the rifle. Storm yanked his t-shirt, pulled him roughly away. Flecks of blood were in the boy's eyes; he was crying blood. Not only was the joint of his left forefinger hacked away, now Storm could see a cigarette burn on the inside of Abdi's elbow. It was time to go. Storm said, "Oh my fucking God, kid."

In about five seconds, he crouched, lined up the shot, and blew the man's brains out.

*

The light is a blowtorch. Dub finds himself in the backseat of a car, upright only because he's handcuffed to a modified suit-hook in the ceiling. He tries to shield his eyes, but can't. The car isn't moving. Light burns everything, makes him feel cocooned in the world's only dark space. His hands and arms are asleep and his head feels donkey-kicked. It's better, he knows, to wake in this blaze than in some gloomy lair. It qualifies as good news.

He tries speaking but his throat is too dry. So he thumps window glass with his elbow, slowly, which is the most he can muster. Stupidly, he thinks how much he'd enjoy a joint right now, and that leads him directly to the matter at hand.

He bangs the window harder. He croaks, "Hey! Hey!" He wonders if he can reach a foot to the steering wheel and honk the horn.

He thinks: *What the hell happened to me?*

The door he's leaning against opens, and he reels out into the open air, dangling like a marlin, feeling the evening's cool. Someone brushes against him, something touches his wrists, and the handcuffs are gone. He falls onto dead wet grass.

"Get up," says Detective Berkshire.

He doesn't. He stays face-down. The world feels good and cool pressed against his swollen right temple. He hears voices: other cops. He says, "How bad is it?"

"See for yourself."

Dub opens his eyes, rubs his wrists, rolls fully onto his stomach. Wyatt Parsons' front yard is professionally floodlit and surrounded by a couple squad cars with their cherries flashing, and orange barricades with nobody on the other side. The red Miata is cordoned by police tape and broken glass glitters like diamonds. There's no ambulance. Nobody is scurrying around trying to keep anyone alive.

Berkshire puts his face close to Dub's ear. Quietly, he says, "I've got you on felony aggravated assault of a public servant and stealing a police officer's weapon. Do anything dumb and I'll shoot you. Now get up."

Dub has no snazzy comeback. He lets Berkshire lift him off the ground by his clothes, sees the other policemen barely take notice. There's a mammoth bloodstain here on the lawn; a few chunks of flesh and hair are strewn, but officials have already bagged the body. A hundred feet away Bodean is still curled as though sleeping. Dub walks rubber-legged to the Miata. The top is up but the driver's window is gone and Kid's blood is sprayed over every interior surface though he, too, is missing.

"You heard it happen," Berkshire says. "Parsons got it over there, Collins right here. What did he say to you?"

Dub touches his temple, feels his own caked blood and the terrible swelling underneath. So only Berkshire can hear, he says, "Kid told me just one thing: 'Whatever you do, don't trust the crooked cop.'"

Berkshire shakes his head and steps away.

It was a split-second decision: Dub took Berkshire, and let Kid tail Parsons. He did it trying to protect his friend. Now it's a source of horror. With roles reversed, he'd have defended himself. He'd have sniffed it out before it happened. Dub puts his palms against his eyes and presses hard. Why make the phone call? Why involve Kid at all? His stomach lurches, every muscle constricts. With only his wind, he says, "No no no no no no no no no no no no no no."

After several minutes of standing bent over, hands-on-hips, Dub walks around the car and reaches for the passenger's side to check the glove compartment.

"Hey!" says a cop. "Get the fuck away from there."

"Look in," Dub says. "Look in there, man."

The cop checks over with Berkshire, who nods. So the blue-suited youngster opens the passenger door, takes out a ballpoint pen and clicks the compartment, revealing…nothing.

"He had a stash in there," says Dub. "I heard him offer it to whoever shot him. But then, you know who shot him."

Berkshire waves the younger cop away, tells Dub: "We'll have plenty of time to talk, you and me. Right now, shut the fuck up."

There's a snoring in Dub's head; he realizes it's the generators powering all this light. The badness has levels. The enormity of death—not unfamiliar to Dub in younger days—is primary, but there's also what it means that Berkshire is walking around here running things.

A forensic team spreads out, looking for shells and the like. Dub stands and watches, wondering why Berkshire uncuffed him. This will last deep into the night. Dub is sick with hunger and maybe a concussion. This is perhaps the darkest day of a dark life. He fights a mounting urge to simply run away.

After waiting a long while, after seeing Berkshire taking measurements and making fastidious notes like an actual officer of the law, Dub's nausea ratchets up in a wave and he steps away from Cedar Elm Street. He just needs to sit. The police are all still working the crime scene and, having assured themselves the little boy still isn't inside, are leaving the rest of Wyatt Parsons' house for later; Dub goes up there and takes five on the front stoop. He looks up and wishes he could see stars, but either the floodlights erase them, or cloud cover muffles everything. He dry heaves into a bush and looks at the enclosed porch behind him. Miscellaneous junk is piled on the floor, including a rectangular bag whose top is curlicued shut. Dub opens the porch door, mind blank, and flicks on the light. The quarter-filled bag has white powder on the floor beneath it, and one word emblazoned on it:

SAVAKIS

"Oh," Dub says. "Oh, no." Quik-Dry Concrete.

Out in the back yard, near the empty above-ground pool, there's a white square in the ground. Prodded by Dub, Berkshire surrounds it with his flashlight; it's a hole that's been freshly filled with concrete.

A man with a jackhammer arrives and spends an hour carefully breaking up this unremarkable patch. It might've been anything, maybe just a sinkhole covered up for safety. At around midnight, they discover Hunter Parsons.

SUNDAY

A black-and-white drops Dub at the Accord. Next thing he knows, he's past his house, driving in the dark on South Lamar. He wonders if he has a concussion, but doesn't make waves with his autopilot. In minutes he's eating a full stack at Kerbey Lane.

"Dub," says Grace, the all-night waitress, "that's enough pancakes to kill a rhino, son. Bet I know what you been up to."

He nods.

"Hey hey." Now it's Manny the cook, back from a smoke break and surveying this restaurant that's only otherwise got a couple drunk college kids dipping chips in queso. "Look what the cat puked out. One of them nights, Dub?"

"Emmanuel."

"If I knew it was your shit I was making, I'd put in some methadone."

Dub chews.

"Fuck, dude. The fuck happened to your head?"

"Crashed my blimp."

"That looks all crunchy, man. You thinking about the doctor?"

"Not as yet."

Manny folds his arms with friendly concern. "I know you're not a junkie, man. I was just teasing."

"I know it."

"I don't get outta here 'til eight, Dub. But you want Grace to take you to the hospital? Hey, you going to the protest thing tomorrow? They're trying to put up that Borders?"

"Yeah," says Dub. "Yeah, man, I'll be there."

"Right across from Book People and, like, Waterloo. Taking out the local institutions one by one."

It hammered you every time, losing a man. He remembers the aftermath of Bruno, and others through the years. Rewinding everything, trying to take control of the memory and change it, trying to make past events different through sheer force of will. Everything else, they controlled via application of the self. But not this, and helplessness wasn't good for a soldier. Then, there were orders to fall back into. Now, tonight: Kid wasn't just another man who signed up knowing the risks. And he is *gone.*

Dub forks home more pancakes.

Other regulars stop by: Stevie, Cowboy Ron, Thin Tony. In turn they give Dub nods, tethering him to Planet Earth. Of course, they know nothing of what's happened to Kid. He plants his bald spot against the back wall and sighs so bad he breaks his own heart.

Back at home he parks on South 2nd, an old mid-case habit in the event someone's scoping his driveway. He walks the alley between Mary and Johanna Streets, passes an ancient swathe of sheet-metal, which in the sodium light is spray-painted with two crucifixes and the word "Forsaken." But it turns out there's a car parked in his driveway after all: a jet-black Mini Cooper that scares the hell out of him when his motion-detector porch light comes on. Sitting at his wrought-iron patio table is Angela Easley.

"I never come down here," she says. Her dog sits

blinking next to her feet.

Dub sits in the other chair. "Where do you go?" he tries to say gently.

"Nowhere." She's paler than ever. She barely moves her head and speaks in a baffled baritone voice, giving Dub the impression she's under the influence of something.

"They told you."

She nods, eyes dry.

"You're in shock."

"Baby," she says. "You have no idea."

They sit still and the porch light automatically goes out while Barney the hound snores. A lonesome Union Pacific train hoots through the neighborhood down by Oltorf. It's the sound of 3 a.m. throughout Dub's childhood.

"I'm…sorry," Dub says.

"They're going to check me in somewhere, I guess. Makes sense: I'm a danger to myself. Look at me. Running off in the middle of the night."

"Under the circumstances, you seem okay."

"I could do anything," she says. "I could jump in front of a moving car. I could hitchhike to Vegas and deal blackjack. I could go feed sick old ladies in Mexico City. That's the thing that makes me so scared: I could do all those things." Her leg bounces minimally; the table jostles, not enough to trigger the light. "It was better when I knew the world was smaller."

"Probably now's not the time to make any big decisions," says Dub.

"It hurts so bad I don't have enough body for it."

Dub just nods, knowing she can't see him.

After a while she says, "I haven't acted great with you."

"Come on."

"I'm a spoiled little bitch. People look at me that way."

"Well."

"But they don't know. All I ever cared about was not being a phony. I was a deb and I wore an expensive dress to prom, and even when I was a mom, I saw myself doing all those things and the most important," she breaks off, husky, "the most important thing is you don't act like a fake. You don't say things just to be sweet. Everybody is so sweet."

Dub waits a while and says, "Yup."

"Not you, though."

His temple thumps.

"You," says Angela, "gave it to me straight. And you lost your friend and I lost everything. We're the two people who lost." She breathes loudly for a while. "Stupid things like he looks up at me playing in the sandbox, holding this chunk of something filthy, looking at me for permission before he puts it in his mouth. But that's…. They told me to remember the good times."

"Okay."

"I mean, I know I can't face it right now. But what good does it do remembering him? He's the thing that's gone. Why would I…what good is it trying to go back there?"

Dub reclines, extending his legs, which triggers the motion detector. The light comes on and he shields his eyes. He says, "It hurts less."

"Maybe better to think nothing."

"No maybe about it."

"They gave me a horse tranquilizer."

"I figured."

He looks at her feet, with these green platform shoes that have plastic daisies across the top, then her skinny legs in snug old jeans, then her black t-shirt that advertises half-an-inch of midriff.

She says, "I'm being punished."

"No. That's not the way it works."

"I've done some really bad things. I don't always mean to."

"You can think however you want to think," says Dub. "But all I know is I'm a lot older than you. And nobody's up in the sky keeping score."

"I'm guilty," she says. "I'm so, so guilty."

"Come on."

The light clicks off again as Dub is watching her face. In the darkness he can see obscure highlights of her cheeks and forehead. He thinks that here may be his orders. Don't let this girl believe such awful nonsense.

She weeps quietly. The dog snores. A long time passes. Dub thinks about Kid, and then he thinks about Abdi.

"I'm so guilty," Angela says again, and this time her slurring is pronounced.

"Let's put you to bed," says Dub, glad to know what comes next, to focus on one small thing.

He unlocks the back door and the three of them go inside, Barney leading the way. Dub steers her through the kitchen, left into what used to be a family room, but his mother put a bed back there for guests and so it's been a third bedroom forever. Angela's feet continue to stride but her balance is gone. Dub touches the bare skin at her sides— it's white as uncooked dough, pliant and warm—and lowers her to the bed.

Dub walks to the bathroom. He looks at himself in this silvered mirror: head swollen, three days' beard, pupils tiny, self-deprivation written all over him. He washes his hands. The simple life is of course no longer possible. Fly free, but the tendrils will latch on.

He steps back through the doorway and Angela is on her side, facing him, eyes quarter-open. He tumbles into a wicker chair.

"I'll get whoever did it," he says.

"I don't really care," drugged, vanishing into herself.

"You will, though."

She falls asleep as he's watching. She gets older in sleep. Now he can see her sister.

Barney's toenails clack a complicated rhythm as he considers whether to jump on the bed. He decides against it, this graying little hound, and instead looks at Dub, his tail a disquisitive metronome. He touches Dub's hand with his freezing nose and receives a few body-scratches; Dub feels little lumps up and down the dog's body. Barney sighs and falls to the floor with a bumping little smack, swallows loudly, and begins snoring anew.

Sometime in the night Dub wakes and she's talking to him from over there:

"…wouldn't do it. You just had to see him one time and you'd know. I shouldn't have married him, but he was the best father. He was such a big baby. The stupidest things made him happy. He liked this candy: Now and Later. Like little taffy Starbursts. They were everyplace, like, he left trails of Now and Later wrappers wherever he went. He ate them and he just smiled and closed his eyes like he was a little kid. You couldn't get him mad, he just popped one in and got this stupid grin on his face like he didn't remember his own name. But now he has a fucking hole in his face."

"We have to figure out who did this," says Dub.

"A vengeful God," she says.

They both fall back asleep and then light sluices through the window, Dub finds himself coiled in a flamenco position, with a serious erection. Angela and Barney and the black car are gone.

He eats at Bouldin Creek and on the way back sees gray-suited Raphael the developer standing across the street, making notes on a clipboard.

"Out here on a Sunday morning," Dub says.

"Mr. Storm. How are you doing today?"

"Can I ask you a question, man? Do you own your company?"

"Well, no, sir," says Raphael. "I'm an employee of the Milton Corporation."

"Pretty big outfit? Irons in lots of different…?"

"Yes, but I can assure you, I have very much freedom in this neighborhood to make deals I want to make. You are thinking about our conversations? There is no crime in cashing out of an up-and-coming neighborhood."

"Thinking very seriously. Like you said, I mean, the tax bill. But who owns the Milton Corporation?"

Raphael's smile fades. "I believe it is a privately held company."

"You know who Thomas Easley is? Because if he's in the deal, that would make it easier to sell."

"I know who Mr. Easley is, of course. But as I say, the company is privately held."

"Mm. All right then."

"Mr. Storm? I must say, this is the first time I have been asked such a thing. Why would you sell your house only to Mr. Easley?"

Dub folds his arms, fiddles with his UT cap. "Tell me just personally. What do you hear about Easley? What kind of guy is he?"

Raphael's shoulders drop a little, but he doesn't respond.

"I mean, is he one of those guys? Do anything to make a deal come out right? I'm kind of just interested in his reputation. Is he a killer?"

Raphael simply shakes Dub's hand and walks toward Polvos' parking lot.

*

Minutes later, Dub gets a phone call from Detective Berkshire and on his instructions drives to a Westlake church. The services haven't started yet, and a four-piece soft-rock band is finishing a sound check. The drummer lets loose with a decidedly devilish roll punctuated by a series of high-hat whacks, then looks around to see who's watching. But the hall is still mostly empty. The crucifix sparkles directly above him, and the organ pipes are silent. The band members put down their instruments while Dub watches the door.

Here comes Berkshire, out of the sunlight. He nods at a couple of older Westlake ladies who scuffle with their walkers, trying to get good seats for the upcoming worship. Berkshire wears a droopy beige sports coat with dark pants, and looks like a cricket umpire. Dub is in jeans and a Squeeze t-shirt, and also the UT cap, which like everything makes him think of Kid.

Berkshire comes over bearing a tight, open-mouthed smile and sits in the same pew as Dub. "It's as good a place as I could think of," he says, "for a come-to-Jesus session." He tries a broader grin, but his lips stick to his teeth. "Anyway, Austin's Finest probably won't be in here." The curtain way up there behind the pulpit is the color of blood.

"Go ahead," says Dub.

"What you saw between me and Wyatt…." He touches his face.

"Undercover work. Really dedicated to your craft."

"We've had a thing for a month. I admit it: an actual, serious thing. I met his boy and everything. Then he called me Friday and told me the boy was missing. I made sure I got the case. So no, it's not a coincidence. But there's nothing…. You know cops, right? You never heard of a cop pulling strings to get an assignment and help a friend? I was trying to help him find Hunter."

"Why should I believe a word?" Dub says.

"Because I could've left you dead in the sewer. Remember that."

Dub nods. "Convenient when your corroborating witness is shot dead."

"Maybe Wyatt was playing me, Storm. Maybe he set up the kidnapping all along. I don't know. I don't like to think so."

Dub bends forward to breathe different air, thinking he can't believe he's sitting here with this guy. But what he's saying is reasonable. Dub's been fitting and refitting the pieces. He placed a dummy call to Wyatt. That sent Wyatt back to New Braunfels. So whoever shot Wyatt and Kid couldn't have known they'd *be* in New Braunfels. It all breaks apart in Dub's mind. Could Berkshire have enlisted someone to follow Wyatt, and kill him wherever he drove? But why? Especially with that poor boy dead in a hole.

"Whoever shot them last night," says Berkshire, "who's to say it wasn't your friend Collins they were after?" He looks around, lowers his voice. "He was a dealer, right?"

"What a coincidence, man. Kid's drug connections shoot him in front of the same house where a missing child's body is hidden."

"I know you're pissed," Berkshire says. "I don't know what to say."

"Tell me why you did the press conference," says Dub.

Berkshire wiggles his jaw. "The family," he says. "The family insisted."

"Who?"

"The mother. The aunt. The grandfather. They all agreed."

"Now that this has happened," says Dub. "Don't you know what it looks like? Hunter gets taken but there's no ransom. Instead, the note says, 'Stop Killing Austin,' which sets it up to look like some environmentalist nutball took him. You hold a press conference saying as much. Pretty big coincidence, since there's an important vote, what, tomorrow? Thumbs up or thumbs down on the next big Easley moneymaker, with those Aquifer Assurance Association people set up to look like the bad guys. Yup, there you are out front, talking into microphones. Go ahead, tell me where I'm wrong."

The detective is ashen. He blinks, assembling facts. He folds his fingers together on the pew.

"Why he winds up dead," Dub says. "Why anybody winds up dead is the fucking mystery."

"…"

"Did you kill the boy, detective? Did Wyatt? Who put

him in that hole?"

"…"

"The easiest explanation," says Dub, "is you took Hunter. You know that, right?"

"Jesus Christ."

They're both breathing hard, overheated. The service still seems several minutes away: parishioners linger outside in the sun, filter in just one or two at a time. Dub checks everyone's face as they enter.

"So it's a setup," Berkshire says, shaking his head. "I mean, someone and Wyatt. All I was trying to do is…help a friend. I mean, you're right, more than a friend."

"…"

"If Wyatt was really doing this, he wasn't smart enough. I liked him but he wasn't that kind of smart. He was doing it with someone else in the family."

"Not the mother," says Dub.

"Agreed, not the mother. The grandfather or the aunt."

Dub leans back and on the ceiling he sees angels surrounding a beatific woman, trying to fend off a dark devil. For some reason the scene sends him to a time in Addis Ababa when he and a couple platoon members stumbled on an exorcism ceremony in front of a church. Chanting children clapped while a skinny man spoke calmly with a priest right until the moment when he began screaming and grunting and writhing, then flipped backward into a crowd of onlookers as though seized, landing on several of the children. Dub hasn't thought about that exorcism in years, takes from the memory an overpowering proximity to evil.

"What can I do?" Berkshire says. "What can I do to prove I wasn't in this?"

"Simple. Let's drive a couple blocks and get another cop on the case. Tell 'em everything we know. You're compromised."

"Fine," Berkshire says.

"Fine," says Dub.

But they don't move. Berkshire whispers: "Goddammit, you know I can't. Nobody knows. Nobody *knows*."

"That you're gay."

The detective nods. "I'm not," he says. "I'm not ready."

"So what's to stop me from going?" says Dub.

Berkshire licks his lips. "I can help. I'm trying to help. I traced that little red car." He pulls a laser printout from his jacket. "It's registered to a company. Antebellum Services, Inc. But I can't find a damn thing about Antebellum. Nothing online, nothing with the state. Collins hooked up with a woman Friday night, and it was her car?"

Dub reads the sheet. "That's what he told me."

"We sweat the family," says Berkshire. "We get the truth out of them."

"There's no 'we,' detective."

"Goddammit, I'm trying. I can't tell. I can't tell anything. Was it you set me up, Storm? Are you this good an actor?"

"I know what I know, and my best friend got killed." Dub feels his face heat. "I won't stop."

"You and Wyatt? And your friend Collins?" Berkshire looks genuinely afraid. "You all set me up?

" . . . "

"A big black guy with a scar." Berkshire shakes his head. "I don't know Wyatt's friends. I couldn't be seen with him like that…." He folds a bit, puts his palms over his eyes. "I can tell from the way you carry yourself," he says. "Under all that stoner bullshit. What were you? Army? Marines?"

" . . . "

"Fell on hard times, got messed up, couldn't get clean?"

"Detective, we both know *I'm* not in this."

Berkshire nods, defeated. "But you know what it's like to come down a long way."

Dub's phone rings. He looks down and sees Heather Easley's number. He holds an index finger in the detective's face, then stands and walks to the back of the church, where several corkboards feature multicolored signage and a giant chain droops down from a chandelier and anchors to the wall. "Yes," Dub says softly.

Heather says, "Have you seen Angie?"

"Last night. She came to my place, but she was gone this morning. I figured she went back home."

"She came to your…?"

"…"

"Mr. Storm, is there something you're not telling me about my sister?"

"Of course not. And I'm sorry, Heather. Please tell your father how sorry I am, too."

"Can I see you?"

Hearing this, Dub's stomach aches. "When?"

"Now. I'm at my place downtown." She gives him the address. "And don't lie to me about my sister. I bet you've never taken a stupid breath in your life. Don't start now." She disconnects.

He walks back to the detective who pulled a weapon on him, who cracked him in the skull, who cuffed him, who tossed him onto that front lawn. In the interim, the band has stepped back up to their instruments and now begins playing some jazzy walking-around music, and a pastor enters shaking hands like the president. Dub's neck prickles like a bulldog's. Time accordions out into the thing he always hated, the complication of politics. Anyone who allows his sense of self to grow too thick. Anyone stuck in everything they ever were or are.

"There'll be lab work on shell casings," Berkshire says. "I'm not sure what they can tell from Hunter's body. Maybe there's other forensics."

"What went wrong?" says Dub, to himself as much as anyone. "Why did they start killing people, starting with that boy?"

"I'll find out what I can. I'll show you the reports."

"So that's it?" Dub says. "Tip of the cap, tell the sucker he should trust you, and that's it?"

"Fuck!" says Berkshire, and though the pre-sermon conversation around them is still audible in this big room and though the band is going through its major-chord paces, the curse echoes hard, causes some of these Methodists to frown and others to smile indulgently. In a near-whisper, the cop says, "The second anyone finds out he and I were together? Romantically together? I get sent to Huntsville and get a needle." He stands.

"Where are you going?" says Dub.

"I told you. I'll talk to the lab guys."

A lady singer with a country lilt takes the mic up front and starts singing a paean to the Almighty. The large congregation warbles along.

"We'll get this guy," Berkshire says. "And we'll kill him." He walks outside.

*

Before driving to Heather's apartment, Dub finds Pete behind a vacant building on South 1st. He's chatting up three older homeless guys who seem about as tired of Pete Bellingham as everyone eventually gets. Dub pulls the younger man aside and tells him about Kid.

Pete cries. Tears run down his sunburned cheeks, he dribbles snot onto his upper lip, sits on the curb and covers his face. He's just filthy. "Who did it?" he says. "Some skeez looking for his stash? I knew people who died. But not Kid. He was golden."

"I don't know who did it," says Dub. "But I'll find out. Did anyone else go in that house on Greenbriar yesterday?"

"Naw, man. I stayed there a long time. Does he…have a family? Aw, shit. Shit."

"His parents left Austin way back. I don't know how to get in touch." Dub softens. "Pete, think back to Friday night.

Remember you saw him talking with some guys at George's? Tell me everything. How many were there, what they looked like, what were they talking about, were they laughing or yelling, arguing, acting weird?"

Pete is on the curb, knees together, looking forlorn. He says, "I think two guys, old guys. I dunno, white guys? They were shaking hands, standing outside in a little circle. Sometimes Kid…he does business-talk really good, he's a regular suit. They were laughing like they didn't mean it. The two dudes, they acted like Kid's clients: give 'em what they want, and they'll be on their…. Maybe he was selling the good shit, that Silver Haze? I smoked a little Haze once and my kneecaps came off."

"Describe the men talking with Kid. Older than me?"

"I don't…. I'm not sure, Dub. Sometimes my memory's not so good. I'm trying to think about it, but I'm just…. I'm in a fucking stagmire."

Dub is tense and straight. He's wrung out. "Did you hear any of them say the word 'Antebellum'?"

"Naw. Naw, man. I dunno."

"I know you loved him, Pete. You want to help me find who did this?"

"Yeah. Shit, yeah."

"Find out where Jeb Sparks is. Remember where you picked up my car? That was his rally. Aquifer Assurance Association. Go hang out with Sparks and his friends and see what they're saying."

Pete rubs his eyes and blows snot through each nostril into the gutter. Dub can't help remembering how when they were young teens, he and Kid called this nasty practice "an Arabian."

"Anyone you meet, write down their name, all right? Don't rely on your memory." He helps Pete up, then steps on his foot with light pressure. "Facts, not memories, okay, Pete? That's how you investigate."

"Yeah, man. Yeah. I'll do it. Ahh. Sorry, I know it's

important to be tough."

"First sign of trouble, get out. Crazy and dangerous people running around here. It's not important to be anything."

Pete whips around his hair. "Nobody would miss me, Dub. For Kid, I'll take it all the way, 'cuz nobody but him would ever even miss me." For some reason he crosses himself, backwards, and lights out for the bus stop at Annie Street. Dub tries to give him a few dollars, but Pete breathes deeply and refuses.

Driving north on Congress to Heather's, Dub removes the hat and checks his head in the rearview. The swelling in his temple is crazy, like stage makeup. His skin is transitioning from maroon to purple, with all sorts of coppers and oatmeals and lemons blended in. His right eyelid is swollen down into his field of vision, making him feel half-blinkered, the aptness of which isn't lost on him. But he doesn't believe anything is actually broken, so he's got that going for him. Over the river, he turns right on 7th and stops at the Omni. The town is mostly dead down here on a late Sunday morning; some brunch-goers hoot and backslap a block south, but traffic is nil. The Omni occupies an entire block and is twenty stories, which used to seem like a lot, but the 600-foot crane working on that glass monster just over there—hefting a passel of steel against the blue sky, doing an aerial glissade that communicates its outlandish size—throws off Dub's scale. He walks past the Mexican restaurant here at ground level, noting that it's good, but not as good as Las Manitas over by the bridge.

He asks at the front desk, then elevators to the top. These highest five stories are condo suites partitioned from the hotel's rank and file. The hallway contains a special kind of luxury quiet. Dub almost feels guilty knocking.

Heather's blonde hair is frizzy with neglect and she wears all-black: an oversized shirt and loose slacks. Dub can only see wrists and ankles, but makes himself believe he can perceive her body moving around in there, and feels overpowered. She says, "Welcome to my private floor. I think I'm the only one actually living here. Everyone else is a dotcom millionaire who's hardly ever in town." The suite itself is huge and chilly, matte-black and minimal. Bookshelves feature deco baubles and glass globes, the kitchen counter bears a vaguely anatomical-looking wooden sculpture with a hole punched through the middle. The front den is sunken, and multiple other rooms branch off in either direction. "I made Bloody Marys," Heather says.

Dub nods, wanting one. Everything is a scrape over exposed nerves. He isn't a drinker, but what he really needs now always came from Kid. Why does he feel so young around Heather Easley? He keeps touching the wound on his head, less because he's concerned by the odd pain and more, he thinks, to keep everything up there from sliding loose.

"So now that we're getting all friendly-like," she says, "what the hell are you doing with my sister?"

"..."

"She showed up at your house in the middle of the night, you know what she's going through, and you don't call her family."

"She was hurting and it was pretty clear she was on something. I got her to bed."

She finishes off her drink. "I'll go ahead and assume you didn't mean that the way it sounded."

"You don't think much of me, Ms. Easley."

"On the contrary, Mr. Storm. You've been on my mind all weekend. I'm not sure what agreement you and Angie arrived at." She flourishes with her empty glass.

"..."

"What I mean is are you finding the person who did this. Are you still on the case."

"Yes," says Dub. "Still on the case."

"Thank you." She sits delicately on a razor-thin leather sofa and begins to cry, covering her mouth with a forearm. A vein in her pink forehead is suddenly just there, pronounced and biological. She says, "How can this be happening?"

Dub stands with his cut-glass tumbler of blood, recognizing the moment's heroic potential, and also feeling terrible for sniffing opportunity. What does he recall about Heather Easley? The fact of her existence hasn't occurred to him in two decades but now it all tumbles out of him: a dozen times watching her climbing in or out of an expensive car all legs and curved neck; seeing her on the sidelines in those white canvas sneakers; talking at a party and discovering she loved *Star Wars* and Pink Floyd; the time she teased him for wearing a puka-shell necklace and they wound up under the moonlight tower in City Park with other friends and a water-balloon fight broke out; the time he stood aside and watched her dance with Austin's other beautiful teens down at Auditorium Shores, doing mock incantations of the Twist and the Watusi and kicking up dust that powdered the trees.

"She didn't come back," Heather says. "I don't know where she is."

"She was calm. Crushed but talking clearly."

"You've known her a couple days, Mason. She's capable of…. You probably think I view myself as her mother."

"She talked about the size of the world," says Dub. "She said she might just drive off and go anywhere. But it was hypothetical. She was trying out the idea."

"She's lucid now. She's up walking around, hell, driving a car. But we've seen her in electroshock therapy, we've seen her strapped to a bed. And it can go quickly. She lied about our gardener raping her, had him sent to jail. She lies about things."

"Forgive my saying so. But there isn't much for her to lie about anymore."

Heather bites both her lips, one then the other, as if testing them for numbness. She looks so beautiful to him, Dub can hardly stand it. He's fairly sure Heather isn't putting out the "ravish me" vibe, though now that he looks around this apartment, every picture frame he can see has been turned face-down. Some part of him finds this promising.

Nevertheless, he says, "Tell me about the city council vote tomorrow."

"No," says Heather. "Nobody cares about any of that now."

"But before last night. How much was riding on coming out of the vote with a go-ahead to build in Sunset Valley? A million? Ten million?"

"We won't build now," she says. "How could we? It's off. It's all off. Every time we look at that place, we'd think about…. Why would they do it, Mason? There's no reason. There's no reason in the world to hurt Hunter."

"I don't mean to be…." He's almost whispering. "Listen, the way I see it, there was exactly one reason to take him in the first place."

She puts a knuckle to her lips and searches Dub, hopeful, plaintive.

"Trying to sway that vote," he says.

Heather frowns, slightly shaking her head, calculating. She's looking through Dub, seeing implications, whereupon some truth strikes and her shoulders pull back, her spine goes straight, and her expression grows exceedingly displeased. She says, "I'm going to stop you right there before you say something we'll both regret."

"I know it's a terrible time for your family."

"I have something to show you," she says. "In a minute. Just…for now, stop talking."

"If there's anything else you can think of," he says. "Just anything that seems strange. Maybe your father. Meeting with people you didn't know. How did he react when he found out Hunter really was missing?"

She rises again, walks to the kitchen, refills her glass.

Dub looks out these picture windows at the state capitol: big pink-granite nipple in some renaissance style. Just behind it is the UT Tower whose inscription Dub remembers, and he says it wistfully: "Ye shall know the Truth and the Truth shall make you free."

"No," Heather says, carrying another drink. "My father is beside himself, same as everyone."

"And do you know a black man with a scar on his face? I mean, trust me. I want this guy as much if not more."

She puts her elbows on a mantel, cradles her head, full glass held carefully above. She's crying again. He doesn't move. He tries to remember what pretty women do, how they work you over, but maybe this isn't that. Anyway his knee joggles and his fingers squeeze this glass, she's just killing him: that cleft chin, that blonde forelock. He thinks: *this grief is genuine, she's not sociopathic.* But he breathes, he looks away, he's had scorned wives weep on his shoulder and press against him hard, he's had exotic dancers kiss him with gratitude, and while none of those evoked his pubescent fantasies as Heather does, they nevertheless could've led to messiness. His housekeeping habits aside, Dub is still sworn off messiness. He must simply *be.* Nor will he be a knight-errant, because that's messy, too.

She says, "Do you want another drink?"

"I do, but I can't. Let me ask you a question. Did you know my partner?"

"The one who died."

"That one."

"Collins. No."

"But you remember him. From high school."

She sits down again, this time flouncing in a strange circular recliner. Her posture becomes recumbent, abject, and her face is streaked in shadow. "I don't remember. It sounds awful but I slept with a lot of boys."

"He told me about this company, Antebellum Services." Her face belies nothing. "I'm just asking."

"Sorry."

Dub thinks through some alternate reality, where he's

here by choice, where he lives here with Heather. She's chilly and vacant, but he can't help it.

She says, "I don't know who to trust."

Dub thinks: *A person who trusts nobody can't be trusted,* but of course, now he doesn't trust anyone either.

"Death," says Heather. "I mean, it's right there."

"…"

"Tell me what happened," she says. "I know your parents died. I was thinking about you last night, and I remembered. Maybe if you told me about that. They disappeared, didn't they?"

"…"

"My mother died having Angie. I was mad at her for a long time, but it goes away. She's always been so fragile. I do have something to show you, Mason. I want to trust you. Please, tell me something. How losing your parents…affected you."

Dub blinks and says, "Well, I'm not doing that."

"…"

"…"

"Then sit with me and enjoy Austin," she says, looking out the window. "I've had enough alone time this weekend."

There's a long silence. How can she be so hard-boiled and so unguarded at once? He can't get comfortable, can't find the angle of repose to view her as anything but alien. He doesn't want love. He just doesn't want it.

Heather's face is turned away, and he wonders if she's asleep. Twentysome years of service—dark, dark service— can rid violence of its power, can shear empathetic flesh from bone. But it never contains a moment like this: unsure whether you want to move, halfway between falling asleep yourself and standing up, shaking the woman awake with a growl. But Heather isn't asleep. The bent-metal line of her jaw reflects sunlight and then she comes to a decision and turns his way, standing up, reaching into a pocket of these pants, coming out with a piece of paper. She hands it over, and Dub reads:

$1 Million
Noon Sunday
Under The Bat Bridge
No Police

"This is new?" says Dub.

"I found it this morning, under the door in Westlake."

"Not even an hour from now," says Dub.

"Yeah."

"Congress Avenue."

"Yeah."

The long-awaited ransom note, two days late. "Whoever left this," Dub says. "How could they think…? Why would you pay now?"

She's doing something with her eyes, something desperate, trying to find something in his face. He tries to give it to her, whatever it is.

*

He parks in the *American-Statesman* lot and waits for noon. The Congress Avenue Bridge looms above, concrete arches that span Town Lake. In summertime, the bridge's underside is home to the world's largest urban bat colony; somewhere around a million Mexican free-tailed bats hide out during the day then at dusk fly into the hill country in search of insects. Their nightly exodus is a major Austin tourist attraction and a source of city pride, drawing hundreds of observers who ogle a seemingly endless bat-column which looks like nothing so much as smoke. Except now it's winter, and the colony has migrated south to Mexico, so nobody will stand in rapt anticipation of what's about to happen here, and nobody will applaud. Dub blends into the scenery, watches a few joggers go by on this trail, assesses angles of approach.

His phone rings.

"I just heard from the coroner's," says Berkshire. "They're assuming strangulation for the boy. They took prints off his neck."

"All right."

"Meaning he wasn't alive when he went in that hole. Maybe that's some comfort for the family."

Dub has his eye on a sandy path that leads to the trail underneath the bridge. A few bike riders hiss by.

"What's the latest on your end, Storm?"

"I don't know how I can be any clearer, detective. I don't trust you."

"They're not my fucking prints on Hunter."

"What's this like? It's like a child tugging your apron over and over, swearing he didn't do it."

Berkshire says, "I got someone I trust tracing that car your buddy Collins borrowed."

"Listen, man, you try to pin any of this on Kid…."

"Like I said," Berkshire answers, "I checked you out, Storm. Not enough to get specifics, but if I can't get specifics, it probably means you used to be a badass. Why the fuck you're a burnout now, I can only guess. But I plan on avoiding your bad side anyway. On your pal, my lips are sealed. Silent Bobby, that's me."

Dub touches his head. Antebellum Services. That little red car. He wouldn't be surprised if Antebellum goes right back to Easley Partners, which would mean the red Miata belongs to the Easleys. Who was the woman who took Kid home Friday night, and then lent him that car? Could it have been Heather? Dub can't figure out why. Why would the Easleys approach Kid, separately from Dub?

"So you're not gonna tell me anything," says Berkshire.

It's five minutes before noon. Dub doesn't want to go down under the bridge first, knows he should hang up the phone, is filled with indecisive energy. He's also been scoping out this parking lot, and it doesn't seem Berkshire is spying on him. Maybe he could be up in one of those hotels. But if this new ransom note—this *post*-ransom note—is from Berkshire, why is he calling? Weak, unfocused, Dub says, "Your name is Bobby Berkshire?"

"What's wrong with that? What the hell kind of name is Dub?"

"I guess you haven't worked Vice. It's twenty dollars' worth of leaf. People call 20-inch rims 'dubs'...."

"I worked Vice in Dallas, you stoner shithead. Forgive me for mostly locking up assholes who deal heroin and meth. But y'know, any time I feel like arresting some Phish fans down at the frat house, I'll be in touch."

Dub still has the phone clamped to his ear, but stops listening. What's the feeling? This is a ridiculous place for a meet. What's to stop the Easleys from bringing the entire APD down on that spot? You'd just trap yourself with the guano under there. Dub gets that prickle at his neck and starts walking the sandy path, his footfalls sounding like a bouncing tennis ball. Left turn into the bridge's shade. He's half-running now. Young mothers pushing strollers meander this way. Dub's eyes adjust quickly, and he peers up at the graffitied bricks that lead to a garbage-strewn darkness where bridge kisses land. There's nobody up there.

"What the shit," says Dub.

There's a neat white stack of something among the tattered cardboard, muddied rags and hypodermics: Dub clears away some of the junk and finds several rectangular little slips of paper, which when he bends over turn out to be five old-fashioned Polaroid snaps, in mint condition. He flips through: candid photos of the Easley clan, one at a time, Thomas, Heather, Angela, Wyatt, Hunter...each with their name written in ballpoint ink across the bottom.

"Storm?" says the voice in his ear. "Storm? Hey, Storm?"

Dub scans his surroundings. Whoever left these pictures here would want to know who showed up, whether they were a cop, whether they brought a suitcase full of money. Across the water, on this jogging path's twin, a few teens zip past on bikes, a couple holds aloft a cell phone to click a photo, and indeed, there's a large man in a dark hooded coat striding away, looking over his shoulder. "Stop!" Dub says, "Stop!" and sure enough the guy starts running. Dub shoves the phone, the Polaroids and his cap into his pockets and takes a running dive into Town Lake.

He pushes air from his lungs and sinks deep, streamlining with his hands up over his head and his legs kicking from the hips. It's probably 500 feet across, and his sneakers filling with water mean his best chance at speed is to stay submerged. The shock of cold water recalls other times, bloody nights. His lungs burn, but it's a wistful burning, not unlike the sting of Silver Haze. When he surfaces he's probably more than halfway across but he can only see his own splashing and the bridge's undercarriage. Indeed, it's too difficult up here so he's back down again, eyes open, seeing vegetation and post-industrial shapes, dolphin-kicking, until finally his hands scrape egg-shaped rocks and he stands having made it across, people are gawking, his suspect went left on this path toward downtown, knowing it would take too long for anyone on the south side to climb up and over, never suspecting a lunatic would swim straight at him. Way down the path, already nearly to the South 1st bridge, the big man in the black coat runs like an athlete and Dub takes off after him, hard as he can go, not quite a quarter-mile behind. He leaks river water, arms thrashing so hard his ribcage feels it. This isn't Wyatt Parsons he's chasing. Dub can go this fast only for maybe half a mile, but better to close the distance and maybe put fear into this guy. Nothing is in his mind, nothing but calculations of distance and speed, status checks on his limbs, possible avenues of escape.

By the time he reaches South 1ˢᵗ, the other man is unseen way ahead and it's impossible to know whether he's stayed down here by the water or taken the steep grade up onto Cesar Chavez and into the city proper. Dub continues on the trail, sprinting blindly. When he crosses under the railroad bridge his hands are shaking a bit and his quarry seems lost, but then he catches a glimpse of his man under the new pedestrian bridge at Lamar and the black-coated man gets tangled up in a crowd by the ramp and takes a leap to avoid these pedestrians and his hood flops off, Dub can see his shaved skull and dark skin. The man looks behind, sees Dub charging, runs under Lamar and finally does abandon the trail, climbs up, but Dub anticipates this and cuts the corner, closer than ever now, they're pounding past the YMCA and the Amtrak station, Dub feels the limits of his wind and wonders how this guy is still going.

They're across the railroad tracks, and the man disappears into a big rusted warehouse, some kind of light-industrial metal works. Dub is about twenty seconds behind him and his gauges are in the red. He stops outside this open door, then gets low and charges in. A gunshot sounds.

A bullet strikes the concrete doorway and ricochets up through the tin roof, so a pillar of sunlight shines down. Dub's evasive action lands him behind some metal fabricator the purpose of which he has no guess. The building is like an abandoned hangar with big sliding doors in each side wall, which have been left open. There are a few rows of workstations divided by equipment and ancient stacks of raw materials; he could play hide-and-seek in here all afternoon. Nothing about the man he's pursuing says "amateur." Dub tries to control the volume of his frantic breathing, stays crouched, listens and advances deeper into the must and rot of this place.

Has the man taken off again through one of these two giant doors? Is he standing inches away ready to pull his trigger? These are the matters Dub has been trained to know by instinct, yet he recalls his miscalculations following Wyatt into that construction site yesterday. The point of this THC-soaked life he's lately developed has maybe been to blunt the impossibly sharp spike at his psyche's leading edge, and it appears he's succeeded. *My confidence*, he thinks fleetingly, advancing, *exceeds my competence*. These things—which way this pro went, whether or not he's about to kill Dub—seem impossible to know.

There's a fleet of sewing machines piled harum-scarum atop one another, some antiquated mechanical bacchanal, and Dub hefts one, feels the coolness of its blue metal case. Like a discus thrower he winds up, careful not to brush the refuse around him, and flings the sewing machine across this hangar. It lands with a clatter that rivals gunfire, but is followed by no other sounds, no more bullets, no inquisitive footsteps. There's a rusted awl on the floor and Dub puts it in his damp pocket.

If it were him, Dub wouldn't run, and he wouldn't react to big sounds either. He'd stay still, gun raised, backed into one of the corners, awaiting the subtle movements of his stalker. Dub keeps advancing down this rightmost side, coming to the sliding door, squinting, peeking into an alley which leads to an empty parking lot. Maybe the man took this escape, and maybe Dub will be prowling around in here alone for an hour, chasing a ghost. But he slinks ahead, low, basically breathing normally now.

He makes up his mind: he grabs a corner piece of some random lead pipe and hurls it hard against the wall beside him, then snatches up some washers, a small motor, a rubber mallet, and begins flinging them everywhere: across the warehouse, high up against the ceiling, back the way he came. He duckwalks forward, picking up any stray tool and device, chucking them everywhere; the clangor is terrific, now a glass jar of screws, now a pencil sharpener, now an electric power strip. He picks up speed as he does this, still low, plowing down this aisle like a power forward, raining debris and covering the sound of his footfalls, and now he's perhaps fifty feet from the warehouse's far wall and the black man slide-steps into view holding out his gun in a relaxed firing position but Dub is closer than he expects so when he squeezes off a round it's too high, Dub can see the muzzle adjust and now it's down on him and there's another explosion…and he makes contact with the man's knees and thinks he sees the gun flying above him. They plow together into a back shelf that smashes through a window, Dub can't hear anything, but he sees the man's fist coming and it pummels that same part of Dub's head, and he sees the gun again and in fact it's still in the man's other hand, and Dub reaches into his pocket and comes out with the awl and drives it down into the man's foot and everything stops for a moment, there's a howling in Dub's ears and he's on hands-and-knees and has broken glass and metal parts raining on him, there's just this man's feet one of which is leaking blood, and then his hearing returns and yes there's a howling Dub assumes must be the result of his proximity to a fired pistol but turns out actually to be the man screaming and Dub stabs again with the awl but misses and the other man's legs are gone.

Dub is woozy and expects a bullet in the brain. But the man is running again. Dub lifts himself and follows bloody footprints into this other corner, then back the other way, into a smaller warehouse, through another door and into the blinding sunshine: there's a sandy scrapyard here and the man is limping through, anguished, he turns to fire again and Dub sprawls belly-first in the dirt and when bullets again start flying he rolls behind an incapacitated land-moving tractor. Dub can finally see the other man's face: a damager's mashed-in visage with a diagonal scar leading from under one eye across his nose to his opposite ear. He finds himself surprised that it's not a face he recognizes. He finds himself surprised it's not someone he knows from Major Partridge's platoon.

The man once again turns to escape and Dub tries to get up and follow him out into a back lane, probably a feeder to West 5th, but his head feels incredibly awful and he can't catch his balance, and he plows into a big reptilian tire. He falls down, this time on his back, and gravity's warm clutches are too sweet.

*

He recognizes this.

It's the release of incapacity.

He looks at a limitless blue sky framed by a tin-roof overhang and a depilated maple, and he revels in insufficiency. His head and face throb. He has still taken too much pride in himself, has gleefully sleepwalked but still viewed himself as a concealed weapon. He was too ready to get back into this, too ready to be a killer again. From this prone position it seems clear he's been living a farce, not actually immersing himself in the underbelly but rather cloaking himself, winking, perhaps waiting. And now that he's been beaten, true prostration comes. There's really, actually nothing he can do. The sky lovingly comes crashing down on him as a three-dimensional object and his eyes close on their own.

He thinks about Kid with the unknown men Friday night, just hours after telling Dub how badly he wanted to milk cash from the Easleys. He thinks about Thomas Easley, initially unconcerned about his grandson's disappearance, with more money than a sultan. He thinks about Heather's quest to get the Sunset Valley construction underway. He thinks of Jeb Sparks sneering, and Angela Easley's frailty, and Berkshire's affair. Hell, he thinks about Partridge, who's capable of anything. Their faces emerge but then fade.

He flops over onto his stomach in the dust. He reaches into his back pocket. His wallet is marinated in river water. He pulls out his license, some postage stamps, a couple faded business cards, an ATM card, a sandwich shop loyalty punch card, a time-ravaged fortune-cookie fortune, and thirteen one-dollar bills, and he spreads them all on the ground around him, seeking to dry them in the sun. The Polaroids are in his other pocket and they're soaked: the names have mostly smeared off, and the pictures themselves have washed out to a yellow, chemical tint. Finally he pulls open the wallet's lining and finds three joints, soggy as dumplings. He doesn't have a lighter anyway. He lines them up in the sun with his other accouterments and falls back again, with his hands crossed over his chest.

*

After a long rest, he finds his UT cap on the warehouse floor, falters back to his car and drives to find Pete. William Cannon is busy as ever, but Brodie Lane is asleep; the only indication of yesterday's protest is a cluster of signs planted like crosses by the Easley gate. Dub reads: "Save Our Springs!" and "Dear Capitalism, It's Not You, It's Us. Just Kidding. It's You." and "The Clothes Have No Emperor." Pete isn't here. Dub drives to South Congress and there he is, panhandling in a yuppified neighborhood that was Needle Central fifteen years ago. Dub honks, interrupting Pete's act, which regularly changes from breakdancing (he's terrible) to singing (he's alarmingly good) to stand-up comedy (he's indecipherable).

"What happened?" says Dub as Pete climbs in.

"I saw that guy, Sparks. He's in Guero's. People are like, coming in to see him. They're talking and yelling."

"Yelling what?"

"Dude, I couldn't hear tons. I got a taco and I paid for it, but they looked at me funny. None of 'em said weird shit. None of 'em, like, ran out the back door."

"It's important, Pete. You get it, right? That first note said 'Stop Killing Austin,' and if it turns out these guys really are involved somehow…."

"That guy Sparks is drinking beer and some shots. It's Sausage Town in there, all dudes. It wasn't happy yelling, but he wasn't freaking out. I dunno, Dub. He said he was trying to set up a meeting with a rich guy, like, he's waiting to hear if this rich dude will talk about water with him. And he wanted hot sauce, he was yelling for some hot sauce."

Dub thinks about this. With Hunter dead, the development is probably on hold, but Sparks and the Aquifer people still think maybe they're getting negotiation time with Thomas Easley? It makes Sparks seem like more of a patsy than ever. Sparks is talking about water while everyone else has moved on to blood.

"Did anyone say anything about a little boy?"

Pete squints and it's ridiculous, like only now is he listening hard. "I didn't hear it," he says.

"And nobody said anything about Kid."

"No way."

"Sparks is still holed up in there? And the people coming in to talk with him…."

"I know some of 'em. Guitar George was there for a little while and then he came over and said hi. Other guys like that."

"Guys like what?" says Dub.

"Y'know, the ones always pissed off about everything."

"Any reporters? Anyone writing in notebooks, anyone with a tape recorder?"

"Maybe?" Pete says. "Sparks was yelling about water. Yeah, I think: 'Nature makes a drought, man makes a beverage.'"

Dub puts the Accord into drive, and the sky is cloudless

again but the sun reflecting off his hood is brighter than the genuine article above. He says, "How'd you find Sparks?"

"Oh, Dubber, trash like me, we got ways, man. Every busboy's my friend. Hey, where we going?"

"Westlake."

Pete plays with the radio, finds a classical music station and cranks up the violins, conducts the orchestra. Dub rolls down his window, thinks about losing his hair, tries to let it go. He feels guilty for this drive's meager enjoyment.

"You hung out a lot with Kid," he says loudly, into the wind. "Was he in trouble?"

"Kid never had no trouble his whole entire life," says Pete. "That dude was so plumpendicular."

Would someone tracking Kid every hour of every day have noticed something amiss? Maybe. But maybe a beguiling future only he saw was enough. Something's wrong with what went down Friday night. Nobody knew Kid better than Dub, and he can't figure it. But the guys he talked with, the woman he took home, the car he borrowed…it feels part of the same marauding chaos that took him down. Dub guesses he's been half-a-step removed from the grief that should be crushing him today because he's developed a very good sniffer for betrayal. He can't decide if he really would've wanted that job: tracking Kid Collins, learning everything a good detective can learn. You can't really get to the bottom of a person, can you?

"You get high today?" Pete asks, sort of angrily.

"I don't remember," says Dub.

They park across the street from the Easley manor and kill the radio. Dub can't see into the garage, but there are no cars in the driveway. He isn't sure who he expected: Heather, maybe, reporting Dub's suspicions. Or the man he just chased. It will come to confronting Thomas Easley, but Dub wants to sit for a few minutes and just think. They wait and watch that huge Easley house, and Pete says, "Maybe they'll adopt me," which makes Dub laugh.

"I chased the guy," he says. "The one who must've killed

that little boy. I had him. But why is he ransoming after the fact? He *has* to know. He has to know the police have already told the Easleys that Hunter's gone." Which means the most recent note isn't about ransom at all, but rather blackmail. And the Polaroids? Proof that this psychopath knows the family personally? Proof that he'll turn them all in?

"It's a yellow brick house," says Pete. "Follow the yellow brick house."

Dub's head feels bad, and he suddenly throws up out the driver's side window. He coughs and spits to get the taste out of his mouth, then leans back breathing hard, clutching the steering wheel. His molars are gritty.

"That's not good," Pete says.

Dub doesn't answer. He rides a hilly nausea that somehow radiates from his brain, thinking if he can withstand a minute or two he'll start to feel better. In his mind, he recites the Oath of Commission three or four times, waiting.

"I guess it's not really yellow, though," says Pete. "The house."

"Close enough," Dub says with his eyes closed.

"It's more like…it's maybe the color of…."

"Saffron."

"I don't know what saffron looks like."

"Like the house."

Pete clicks his tongue. "No, you know what? It's the color of tofu scramble."

Dub opens his eyes. Pete's right. It's the color of tofu scramble. A long while goes by. The sun-stippled neighborhood is intensely quiet; even grackles know to stay away. Recycling buckets squat beside topiary, ivy creeps over short stone walls, a fire hydrant pokes extra-tall out of a dirt hillside like a polyp, and nobody drives in or out of any of these gated driveways.

Pete says, "I'm really hungry."

Dub doesn't answer.

"I think there's a Whataburger over there."

"There's no Whataburgers in Westlake."

Pete sighs. "Kid used to say, 'You know who eats at Whataburger? Poor fat people. Eat like the person you wanna be.'"

"Mm-hm."

"'It's about your class, like smoking and NASCAR.' And I was like, 'But those are three things I really love!'"

"Pete."

"I'm just tired of a fish taco costing five bucks. I mean, I can go down the street and get three for three bucks!"

"Pete. You have to stop."

"Except I guess the place down the street actually closed down."

Dub puts the radio back on, and finds a Postal Service song that smooths everything out: uptempo but quiet electronica that's exactly Austin at this moment. It's followed by a new Pearl Jam song about the president. Finally Dub hears a super-quiet and amazingly sad Reindeer Section song called "Will You Please Be There For Me" and Dub says, "If I was the one who got out of the car Friday night, instead of distracting those idiot cops. If I got out and walked up to Wyatt's house, instead of making Kid do it. If I did. I mean, I should have. And then I'd have looked in the window, and I'd have seen the Savakis bag. I would've known what it meant, and all this wouldn't have happened."

"Car," Pete says, and glittering chrome blinds them, they duck instinctively though the car turns before it ever gets to them, and it's Berkshire's Altima.

"Goddammit," says Dub. He waits a minute and gets out, sidestepping his vomit. Pete follows, and they walk directly to the Easleys' front door, which is ajar. Dub doesn't ring the bell. They step inside. The air conditioning is on. He hears a voice down the hall and just strides pissed-off in that direction. He rounds a corner and walks in on Berkshire holding Thomas Easley at gunpoint.

"Jesus, what the fuck," Berkshire says. "I almost shot

you." He's standing and Easley is sitting, and two gigantic televisions are muted: one shows footage of explosions over Baghdad, and the other shows the Longhorns playing Purdue.

"Mr. Storm," Easley says. "Y'all have very good timing."

"Shut up, asshole," says Berkshire. "Dub. I figured I'd find you already here." On his face, Easley's hopes for rescue are markedly dashed.

"Hey," Pete says, looking at the TVs. "What's blowing up? Is that PlayStation?"

"Like I was saying," Berkshire tells Easley, "I'm here for the motherfucking truth."

Easley takes a moment to calibrate, looking back and forth at the standing men. He says, "I admit, knowing the truth would be nice."

"Save the act," says Berkshire, and he steps toward the older man and places his gun barrel on Easley's right thigh. "We'll skip the part where you dance around and I pretend like this is a polite inquiry."

"That little boy is dead, is all that matters," Easley says. "Shoot me. Shoot me wherever the hell you want."

Dub says, "Let's everybody just."

"True or false," says Berkshire. "This is all extremely good for business. Pin it on a couple dim-bulb protestors. You cooked it all up, told Wyatt to hide the boy."

". . ."

"Go ahead. Tell us we're wrong."

"Y'all think I'd tell somebody it's okay to take my grandson."

"I not only think it," Berkshire says.

Easley looks at Dub, a modicum of fear in his eyes.

"You can't help yourself," Berkshire says. "Guys like you can't. It's never enough. If you sat in your mansion and *didn't* try to fuck everyone that crossed your path, you think the world would be disappointed."

"If this is what I did," says Easley, "why is my grandson dead?"

"You don't care," says Berkshire. "What the fuck do you care? Look at his parents. What the fuck chance did he have? Better to end his misery early on."

Easley is shaking now, gripping his leather armrests. Dub looks at Pete, whose mouth is open listening to all this. On the leftmost TV, file footage of Saddam Hussein giving a speech intermingles with live coverage of a peace protest from Vancouver. "What I don't care is if y'all kill me," Easley says. "I'm the one who'd be better off."

"Sounds like a guilty man to me," Berkshire tells Dub.

It's like Easley has touched his foot against some deep unseen electrical source that shocks him into a palsy; his eyes get big, his vibrations are vehement. "What do y'all want me to say! There's no reason for any of this! We were gonna win the council vote! Y'all want money! That's all y'all want from me!" Berkshire is about to say something in response and half-waves his gun, on which the safety is most decidedly not engaged because the gun goes off. A bullet slashes through an end table causing a lamp to topple, and thuds into the baseboard of this wall, not five feet from where Dub stands.

"Jesus, detective," Dub says. "Maybe this requires just a little bit of finesse." He bends to pick up the lamp, and sees a novelty placard that's fallen off the table which reads: 'A Man Is As Big As The Things That Annoy Him.' "Mr. Easley, nobody wants your money."

Easley looks at Berkshire, eyes wide and frightened.

"I've got something to show you," Dub says. He comes out with the waterlogged Polaroids, hands them over. "Do you know who took these?"

Easley scans them, lingers over the one of his grandson. He drops the others in his lap. "No."

"I find that hard to believe, man. People run around snapping Polaroids at you every day?"

"I remember *when*," he says. "It was a party here, in the backyard, maybe a month ago. I just don't know who. Someone. A guest, maybe someone with the caterers. He took pictures of everyone. I didn't think a damn thing about it."

"The fuck?" says Berkshire, snatching the photos. He flips through. "Here you are right here, Thomas Easley, you slick asshole. Look at you. Guilty as shit."

"A name," says Dub. "Or what did he look like."

"We're throwing you in a hole," Berkshire says. "We're losing the key."

"I don't know. Just go. Just get out of here."

"It was him," says Dub. "Whoever took these. He killed your son-in-law, and he strangled your grandson, threw him in a hole and poured concrete over him."

Easley fidgets. "Y'all both are *evil*."

Berkshire runs a hand through his hair. "I'll blow your fucking foot off. Every lie you tell, I'll shoot off another toe."

"Y'all both are evil, coming here like this into my house, after what happened to that boy." He stands half out of his chair to reach for Berkshire's gun, drags it with both his hands back down against his knee. "Go ahead and do it. Do it!"

Now Berkshire growls and lowers himself, nearly straddles Easley's lap, takes hold of the older man's face and head-butts him, hard. Dub grabs Berkshire from behind and shouts, "Pete!" and the two of them pull the cop away. Easley's large, masculine head lolls in his recliner.

"Go!" Dub says. "Get out of here, man, let me talk to him. Pete, show Detective Berkshire your rock collection. Outside. Now."

Berkshire's own dome is bleeding and he steps disgustedly from the room. Pete follows, looking like a spooked-out 10-year-old. Thomas Easley, this powerful, timeless personage whom Dub feared two decades ago, is a mess. Blood from his forehead covers his face. Dub finds him a golf towel hanging from a hook, but Easley just holds it.

"Villains," he says. "Y'all are goddamn villains."

"Did you do it?" says Dub. "Did you ask Wyatt or the man who took those pictures to hide Hunter away for a couple days?"

"Of course not." Easley is still shuddering, but now with tears. "I don't know what your game is."

"Just tell me everything."

But all the old man does is cry.

"All right," Dub says. "Listen. Take a minute. In the meantime, tell me about Antebellum Services."

Easley places the towel against his forehead, sniffing. "What?"

"I know about Antebellum. You had those guys talk to my partner Friday night."

He shakes his head and coughs. He says, "I don't know from any Antebellum." He's looking Dub squarely in the eyes, but Dub has seen a photocopy of the car registration. Someone is lying to him, and lying is the grand unified theory, it's the mortar binding everyone to everyone. It's not news, of course, but for some reason just now it hits Dub hard. He sees them all hanging from the city, feet kicking above a chasm, desperately holding fast by virtue of the construction matter pouring from their mouths. Without the lies, he doesn't have a job, certainly. The only alternative he ever knew was in the platoon, until Kismayo. And then he probably ushered in the contagion himself.

"I'm just trying to get to the bottom," Dub says.

"You think I'd do this to my family. Why can't it just be a stranger? A thousand people hate me."

"…"

"Your bastard partner. You think…you think *he* wouldn't pull off something like this?"

"Berkshire's not my partner, Mr. Easley." He looks at the TVs. They're showing Al-Jazeera footage of injured children crawling from rubble, and it's midway through the second half, with Purdue up one. "Why do a thousand people hate you?"

Blood has dripped down into Easley's eyes, and he's ruefully done crying. He gestures with those massive hands. "Some of 'em are jealous," he says. "The others think our family got here on their backs. We're wrecking the city by building it."

"And you don't think so."

"What do you imagine they're fighting for?" says Easley, motioning at a few Third Infantry soldiers trudging out of an Abrams tank, possibly from training footage. "Is it all revenge? Is it all making sure we get our oil?" He pats his injured forehead, and winces. "Y'all aren't stupid, Mr. Storm. They're fighting for *our* hearts and minds. Are we gonna be scared, or are we gonna keep living. Are we gonna march ahead, or are we gonna retreat. So let's go win an easy one with a professional military, skip the draft, prove to ourselves it's painless to keep going higher and higher. Good goddamn, I believe my head is broken."

"You don't know a guy with a big scar across his face. Wasn't he the one taking all your pictures with that Polaroid? This dude *knows* you, man. Come on."

He looks down, shakes his head at the bloody towel.

"What could he have hanging over you anymore? Give him up, Mr. Easley. The guy who took those pictures of you and your family just out there in your backyard. It's the same guy who shot Wyatt and buried that little boy last night."

Easley is still looking down, still shaking his head.

"Thomas. Please. He killed my friend, too."

He examines his blood. "I remember. A scar on his face, with a camera. I ain't seen him before or since. Now y'all keep that sumbitch cop away from me. I won't give him anything else."

"Did you set up a meeting with Jeb Sparks to talk about his protest down there?"

"No. Uh-uh."

"One more," Dub says. "Your grandson is dead, and I'm sorry about that. Have you talked to the press today?"

Easley's gaze is fixed a thousand yards into a future only he can see.

*

Dub steps through the hallway, back out the front door. The light kills him, sends pain through the beaten up side of his head. He looks around at the sprawling front yard, the faux-aged stone wall, the preschooler's Technicolor toys lined up at the side of the house. He wants to feel rage, that's what this cusp of emotion is. He wants to look at this privilege, these homes set apart from the city in their unspontaneous enclave, and be disgusted. But he's tired and actually a little buoyant, a bourgeois feeling that often comes when a case is on the border of wrapping up. The possibilities are narrowing. He wants revenge for Kid, and he'll have it. Right now he can't get behind toppling the rest of the world's injustices, he just can't. Men will always live in houses like these.

He doesn't immediately see Pete or Berkshire, though the Altima is still parked in the driveway. He walks closer to the street, and hears masculine burbling. The two of them are sitting on the curb, smoking weed.

"Here he is," says Berkshire, who has a driblet of drying blood running from his forehead down around his nose. "The voice of reason."

"Don't worry," Pete says, reaching into his hair. "I got a little something for you, too, Dubber." He comes out with a third pinhead.

"No thanks," says Dub.

"Judgment in his tone," Berkshire says. "He always a judgmental prick?"

Pete says, "The Dubbermeister is okay, believe me."

"Just made a phone call," says Berkshire. "The guy

tracing Antebellum. He hit one last wall. One database back to another one, which I guess isn't too uncommon when the bad guys are trying to cover tracks. But the registration on that little sports car? Just drops dead. Goes into a database I guess he can't see."

Dub sits on the curb, elbows on knees, the third monkey in a row. "He called the press. He called and told them Hunter's dead."

Berkshire French inhales, spits into the street. A while later he says, "Fuck."

"Yup."

"Can't lose that council vote now."

"Yup."

Pete says, "So what, that dude just gets everything he wanted anyway?"

"He does," says Berkshire.

"And he doesn't even get, like, arrested?"

Berkshire looks at Dub. "Because there's a chance he knows a couple things I would rather not get out, for the moment he does not."

"You ever seen him before, Pete?" asks Dub. "He wasn't one of the guys talking to Kid at the party, right?"

"Naw," Pete says, shaking his dreads. "Naw."

The day has suffered its mortal wound, and here comes dusk's big conceal. A creeping chill rises, the hairs on Dub's forearms pleasantly crawl. Acacia bushes across Michaels Cove are gnarled and jagged, without bloom. A boat jeers by on unseen Lake Austin, probably not 500 feet away.

"So you were holding out on me," Berkshire says. "Those Polaroids. How'd you come by 'em?"

"Quite a performance in there," says Dub. "Beating up an old man. Let me ask you this. If we got in there five minutes later, would Thomas Easley have a bullet in his brain?"

Berkshire sighs, sucks again on his skinny cig. "Easley won't get away. Cocksucker jerked around the wrong cop."

He laughs unhappily. "No, okay? He wouldn't have a bullet in his brain."

"I dunno," says Pete. "You went pretty fuckin' mental, dude."

"But it was a different kind of mental," Dub says. "Icy cold to burning hot in five seconds flat."

"You kidding me? What that fucker did? What that fucker did to *me*?"

"What did he do to you?" says Pete.

Berkshire smokes and snickers again. "He knows I'm a sucker for romance." Blood has also dripped onto his jacket lapel.

Dub clears his throat. "I believe him," he says. "I don't think he set any of this up. He wanted you to shoot him."

"Jesus," says Berkshire. "That's your proof? He's a titan of industry, and they're the best actors. Seriously, where'd you get the Polaroids?"

Dub fingers the frayed cuff of his jeans, closes his eyes with resignation. "I had a run-in with the mystery guy. Our man with a scar. I chased him. I almost had him."

Berkshire reaches in his sports coat and comes back out with the Smith & Wesson Dub took off him yesterday. "Next time," he says.

"You're offering me your piece?"

"I'm suggesting you get one of your own. A lot less chasing required."

"Dub's badass," says Pete. "He don't need it."

"He's lucky it wasn't me," Berkshire says. "He'd have got his wig split."

Dub says, "I'm sort of still sitting here waiting for you to leave, detective. No more beating the crap out of old men, right?"

Berkshire puts his gun away and thinks about it, then nods.

Several minutes pass unadorned. Then Pete says, "This is my last one, Dub. If you don't want it…."

"Well, hell, give it here, son," and Dub takes the pinhead and looks at it, rolls it between his fingers. "I'll hang onto it."

"What," says Pete, "you think you can't smoke when shit gets serious? Dude, everybody knows that's, like, the *best* time."

Berkshire says, "When he's right, he's right."

But Dub still just looks at the joint, feeling his heartbeat shove something forward in his mind, some thought getting thumped and nudged further and further toward the end of the shelf.

Pete says, "Remember the time when Kid got that White Widow? Compared to that, this shit's ragweed. We drove out to Salt Lick and ordered cobbler before it all got taken, right? Then we stepped out into the cow patties and fired up and I saw Jesus Christ. He was out in the field talking to a sheep, trying to get the sheep to agree to a little hide the holy sausage. And then we ate ten plates of brisket and the cobbler and Kid paid for everybody."

"What's that place on Greenbriar?" Dub asks Berkshire.

"Foreclosure for tax nonpayment," Berkshire says. "Officers on site to forcibly eject. So now it's an honorary safe house."

"Honorary just for you, I'm guessing."

Berkshire grins unhappily. "My oh my, aren't you a pretty asshole."

Dub thinks that the supermarket was always going to get built. Strings are dangling from the sky, jerking limbs, knocking over trees, pulling fresh new buildings up out of the ground.

"What comes next?" says Dub.

"I was about to ask you the same question," Berkshire says. "All I know is life in prison is too good for some people. Next time you see whoever this motherfucker is, take the fucking shot." His pants pocket begins to ring and he stands up, fidgets with his phone, says, "Office calling," but doesn't answer. He drags hard on the remnants of his pinhead and tosses the final millimeters against a thoroughly unsoiled gutter. "Take it light, boys. Here's to finding the sick fuck and ventilating him."

Walking back to his car, Dub realizes the sidewalk is covered with snails: little orange pasta shapes trying to slink out of the dying sun. He makes sure to avoid stepping on them, but knows he must have killed many already.

*

It's dark. He and Pete go back to the house on Johanna and eat anchovies from the jar. The old place feels heavy with ghosts, the kind that might not even belong to you. Pete makes noises like maybe he should leave, and Dub says stay. They turn on the 14-inch that's still hanging in there after at least a couple decades, play with the rabbit ears, and it turns out the Academy Awards are about to start. The plan is eat something, rest his head, then get back out there and hunt for the killer. He won't get anywhere else with the Easleys. He needs to find the man he chased, get the story from him.

But he creaks into one of the rocking chairs and feels ten years old, a sad smile breaking across his face. He can't really see through the static, but it sounds like Steve Martin welcoming everyone.

Well, he could fall asleep. It would be nice. Why his heart isn't heavy is a mystery. He's not even high. He realizes maybe more than anything he's turned into a forgetful man, and maybe he likes it that way.

But Pete says, "Hey, it looks like we're surrounded," and that's how Dub understands his eyes are closed, and he fills with panic. His every muscle tenses, he's alert as a panther. Pete has only meant the crazy furniture in this living room, all the old chairs, literally surrounding them. Yet Dub feels he's right. Sleep isn't possible and orders are always coming from somewhere. *My God, Kid is dead.* It's always been time to wake up.

Perhaps ten minutes later, Dub is in the kitchen fetching frozen waffles, and he hears Pete say, "Who's the slice in the black giddyup?"

Heather Easley is standing by the front picture window, hesitating to step forward and ring the doorbell. They watch her perform some mental or emotional gymnastics. She's psyching herself up. Then she realizes she's being watched, presses against the glass to see past the very old linen curtains, waves hello with chagrin. Dub lets her inside.

"Angie called," she says. "I finally heard from her."

"Well, good," says Dub.

She paces across the room and sits in the same wing chair Angela chose two days ago, when Dub was happily high and waiting for this bedlam to alight. "Maybe not. She's in San Antonio."

"There used to be this pot bar in San Antonio," says Pete.

"You didn't get him," Heather says. "The one who left the new note."

"No."

She crosses her hands, ladylike. "I pleaded with her to come home. I talked to her for an hour. All I could picture was her driving straight into the Alamo while she wasn't looking. She wants to come back, I know it. She wouldn't answer the phone otherwise. Mason, I'll pay you more, just please get her back."

"Ms. Easley, there's something else we have to...." He turns off the TV. The pinhead that's still in his jeans pocket cries out his name. "I can't tell if you're the world's greatest actress."

She blinks, and looks from Dub to Pete, back again.

"I'm guessing you haven't checked with your father in the last little while," says Dub.

"He wouldn't help," she says. "Angie doesn't listen to

him."

"The guy I chased today. He knows you. He's been around your family. He had pictures of all of you, taken up close."

"…"

Dub says, "Is there something you want to tell me?"

It's like something in here is ticking, but there are no clocks on the walls.

In a tiny, wrenched voice, Heather says, "Fuck y'all."

Dub says to Pete, "Will you give us a minute?" and Pete plays good soldier, even gathers up the dirty dishes and beer bottles, retreating to the kitchen. On his way out he says, "I'm on a train to the big adios." The back door slams and Pete is gone.

Dub sits in the rocking chair directly beside Heather.

"You didn't want to do it," he says. "You fought against it, but got overruled."

"This is just…."

"You played a part because you thought you had to."

"…"

"The only piece you liked was making a fool out of this guy who had a crush on you back in high school." He hears himself say this, is how he knows his heart really is broken. Old, buried, fractured friend.

"You think I took Hunter. You think I…killed him."

"I think you set it up," says Dub, not sure if he believes it. "I think it went bad."

She breathes so deeply it sounds like she's wheezing. "Am I under arrest?"

"I got a feeling it's coming down the pike."

Her eyes brim. The night's doubleness is palpable, its innocence and ill intentions. It's above them, now that they're down here at the bottom of everything, as strangers. "Angie," she says. "I just want Angie back. She's ruined. She'll never be the same, she'll never get right. Do whatever you want to me."

It's not Heather he really wants. He remembers who she was by the end of high school. He remembers discovering she was foolish, that she treated her friends badly, that she slept around. She had the simulacrum of a personality, produced commotion—forgotten dates, awkward encounters, a famous episode involving a young science teacher who was fired for his attentions—as if by breathing. Hell, by graduation, when the local army recruiters knew him by name, he rather pitied Heather Easley. But just now it hurts looking at her.

"You had no way of knowing," he says. "You figured Wyatt would keep him safe."

"…"

"She'll find out. Eventually Angela will find out."

Heather's eyes become hard. "You think I'd take her baby away for one minute, knowing what it would do to her?"

She's this close. "I do," he says, his voice changed. "I honestly do."

"No you don't."

"…"

"I'm sorry," she says, and she kisses him, they kiss, her porcelain face is against his, and he opens her dark clothes. They walk to the front bedroom and she pulls him out and she rides him. He tightly wraps his arms around her waist and he pounds into her from below, rapid fire, hard enough to hurt. Her body is magnificent and fearful and she comes wordlessly, gouging his chest, as he thinks *why why why why.*

*

He turns on the radio beside the bed.

"…*were shown on local television as prisoners of war, while four others were shown dead. The convoy was ambushed outside Nasiriyah, taking fire from Iraqi tanks, rocket-propelled grenades and small arms. Mortar and tank fire also killed several U.S. soldiers near a canal, which is a key entrance point to Nasiriyah. Meanwhile, American and British forces took the airport outside Basra, but the battle for control of that city rages on."*

"Do you know how I remember the Gulf War?" Heather says. She's on her stomach and facing away, the black dress pulled up over her hips. "It was the morning I smoked crack for the first time."

"Yeah?"

"It was a Thursday right before my 30th."

"..."

"When I drink like today, I remember the feeling. Getting liquored up then driving around. I'm a savant when it comes to finding good stuff. Put me in any city, I'm a cocaine bloodhound."

The bedroom is dark but the door is open; her body is twisted unnaturally, and the hallway light reflects off her naked bottom.

"You know what it's like?" she says. "What you're chasing? They're not kidding: the first time is the best. Addiction is like being the most homesick you ever were, you just always chase that first perfect time. But it doesn't exist anymore."

He clears his throat but doesn't say anything.

"Almost six years clean," she says. "But I mean, I want it so much right now I'd do anything."

"..."

"Just so I don't have to feel this."

A heavy weight passes up through Dub's groin, past his stomach, into his chest and head. Elation. But because nothing lasts, it cracks and he leans back and closes his eyes and begins talking:

"My parents went to see the Stones at the Cotton Bowl. Halloween '81. I wasn't in the States, and I guess we didn't talk. Gone more than two years at that point and maybe I called twice. They didn't understand why I was so distant and probably angry, I didn't understand. I still don't understand.

"They knew musicians. My dad knew the Fabulous Thunderbirds, from Antone's. The T-Birds opened for the Stones, said come watch in Dallas, so they did. People saw my parents there. Afternoon show and it rained so bad people were almost getting electrocuted. They're fortysomething, jumping in somebody's car and driving up.

"On the way back from Dallas the car got all the way to Round Rock and the driver was high and couldn't see in the rain and he broke through barricades and fell off the highway. I imagine a long fall, like in a nightmare. Nobody even saw them go. The car landed in some runoff, some flooded sinkhole filled up with, I dunno, leftover tar and whatever from the highway expansion. Everyone's body vanished except the driver, who got his head wedged in the steering wheel. Everyone else floated off and never got found.

"I had an uncle who swore they never got in that car. He interviewed people at the show. He talked to the T-Birds, for years he tried to talk to Mick Jagger. It was Halloween and people were in costumes. People got mixed up. For years when my buddies in the service asked, I said stuff like they were trapeze performers who died in each other's arms, they got vaporized by a jet engine, they were mob informants.

"That was a fun one. Something you can always count on, a soldier knows *The Godfather* backwards and forwards. There are nights you're belly-down with IEDs everywhere and you can't move until someone comes forward to sweep, and you'll hear guys whispering favorite lines. Any time someone's got a beef, they're going to the mattresses, like that. So when I said my parents got hit by the mob, they ate it up. I had this story going in my twenties. Mom's ex-boyfriend was a button man in the Lucchese crime family and she saw some things, they thought they killed her in a Miami hotel but it was another girl and my mother got away, she made a new life in Austin with my dad who didn't know anything about it.

But after twenty years they found her…and I had an elaborate story for what happened next. This is before I learned to shut up. Now with the Internet they'd know I was making it all up. But maybe it made me popular, being the guy with this sordid tale."

He realizes his fingers have been touching her cold hand.

He says, "It's true right? They basically did vaporize. And they were good, and maybe they died thinking I didn't love them." He stares clear-eyed at this ceiling, finding in it the same crenellations they did. "Pretty cold to make up stories for years about how your parents died."

His eyes are dry. He feels outside himself, like all those times, so many times standing with a rifle on a hill, leading a group into an enemy camp, adding and subtracting numbers and feeling nothing. "I saved it up, and it's not even a very good story," he says.

Heather rolls over, presses her breasts against his arm, eyes shut tight.

*

In the living room, her phone rings. It's a small noise but they both wake. She pulls herself up from the bed and walks out. His head hurts terribly. He hears her voice from a distance, staccato, like police dispatch through a faraway scanner. It's been a long time since he's done this—this kind of drama—and he's never done it in this room. It feels ridiculous to consider it a frontier, to be scandalized even slightly. Mostly staying in his same old back bedroom is practical. Here at the front of the house, the neighborhood construction that surrounds him is much louder.

He pulls off a blanket and zips up. He smells his armpits. There's an old desk against the far wall, and he always forgets it's there: it's so small, like an artifact they'd display at George

Washington's house. How did his mother ever squeeze her legs in? He knows what's in the drawers, the knitting needles and potholders, the matchbooks and malfunctioning pens. Junk, Dub is sure, his parents would be mortified to know is still around.

"She's on her way," Heather says, stepping into the doorframe, having reassembled herself. "She decided to come back. She's driving back."

"All right." He has to look away from her. He sees holes in this room's chintz curtains.

"I have to go back to my place. She'll be there in an hour."

He can see his reflection in a full-length mirror beside the closet, and he feels hatred.

She says, "Will you…please come with me?"

"I want you to do something," Dub says. "I want you to go into the kitchen and find one of those old-fashioned rolling pins. You'll find it, it's in the drawer by the stove. And I want you to go fuck yourself."

She frowns, then smiles. "You're dying because I have to go."

"Nobody's dying here," he says.

"If I stay for another round, will everyone's feelings get better?"

"If you stay for another round, I'm pretty sure I'll wake up with scissors sticking out of my neck." He's kidding, but he's not kidding.

She comes all the way back into the bedroom. He's seated, and she approaches, his skin is charged by her proximity. She puts her stomach against his face and lightly hugs his head. "We were impulsive. I'm sorry."

He smells soap and violets in her clothing. Softly he says, "You're under arrest."

"On what charge?"

He doesn't have an answer. He lets his hair be stroked, and he only thinks fleetingly about his bald spot. His weakness has tumbled in on him all at once, but it shouldn't be a surprise.

He drives her home. It's not ten o'clock, but South Austin is asleep. One minute Dub wants to believe she's got nothing to do with all this. The next minute he very much wants to believe she does.

"Come upstairs," she says, and he follows. They take the special elevator and stand far apart waiting for the doors to open. He looks at her calves, these tensed, muscled legs like a bird of prey. She says, "You're keeping a close eye on me."

"One false move."

"I don't know what you want me to say."

"I'll get the guy. He'll tell the truth about everything else."

"..."

"Don't let this handsome package fool you," he says.

The doors ding. She looks at him like she wants to continue the banter, but as she walks out, her cagey grin folds into a flushed half-grimace and she snatches his hand, interlocking their fingers.

Inside, she walks around flicking on lights. He stands beside the bookless bookcase; each switch is an echoing plastic bang. She could shoot him. It would be easy for her to come out with a gun and put him down, but he just stays here. It's a domestic little moment. He finds it easy to imagine this weekend hasn't really happened.

"I think this is one bad person stalking our family," she says from a far-off room.

He doesn't respond.

"So he took our pictures. What does that prove?"

Keep talking, he thinks.

"You don't know my father. I mean, beyond reproach, that's his thing. He never wants to give them a reason."

Yes, he's expecting a gun. She reappears in this front room and he's ready. But her hands are empty and she's wearing a long silk robe.

"You look terrible," she says. She approaches and gently pulls up on his cap brim, to look at his temple. "Maybe we should go to the hospital."

He puffs out his cheeks.

"Is it better to know a terrible thing for sure?" she says.

"I don't know. Probably not."

"I don't want anything to change," she says. She releases his ballcap, checks the clock, steps to the kitchen and runs the tap, filling a steel kettle.

"Let me look at your eyes," Dub says.

"What?"

"Come here." He joins her in the kitchen, beside the tap-water hiss. She demurs, he presses close, gently straightens her shoulders.

"Mason…."

"Let me see."

The green rings of Heather's eyes are down to the thinnest halos, and her pupils are beautifully shiny black gyres.

"Either you snuck out to the ophthalmologist," he says, "or you just got high."

She smiles brightly. "Don't be crazy." She turns on a gas burner, deposits the kettle thereon.

What Dub wonders is: did he miss the dilation when she knocked on his front door a couple hours ago? He says, "Too late."

She says, "Then don't be cruel."

This time he kisses her. She answers. It's a long, slow affair, and she reaches up with one hand to hold his neck. As they gasp, she gives off shrill notes, straining against him and recoiling as their faces roll side to side. His hands touch the cool robe, then press in further and land on her ribs and she's so thin and solid, it reminds him of everything wonderful he fears. She's emboldened by his touch, with her free hand begins to pluck at his waistband. They breathe, her face is against his neck, he kisses and licks her ear, she has him out in her hand, and he spins her around, pulls up the robe, bends her forward against the counter. He cups her breasts from behind. Her head tips back. He thrusts, she returns, they gain a rhythm and it lasts much longer. She moans; he can see her smiling in profile. It goes on. The kettle whistles behind them.

There's a rattle in the living room. It's the front lock; the door flings open, Angela Easley steps inside. She drops everything. Something shatters, keys chime, coins roll on hardwood.

"At least nobody bought me sympathy flowers," she says in a shellshocked voice, and Heather makes a wordless noise, not a name, not an orgasm, she's gone from him and her robe rolls back down her waist like a curtain. She stumbles partway to her sister, realizes the robe is open, turns back toward Dub wearing an aggrieved expression, covers her hips, her breasts, and she strides back to the stovetop and turns off the gas.

"Darling," says Heather. "Why don't you lie down in the bedroom and I'll bring you some tea."

"What the *fuck* are you doing?" Angela says. "You phony fucking maniacs."

"Come dear, you've just dropped some things…."

Angela looks Dub in the face, then slides her eyes down his body, where his hands cup his genitals. Listless, without a smile, she says, "I wouldn't be surprised if it was the two of you."

Heather issues disclaimers and tut-tut noises, helps scoop up her younger sister's bag, hustles her down a dark hallway. Dub remembers feeling like this: it's a feeling the service taught him, a feeling the platoon bred. Back to mastery, back to the bleeding edge and stepping over, maybe doing what's necessary. The snoring that's been in his head for four years has stopped. Right now the more shameless men he used to know—Barnett, Nelson, maybe Odom— would think about walking right into that bedroom and having both sisters at once. Barnett bragged he hadn't been in anything but a woman's asshole for years; Nelson usually commented that Barnett had a loose definition of the word "woman." Well, sex is tied up in the most dangerous things men do, just as it's maybe tied up in building a city from nothing, or from very little. Dub zips himself up again and runs water over his face. He's fracturing, was apparently ready to fracture, was just waiting for the right client. But he feels a nub in his jeans pocket and comes out with Pete's pinhead. Orders in his mind say enough is enough, wash it down the sink. Dub stoops at the stovetop, clicks the electric switch, and gets a faceful of blue flame, inhales, and it feels all right.

In the living room he's subsumed by darkness; even the recessed lighting doesn't stand a chance, only reaches a few feet from the ceiling before giving up. He blows smoke. He hears a woman sobbing behind a closed door. Out here everything is still. The heat of this Silver Haze for some reason puts him in the mind of Africa, where he never once lit up.

On tables and shelves he sees those picture frames, still turned face down, probably ten of them.

Something coheres.

Jesus.

He knows it: he's going to pick up one of these frames, and a smiling Heather Easley will be alongside…a strapping black fellow with a scar across his face. And Dub will feel ridiculous because if he'd only looked the first time he was here. Or it'll be Heather and Berkshire. Or it'll be Heather and Kid Collins. Dub's hand pauses, outstretched.

It actually occurs to him for a few moments not to look at all.

But he does. He reaches for a large silver frame and lifts it into the light. Heather is hugging another woman, someone Dub's never met.

He reaches for a smaller frame, and the same two women smile out at him. The other woman has red hair, looks younger than Heather, is nearly as lovely. Dub plays out this calculus, tries to fit in the redhead. Some family member? He keeps turning over frames, walking around this room that overlooks the state capitol which at night is no longer brown but rather glows white like the moon. In this one, the redhead is alone. In this one, she's eating a hotdog and giving a peace sign. Here's one where Heather and this mystery woman are standing beside shrubs fancifully trimmed into the shape of a dragon, though it's clearly not the Easleys' Westlake house in the background. And finally in this one, she and Heather appear not to know a camera is nearby, and are sitting together in a hammock, naked from the waist up and locked in a passionate kiss.

Dub's phone rings, albeit with a waterlogged tone.

"Got a call," says Berkshire. "Damnedest thing."

"…"

"Storm? You there?"

"Yeah."

"What's, ah. Everything all right?"

"Sure." Dub sits in the weird circular recliner, and his feet come up off the ground.

"I get it," Berkshire says. "You and your hoodrat buddy are partaking."

Dub tries to think, with the night on top of him. It takes him a while to say: "I'm at the daughter's place downtown."

"Like I said, my phone just rang. It was the other sister."

"The…."

"Angela Easley. She came clean, Dub."

Dub ignores the telecommunications hiss in one ear, can still hear faint crying from the next room. "When was this?" he says.

"She knew the kidnapping was coming, man. It's probably why she's so flipped out that it went so bad."

"…"

"This is some deep shit she agreed to, right? I'm thinking maybe we rattled daddy's cage, the whole mess started falling apart. I can't say I expected it, but cases like this, I mean, up the food chain, down the food chain. There's a natural progression."

"She called you and just…confessed."

"I'd love to take credit."

Dub doesn't hallucinate when he's high. But he has suspicions right now. He kicks his legs a little and says, "All right, man."

"She wants to come in. She wants to make it right, and I mean she never thought it could get crazy like it did. You can go get her for me."

"Allllll right…."

"She knows who he is, the guy you chased."

"Hang on a second."

Dub gets up. He walks through the living room, into the dark hall. He stops at this first bedroom, phone against his ear. He frets touching the doorknob. Now it's quiet in there, it's quiet out here, Berkshire isn't saying anything. Dub holds his breath, reaches…turns…pushes….

There are bodies on the bed. Four feet, a turned-away back, a paisley blanket. Heather's lovely white face in a tangle. Her eyes unblinking, reflecting a bed-stand light, pupils enormous. He wonders how he could feel so much after a three-day reunion, but his pulse is crashing, tidal. A hand—whose hand?—poking out beneath the coverlet. One of the feet moves. A knee shifts, the whole blanket's texture folds, there's a jerking movement as someone flinches and Heather does blink, she smiles a little and pulls aside the coverlet to show Angie sleeping on her shoulder.

Dub steps back into the hallway, closes the door. "She called you exactly when?" he says.

"Exactly?" says Berkshire. "Exactly fourteen minutes past your scrotum getting caught in a chainsaw."

"Like you hung up on her, and right away called me."

"Something like that."

"And where is she?"

"Frost Tower."

Dub says, "I don't know what that is."

"The new one they're building. The tall one."

"And she told you who the guy is. The killer."

"All she said is she knows who," says Berkshire.

Dub is out the door. He's down this hotel corridor, calling for the elevator. "It's interesting," he says. "Tell me what else."

"What else. There needs to be something else?"

"There always is."

"For a high little motherfucker, you sound like you know something."

"Truer words," says Dub, and the elevator rings its elegant angelus. "See, I was just looking at the younger Miss Easley about thirty seconds ago, sound asleep. And I'm about to lose you, detective," stepping into the red velvet lift, "but feel free to give me a call back."

"…"

Sixteen stories glide by as Dub's ears pop. He bustles through this atrium lobby as glass partitions shimmer all the way up the hotel's spine, a moiré effect whose gloss dazzles in darkness. His phone rings again.

*

Dub answers. "Who hired you?"

Berkshire sighs on his end. "You know who."

Dub walks west on 8th, turns south on Congress. He says, "Thomas."

"Come on," says Berkshire.

"Both of them," Dub says. "All of them."

"You are a big pain in my ass, Storm. I can't say it wouldn't have gone bad without you. But it surely would've been easier to extricate myself."

"The fuck does that mean?" says Dub.

"I had to know what you knew, keep everyone running around until I could figure a profitable exit. In some ways, I guess you're too smart for your own damn good."

"..."

"She's a sweet piece. I'm guessing you also know that by now."

"So you're at the top of that tower. You want to lure me up there so you can what. Throw me off, make it look good."

"Son, I'm on the road. What am I, some James Bond bad guy who tells you my plan before it's finished?"

"But you are a bad guy."

Berkshire says, "I guess I am. But not the worst one."

Dub has stopped beneath the Paramount's flashing marquee. Nobody is out here and the sidewalk is oddly pristine. "Here comes the full confession," he says.

"I don't know the answer, Dub. I can't understand why it went down like this. The little boy wasn't supposed to get hurt, and poor Wyatt didn't know a thing, he thought the kidnapping was real. The one you want is Pilgrim."

"Pilgrim."

"Your facial-scarred individual. He did 'em all. For the life of me I can't figure out why."

"Who is he?"

"Ex-cop. Dallas. All he has to do is sit with the boy, I had him set up at the family's house out at Dripping Springs. It was a good plan. Easy fucking money."

"So you weren't trying to force any truth out of Thomas Easley this afternoon. I walked in, you were blackmailing him."

"After that poor little boy was dead, seems Pilgrim and I had the same idea. He had a note and some Polaroids. I had a gun. I just called him for the first time since it went bad. Told him I'd bring him some of this here money. That's why he's way upstairs in that tower, waiting for me. I'm pretty sure he's got plans to shoot me between the eyes. I have to figure I'm tops on his hit list. Why the fuck he even *has* a hit list."

Sweat dries off Dub's body as though he's marooned in the desert. For a few instants he believes there's literally nobody out here on Austin's biggest, busiest promenade, that he's trapped alone in someone's vacant game-scape. Then a few locals shout happily down Colorado, kids just glad to be out on a school night. The moon is tiny and bright, in transit. There's a trembling in the air, silence resumes, Dub gets a sense of great distance—the capitol, south to the bridge and beyond—and he thinks maybe the explanation for this silence is in the shapes of buildings and structures as the night deepens and they lose their outlines. Everything kind of slipping away. But this waterlogged box in his hand hisses.

"You could've put one in me," Dub says, "and dropped me in the sewer."

"I could've," Berkshire says. "But maybe you think too much of me. I'm not a killer, Dub. I mean, Jesus. I don't just fucking kill people."

"That's flat-out heartwarming."

"And the truth. I don't know why Pilgrim went crazy."

"You're the one who started it up with Wyatt."

"It wasn't tough," says Berkshire. "He was beefcake. I genuinely liked the guy."

Dub's footsteps are instinctively silent. The lights in these storefronts are off.

"Maybe she hooked up with Pilgrim," Berkshire says. "Maybe she showed him that rocketship of a body. I can only speculate. I mean, she's still alive."

"You want irony?" says Dub. "Pretty sure she's gay."

" . . . "

" . . . "

"That freak you out or something?" says Berkshire.

"I don't care what people do."

"Funny, I think you do, Dub. Oh, I don't think you care who people fuck. Or what gender they fuck or whatever. But don't try and tell me you don't see a sewer everywhere you look. Don't try and tell me you're not a moralizer. You can't kid me. Every white knight looks down his nose at the world."

"…"

"Anyway," Berkshire says. "Two things. One is Pilgrim's up there if you want the satisfaction. Call the APD, talk to him, kill him. Up to you, but given recent developments there's a pretty good chance that gung-ho motherfucker will try and shoot his way out."

"What's the other thing?"

The detective pauses. "I really, truly am sorry about your friend Collins, man. I wasn't kidding about tracing the car. That was all true."

Dub says, "So this is one more dance I should do for you people."

"Oh, buddy. Don't beat yourself up, right? The service door in back of Frost Tower is propped open."

"You've been a cop a pretty long time to make detective. And you're throwing it away for a few grand?"

"I admit it's not optimal. Things sounded so simple. But the hand that's dealt, right? Sorry I had to lie to you, Dub. You did right by me, and I didn't like doing it."

"So you're off to Mexico?" Berkshire doesn't answer. The line is dead.

Dub stares up at this stiff-chested tower. Its windows are dark; it looks gothic in the moonlight. The flag of Texas waves limply alongside its U.S. counterpart, and these Congress Avenue doors are bolted shut. Dub walks around onto 4th and sees the loading dock, unguarded and open-mouthed. The idea that any of this exists in Austin outside an architect's fever dream is bizarre; for most of Dub's life, downtown was a squat wasteland at night, as the government worker bees left for suburban sprawl. Now this tower is flanked by a giant L-shaped hotel in one direction, and a white swaybacked office building in the other. After this weekend, it's hard not to view all this construction less as progress, more as virus. He pushes through an unlocked fence and steps into this municipal cave. An empty security guard's chair is pushed up against a concrete wall. A wedge of plywood is jammed into an emergency exit, revealing a sliver of electric light. Dub feels exposed, looks around, steps inside.

There's no choice. Orders.

The Frost Tower basement is mostly finished and the service lighting is on, but there's no signage. He wanders around in a box pattern for a few minutes, finds a dark room containing several silhouettes. Gingerly, he tries the light switch and discovers about twenty sewing dummies in military rows, and realizes his pulse is doing a drumroll. The faceless army stares at him, or through him, or past him toward what's coming next. He continues through the basement and discovers an elevator. It hums, halts and hovers. There's nothing else to do. Weaponless, he presses the topmost steel button that reads "33." His legs grow heavy. The red digital readout doesn't change until it flips from "1" to "22," then his head feels light and the elevator chirps for each of the final floors. The doors open on a yellow-walled room with a black-and-white floor. Dub steps out, sees nobody.

He moves into a hallway that ends in a glass wall, through which Dub can see the massive crane arm, out there in space like a giant robot about to grab the building. Night air is blowing in, though things look fairly finished up here. He steps into an office suite which hasn't been outfitted with equipment yet, but which is clearly meant to represent penthouse luxury. Windows jut at intersecting angles, offset by metal beams that make this feel like inside the Statue of Liberty's torch. Dub moves silently, gets a view of adjacent offices through this series of window-pods. He can't see Pilgrim and he doesn't want to be the first to speak.

Further from the elevator, the walls have no paint, the floors have no carpet, and several windows have yet to be installed. The breeze is stiff 400 feet above the pavement.

Workers have left a few kits lying around, but nothing so convenient as a nail gun. Dub rifles through these plastic packs, and the best he can do is a straight-edge razor that's about six inches long with no handle. He finds a heavy screwdriver and some industrial double-sided tape, and makes a clean job: the razor snugly fits in a slot along the screwdriver's base, the tape secures it and gives him grip. He puts it in his waistband and keeps moving.

In a dark office he creeps away from the windows, listening. The thought occurs: Why would Berkshire suddenly start telling the truth now? What would he gain with Dub out of the way chasing phantoms? Dub feels he's made nearly a full pass of this topmost floor. He puts his back against sheetrock, listening, hearing only that howling wind. Then there's something beside him, along with a sound, but Dub is busy processing the thing that's beside him, this sudden illumination, and doesn't quite relate it to the sound, which now that he thinks about it was kind of a loud clap, and the thing that's beside him—just next to his right arm—is a light beam that emanates from the sheetrock that's against his back, there's a *hole* in the sheetrock, and light is suddenly punching through into this room. All of this takes fractions of a second, seeing a white, gaseous cylinder, knowing that it's been caused by a gunshot. Then there are more. Dub starts to move. More holes bang through this wall, more shots, more tubes of light, tracking him as he heads for a doorway that isn't yet a doorway. He gets low, more holes perforate the wall above him, he stumbles on, holding his cap down tight.

This Pilgrim is not a talker.

Dub is back in the hall, sprints away from the gunfire. There's a body behind him, taking aim. A bullet zings by, Dub turns a corner, there's a stairwell door here and he kicks it open but doesn't enter. Instead he backs away, into another office, giving himself a view of what's coming. He doesn't hear Pilgrim reload, which qualifies as faintly good news:

assuming this is the same gun from earlier today in that warehouse, it's a Glock 17, meaning seventeen-round magazines, and he's probably just fired about twelve. Of course, the asshole may have ten more magazines in his pocket. Or he may be using a different gun. Or he may be holding more than one gun.

Here he comes. He's made a wardrobe change; he's out of the hooded coat and dressed all in black. He's maybe six-foot-three and 220 pounds. The scar is a thick straight line across even features, and his expression is disarmingly unaffected by this pursuit. He's limping. He holds the Glock in both hands, he's neither frowning nor breathing hard. He doesn't see Dub but doesn't chase recklessly, quietly pushes open the stairwell door, takes a few reserved steps in, looks down. Dub runs back the way they came, and Pilgrim fires two more rounds. It's been a long time. Dub has done the close-quarters thing in African catacombs far less symmetrical than this. Of course, he was almost always the pursuer.

He enters a suite whose lights are on but many of whose windows are unfinished. The wind is loudest here. There's a tall pane of glass resting diagonally against a wall and Dub hoists it, waits for Pilgrim to enter, slaps it across the larger man's body and Pilgrim turns away, accepting the blow on his shoulders and squeezing off another round, then Dub thinks he hears a click mixed into the sound of glass breaking and he'd better be right, the Glock had better be empty, because Pilgrim turns toward Dub, about seven feet away, serene misrule in his face. As Pilgrim takes a moment to aim his kill shot, Dub trusts everything they ever taught him—the level of *belief* is what's so jolting to experience, the degree of trust flaring amidst this "now" of unseen deals and weak relenting—and accepts that if there's still a bullet in the chamber, he's dead. He drops the window's remains, pivots and swings, Pilgrim's trigger jerks, Dub's open hand connects, no bullet spins, he pounds Pilgrim's arms, feels something give and it's a sweet shot, nobody could keep a gun in his hands under such circumstances. The Glock thuds away onto the floor.

"Tell me!" Dub says in these whirling, whipping-sky sounds. "Why'd you shoot them!"

Pilgrim reaches in his pocket and comes out with a switchblade.

"You're a cop!" says Dub.

Pilgrim clicks a button, and the blade swings out silver.

"There was no reason to kill the boy! You were about to get paid!"

Pilgrim looks at his gun on the floor, apparently decides not to retrieve it.

"Why'd you kill the boy!"

Pilgrim points at Dub with the index finger of his non-knife hand. Dub helplessly feels his adrenaline curdle. He pulls the razor contraption from his jeans.

Limping less now, Pilgrim lifts a stray metal strut, a spare part from these window frames, and swings it Dubward, Dub backs off and feels how close it came, sees it return in reverse aimed directly at his eyes and also sees Pilgrim's knife-hand make an upward slash—the strut is meant more for distraction than actual attack—and Dub feels the blade touch his t-shirt. He finds a big shard of glass on the concrete floor and backhands it at Pilgrim who dances away but catches it in the shoulder with not enough force to embed glass-in-flesh, but enough to hurt. Now they circle one another, crunching broken glass, Dub knows his chest has been cut but doesn't know how badly, he sees that Pilgrim's shoulder looks wet. Dub recoils against a pane-less window and feels the cold. Pilgrim's strut arrives again and bounces off Dub's ribcage, and here's the knife again, the knife is really all Dub's looking at, and as Pilgrim thrusts Dub dives away, steering clear, slashing backwards with the razor and hoping for contact.

To get close enough to strike means being close enough to be struck, and Pilgrim seems content with this equation. He advances, and Dub knows he has to get that strut, because one sharp blow to the head and he'll be down, and then he'll be sliced open. He feints and presents himself as a target, but lunges backwards with terrific quickness, nearly boneless, avoiding the strut then the knife, the strut then the knife, and on Pilgrim's last swing Dub counter-strokes with the razor and feels it drag along Pilgrim's arm, and the strut goes clattering away. Blood sprays the floor and Pilgrim shows his teeth.

But before he can register it, Dub feels his own shoulder lacerated, Pilgrim is quick and his arms are long, Dub can only counter-slash but he misses, and for his trouble he takes another cut on the same shoulder. Pilgrim is close, Dub can feel the heat coming off him, and as they dance apart Pilgrim swings with his bloody arm and punches Dub across the mouth, Dub swings up with the razor and makes contact with Pilgrim's chin, something comes off of Dub and for a moment he thinks maybe it's his ear but it's the UT cap which gets sucked toward one of the unbuilt windows and soars out: his fedora gone into the night. Pilgrim is too fast, faster than anyone who's ever wanted Dub dead at close quarters. The knife keeps coming out of the distance, it sticks him hard in the right biceps and Dub can't feel it, he just whirls away balletic and spins back pushing the razor through this fizzy air, blood trails are coming off Pilgrim now as they are surely coming off Dub.

Death is grinning with mechanical teeth over in the corner.

"All that trouble!" Dub says in the wind. "All that planning! And you choke the life out of a three-year-old boy!"

"Rrrrrrr!" Pilgrim says, lunging again.

"Why'd you kill him!"

Dub can feel his makeshift blade coming apart, as the mount made of double-sided tape begins to wiggle. Pilgrim comes forward with hatchet strokes of his knife, trying to end it, getting a glancing blow on Dub's cheek and as they separate Pilgrim slashes once again and again makes contact with Dub's chest, but this one is at closer range, and feels different. It almost feels sweet, a sick sweetness that Dub meets with a smile.

Then Dub's limbs collapse. He and Pilgrim are in the center of this blood-spattered concrete floor and Dub loses his balance, topples backward, lands on his back with his hands on his chest, instinctively trying to cover this horrible parcel that's just been carved out of him. And then Pilgrim smashes one knee directly atop Dub's blade hand, causing the contraption to break and his hand to suffer a terrible cut which is the first thing Dub experiences purely as pain, and he shouts.

"You think I'd kill a little boy!" Pilgrim says, from above. "Y'all set me the fuck up!"

Pilgrim's knife comes toward Dub's neck and Dub claws at the floor while at the same time kicking hard at Pilgrim's injured foot. He kicks again, and this causes Pilgrim to wince and hesitate and meanwhile Dub's hand skitters across the floor and finds the straight razor, now detached, and he lifts it by instinct and jams it sideways into Pilgrim's throat, into the hyoid bone, and Pilgrim's empty hands fly up to protect him from something that's already happened, and Pilgrim's blade falls out of his hands, butt-first against Dub's chest, and Dub picks it up with his good hand and turns it around and tries to stab Pilgrim in the left side of his ribcage, halfway up, aiming at his heart. But Pilgrim grabs his wrist. Dub's final stab is halted. He feels Pilgrim squeeze his forearm, harder, until he can no longer hold the knife. It falls again. Pilgrim has one hand on his throat, and with the other he snatches up the knife and readies a final stroke. Dub tries to look around, tries to get this big man off him, exhales hard and sees a cloud of red. There's no joy in Pilgrim's expression.

But then everything stops.

Dub looks up at Pilgrim. Something has happened to his face. Half his mouth is open, his eyes are fluttering. The weight atop Dub's chest grows less urgent, less directed.

Pilgrim still grips the knife in his hand, but he begins to sway. His head lolls forward and as it tips, Dub can see part of his skull is missing. His brain is gray and exposed. His body descends and Dub rolls away. Pilgrim lands with a wet smack.

Berkshire stands in the doorway still aiming the Smith & Wesson.

Dub inches in Pilgrim's direction, crawls alongside him, says into his staring eyes, "Tell me why."

MONDAY

White ceiling. White ceiling white hand. White ceiling off-white tube. White ceiling white face. White ceiling.

There comes a time when his mind understands that life isn't actually a series of still pictures, even as his eyes are busy perceiving his surroundings thusly.

White ceiling woman's face white hat. White ceiling wristwatch clear plastic bag. White ceiling white hand diamond ring. White ceiling hairy knuckle brown tube. White ceiling talking man white hair. White ceiling talking man white hair. White ceiling talking man white hair.

"There he is," says Major John Partridge. "There he is."

Dub hears these words, but any time he opens his eyes comes this time-lapse overlay of photographs.

"The last modern thing I liked was the miniskirt," he hears Partridge tell someone.

Explain everything to me, he tries to say.

"Have you ever heard of 'appoggiatura'?" Partridge says. "It's the little extra notes a singer sings climbing between notes. They say it's what makes a person cry listening to music. But alas, you and I, we live our lives without appoggiatura, don't we?"

What am I doing here? he tries to say.

"It's halftime," Partridge says. "Come on out for the second half."

He's aware of his arms; they've been jabbed with IV needles. Something is wrong on his right hand: not painful, just wrong. He blacks out, and when he wakes he's relieved to view the world in motion and he feels fine. Nobody is in his hospital room. He moves to sit up and suddenly his chest is coming apart. Blood rises out of him, he thinks he can see one of his ribs. He feels this must be a dream. Then people rush through the swinging door and shove him down, now the white ceiling is a background for these stern faces who call out to one another, pressing up on his chin so he can't see his body. He blacks out again.

"You're shot full of morphine," Partridge's voice says. "Don't be a damned fool."

Awake again, eyes closed, he nods.

"If you stop moving, you'll stabilize and they'll finish stitching you all the way up. Your hand surgery will have to wait."

He nods.

"To think: I was your emergency call, Lieutenant Storm. That's very flattering."

The last thing Dub remembers: asking Berkshire to make the call.

"You'll be fine, young man. The only thing these doctors are really worried about is your head. They keep talking about brain damage from that blow you took right there. Eventually you'll have to prove to them you can still talk."

He opens his eyes. Major Partridge is in uniform. Yes, this is a military hospital, which means he's not in Austin. He could be in San Antonio, or even El Paso. Above him are a bag of blood and two bags of clear chemicals, feeding his veins. Nothing hurts. His right hand is rigged in some kind of heavy plastic immobility device and he can't wiggle his fingers.

"You seem to have gotten yourself in a pickle," says

Partridge.

Dub falls asleep, a different sensation than blacking out. Why did Pilgrim do it? He thinks about the frightened little boy hiding out in the summer house at Dripping Springs, not knowing he was about to breathe his last, and then that moment of terror, hands suddenly around his neck. Dub wakes, incapable of telling how long he was gone.

"...kind of thing is bound to happen when you don't take care of yourself."

"Yes sir," Dub thinks he says. His voice is a croak. The room reveals itself in sharper focus.

"He speaks. This is good news. You had us worried."

"..."

"Don't look in a mirror just yet," Partridge says, walking out the swinging door. "They shaved off your hair."

He remembers: Heather. Heather holding his face in her palms.

Partridge comes back in carrying a notepad. His reading glasses balance fussily at the end of his nose. "It seems another man was found with you?"

Dub nods, or thinks he does.

"Anything you should tell me about him, lieutenant?"

"..."

"I admit I can't tell whether you're having a difficult time communicating, or whether you're giving me the silent treatment." Partridge finds a chair, sits close to the bed. "No matter the circumstances behind your...current health, I'm sure you're experiencing a mix of emotions. Not least of which is knowing you've let your country down."

"..."

"I could tell you were conflicted. It's why I insisted, because I once knew you so well. Unfortunately for both of us, it's too late now. We deploy...imminently. I can't get more specific than that. You'll need weeks in a hospital bed, and you may never regain full use of your right hand. Obviously you're in no condition."

Dub closes his eyes. He tells himself it should be easy to shake off the weekend's events, but then he thinks about Kid Collins. He wants to be knocked unconscious.

"I can't help feeling," says Partridge, "that if you'd only listened."

Keeping his eyes closed is its own communication, mutually understood. He hears the major gather himself. Dub sees an awful splotch in the blackness, set off to the right, continent-shaped, scab-yellow and throbbing. There's an undercurrent that beneath the drugs, his head would be the worst pain of all. What a wretchedness he feels, what complete humiliation. In his years of service, he never went so far as to enunciate the thought but now it seems as true as it is trite: Partridge was or is a surrogate father, someone not to be let down. And telling him no over Iraq has been a repudiation, and maybe Partridge feels that too. Maybe it explains the major's perseverance. Dub knows Partridge is judging him for whatever carelessness landed him in this hospital. Or no, this may all be a fiction jarred loose by Dub's own thoughts about his long-gone parents. Suddenly, though, something has snapped into place when Dub wasn't looking. He feels his eyes must look crazy, flapping open like window shades.

He says, "Antebellum Services."

Partridge grins with half his mouth. "What's that?"

"Police couldn't track it."

The major sits back down. "History is made," he says, "when desire reaches a grand enough scale. And of course we are the implements of that desire. This is all I've been trying to tell you."

"..."

"I just didn't want to go to battle without you, lieutenant."

Dub nudges himself slightly higher in bed, careful not to pull anything loose. "You're Antebellum Services."

"..."

"My friend died in *your* car."

Again Partridge looks down at his notepad. He scans writing Dub can't see, vaguely shaking his head.

"Antebellum, major."

"It's true," he says, "that your friend Mr. Collins had a talk with a few of my newer soldiers. They offered him a reward if he could help convince you to come to the aid of your platoon."

You getting an itch to jump back into some camouflage and crush it again?

"One of these new soldiers is a woman?" says Dub.

"Corporal Strauss, yes."

"And you told her to fuck him?"

"…"

Dub feels his brow become pinched. How many more loose threads can he pull, and will they all lead to Partridge?

He breathes. He wants to get high, then realizes he *is* high, at least on morphine. He thinks about his mother's face, leaning over him during a childhood fever. He remembers his father telling him to watch his tone, not to talk to his parents like buddies. He convinces himself they *are* alive, and that Partridge knows where.

"Help me with something I don't understand, lieutenant. I never understood what made you leave in the first place."

"…"

"The unpleasantness in Kismayo? One wrong man shot, and a child molester at that? One of ours wandering off and getting himself killed for love? You'd seen worse. We've all seen much worse. I don't think you were close to Corporal Bravo, were you?"

"Bruno."

"I don't believe this is a case where your value was never impressed upon you. Lieutenant, you are the only inactive soldier whose services I requested who refused. No matter what the politicians say, thousands of Americans will die in Iraq and Afghanistan because we're dealing with an enemy who will dig in and fight forever. Despite your coy act the past week, you know one thing with certainty: where the platoon goes, we save American lives. We are two men out of a select few who are uniquely capable in this way. We are life-saving machines, and when our country decides it needs us, we act."

Dub says, "It doesn't matter anymore."

"Tell me why," says Partridge.

"…"

"I would never have believed you had such dissolution in you, Storm. You among all the others. But perhaps it's those of us wound too tightly in one direction who must snap back furthest in the other."

Quiet settles on them. Dub closes his eyes and feels a fleeting nostalgia for that short time ago, when all he could see was still-lifes. Then for some reason he remembers a jeep ride from the distant past: a caravan blowing a straight line of dust down an ancient desert road, six men to a jeep, helmets joggling like eggs in a carton. This was early in Dub's first tour, long before Major Partridge found him. One man in Dub's jeep began singing: "Like a rhinestone cowboy! Riding out on a horse in a star-spangled rodeo!" and soon everyone else had learned the words and they were all belting out, "Like a rhinestone cowboy! Getting cards and letters from people I don't even know!" and looking at each other with that unashamed expression of serious singing and the hint of a smile, and Dub remembers thinking that even though the jeep engines and crunching tire sounds probably covered over their voices it was still pretty stupid to potentially call attention to themselves out in the open like this, but then he thought it didn't matter, it was fun. He can't place those five other men. The one next to him had a pencil-thin mustache. At some point up the road a VS-50 mine blasted their jeep to hell, and Dub found himself seated in the sand, thrown loose while the five other men in his car died charbroiled deaths. He sat blinking—the sound of rifle fire all around him—

humming "Rhinestone Cowboy." Later they told him he'd been concussed, but that quiet feeling, the release of one's fate to a great lottery, is something Dub recalls with incredible clarity, though until just now he'd forgotten the entire episode had even happened. It's the same feeling here in bed, morphine doing its gentle slosh.

The major stands, removes his glasses. He leaves his pad on the bed, locks his arms behind his back. "This is goodbye," he says.

"Who was he?" says Dub.

"..."

"Who was he, major?"

"Am I expected to know what you're talking about?"

Dub is awake. He tastes blood in his mouth. The words come not from his damaged head, but elsewhere. "The last man I ever killed for you," he says. "The one in Kismayo."

Partridge gives the softest, most believably searching expression imaginable.

"You and I were lying to the rest of the platoon," says Dub. "And you were lying to me. You used the embassy bombings for cover. And set me up."

"..."

"Who was he?"

"This is paranoia," Partridge says, with great concern.

"I couldn't figure it out, except probably I already had. His eyes. We were only across the street so the scope brought him right up close and he had blue eyes." With his left hand, Dub reaches up and touches the right side of his head—it's numbed, like he's feeling an eggplant—and he also paws his warm bare scalp and groans. Partridge's face belies nothing. "And you're bad with names, except you always knew Abdi's name. You always got *his* name right, every time."

The major waves a hand dismissively.

"What did you do?" Dub says, "What did you do to Abdi? You hurt him."

"Lieutenant."

"You staged it. You beat a local boy. All in the name of, what, convincing me to pull the trigger?"

"…"

"When did I ever say no to you?"

Partridge squints one eye.

"Did you personally take off that little boy's finger, major? Did you punch him in the face and cut an ear halfway off?"

"…"

"I'm guessing probably not. Maybe it was someone else in the platoon. I know: Corporal Bruno. And then it was easy enough to cover up that trail."

Partridge's face loses all amusement. "It's a child's mind that looks everywhere for conspiracy and a final verdict."

"If you couldn't tell me about it, then he wasn't just some local al-Qaeda hack. And all the sneaking around, all the lying to our men, all that risk…he had to be important. If you wanted him dead that bad, maybe he knew something about you personally. But he sure as hell wasn't an embassy bomber. And he wasn't some abusive father. I guess I've always been your dancing monkey."

"'*Our* men?'"

Four years feels like nothing and an eternity. What is time? How can we gain an inkling of what time is, as it carries us forward? Just staying alive to ride time is a progress all its own. But a man like Partridge. What he builds along the way. "You won't tell me who," Dub says. "But just tell me I'm right." He tries to take accusation out of his expression, tries to replace it with plaintiveness. "Then we'll both have our answers."

"I'm beginning to realize," says Partridge, "it doesn't much matter what I say. You're too far gone. Believe what you will, paint yourself a picture in great detail and then live inside it."

"Who was he, major? Please. You owe me that much."

"I don't, Mr. Storm. I really don't."

"But I'm not wrong."

"..."

"Tell me I'm wrong."

Partridge is careful not to move a muscle.

"Well, what if maybe I called some journalist in here and gave him this story?"

"Fuck son," says Partridge. "Be my goddamn guest."

Dub rages inside. He sees suggestions of malevolence spidering from Partridge, and it isn't particularly the morality or lack thereof that animates him. It's the awareness. There are players and there are played, something he's always known: but for these past four years he's merely been posing on the supine side of that divide. Now in the past few days he's grieved from the inner core of his peach-pit heart, he's confessed crushing guilt, he's had sex with a ghost, and he's nearly died. Is drama just another word for all this clarity?

He says, "Before you leave, could you put on the TV? Leave it on anything with war coverage. I just want to make sure I see you die."

This makes Partridge laugh robustly, from his heels, so he has to stoop over and catch his breath.

RECOVERY

The hospital's lighting had no nuance. The place was either ink-dark or blanched white. Dub desired infrared or sunglasses at all times.

He stood in his robe watching newborns wrapped like pre-dinner baskets of bread: three white ones, two brown ones. They kept yawning cynically. They weren't crying; they never seemed to cry. It was a game, guessing which would yawn next.

He swore he saw a prostitute take a young leukemia patient into a supply closet, while the boy's father looked on. She was thin and tall, Asian, dressed in maroon velvet with her hair in some wild old-fashioned swoop. Dub vainly sought alternate explanations. The father's beaver-brush mustache twitched and fiddled. Dub hoped to stick around long enough to watch the couple emerge into ensuing complication—shame, political smiles, the exchange of cash—but his appetite had returned, and lunch beckoned.

He hadn't phoned anyone about Heather Easley. It wasn't a final decision; it was just something he kept not doing, every day.

Instead he looked forward to Ramiro's shift, which began at eleven every night. Ramiro was a night custodian

Dub met his second day out of ICU, a late-coming Mexican immigrant with slicked-back hair and quarter-shaded glasses whose frames were hopelessly large and out of style. But the lad was fairly sure he hung the moon, walked around the hospital corridors with a jive-step, bobbing his head. Maybe he was eighteen. Dub first encountered him while changing his hospital gown; he shrugged off the dirty one and stood naked in his small bare room trying not to see his reflection in any surfaces, when those stupid progressively shaded glasses peeked out from the bathroom. Ramiro had concealed himself in there, wanting to catch a glimpse of Dub's scars.

"Man, they oughtta slice you diagonal the other way, too," he'd said. "That way, you got a big 'X' across your chest."

Surprised by the boy's stealth, Dub had no snappy comeback. The plastic apparatus that held his right arm straight and his right hand still after surgery, it had scratched his privates as he'd tried to cover himself.

"Don't worry man," Ramiro had said, "they do a security check on everybody. If I was here to rape your ass, they'd already know about it."

When the hall lights dimmed and everyone was supposed to be asleep, Dub stood at his door thinking about machines, all the machines in this place keeping hearts pumping, lungs inhaling, keeping air moist and cool, humming and blooping a symphony that complicated the gumshoe's straightforward solo. He patted his chest, the crinkling gauze and tape over his stitches. Then came a multi-wheeled rolling sound and Ramiro rapped the wall just outside, Dub stepped through his door, and together they pushed the janitor's cart to the elevator and went up to the roof to get high.

The night air was hot but felt good moving around on his face. The weed was awful, tasted like soap and dirt. But apparently Dub still had a talent for attracting free supplies.

They sat on the roof, either looking down at the parking lot and the anonymous sprawl beyond, or just staring at the tar and cinderblocks up here, the shadowed pipes peeking up out of the hospital only to bend back down again into the belly of the beast. Ramiro's jeans were comically tight, and he wore cowboy boots; only a blue uniform top marked him as an employee. His hands were soft, his mop handle basically untouched.

"They told me now I got to keep the water coolers filled," he said, "that's another job for me on the night shift, man. But them jugs are heavy, and they keep 'em way down in the basement. That's too much work. So whenever one of the coolers is empty, I just fill it from the tap. People can't taste a thing, and the manager, he loves it."

"Don't they notice," said Dub, "that none of the jugs in the basement ever get used?"

"Naw, man. You think I'm stupid? I bring up *some* jugs, bro. Half the time, the lower floors. The manager loves me. He's spending half as much on water as he used to, and he doesn't care why. I'm a fucking genius."

Dub's own lack of curiosity surprised him. He didn't ask what city the hospital was in, he didn't confirm the hospital's name. It was military for sure, too many uniforms and buzzcuts walking around. But there was no base surrounding them. It could be anywhere. He didn't want to know. His phone had rung for a couple days then the battery ran out and he didn't ask for a charger.

One night they tripped down from the roof via the stairwell and arrived on Dub's floor as a crisis was unfolding. EMT guys were wheeling people around on gurneys, madly explaining vitals, and sleepy residents in lab coats bumped around, pagers blaring. There appeared to be bullet holes in several of these incapacitated men. Ramiro strode over to one, who'd been left in a corner with an IV bag dangling above him. He crouched against the wall and whispered with the wounded man. Dub was fascinated by the hubbub. The high from Ramiro's stash was pitiless and abrupt, borne out of smoky, smelly pinheads that made toking feel like a job.

But Dub was fascinated by the streaks these doctors left in the air as they ran from patient to patient. He thought he saw Partridge by the ward desk, but it was an intern crying in a chair. He heard slivers of conversation, heard the words "gunman" and "barracks" and "wounded" in the air, but mostly he stared like a ghost, sadly unmoved.

Ramiro came over, and Dub asked what he was talking about with the wounded man.

"I asked if he got high."

"What'd he say?" said Dub.

"He said of course, but he likes acid, and I'm sorry, that shit will fuck you up."

"Did you tell him that?"

"Of course I told him that. I gave him a couple joints and a jar of pills I found in the supply room."

"What are the pills?"

"I don't know," Ramiro said. "But I think he died anyway."

The doctors requested Dub stay in bed, because they were still concerned about his brain functions. He had vicious headaches behind his right eye, bad sensitivity to light, and intermittent slurred speech. So Dub stayed put during the daytime except for cafeteria lunch. At night, he tagged along for Ramiro's adventures. That was something great about the kid: everything was exalted and worthy of narration, every story. Ramiro came to the hospital every night planning mayhem, whether it was sassing the old desk nurse on Dub's floor or wooing her subordinates, finding alleged secret patients being subjected to military experiments, or keeping a broken vending machine that gave out limitless candy top secret. Dub rarely slept, and suspected some of his sub-optimal brainwave performance was a result.

For what seemed like more than a week, Ramiro talked about bringing in a bong and some ecstasy tablets, and camping out on the roof. He grew obsessed with the idea until Dub was obsessed, too, and they spent the small black hours planning what music Ramiro should steal for his iPod, what munchies Dub might buy from the cafeteria and hide until the big night. Dub crashed in his bed late one morning, so tired he couldn't see straight, and half-dreamed various Easley family members would show up on the roof, asking to partake. He knew none of it was real and tried to force himself awake, wiggled his legs and feet, but it was a ladder he couldn't climb, death held his ankles. He felt hot and cold as Heather kissed him. Why did Pilgrim move from Dripping Springs to New Braunfels?

"The council will let them build," Dub said in a whisper. "They probably would have anyway."

The ceiling blew off his room and the sky was Africa's sky. Or was this Iraq?

"Just a footnote," he said. "Not even a footnote when they write the glorious history of Austin."

It was nighttime. He hadn't moved, hadn't eaten, hadn't relieved himself. He remembered such want from his platoon days; there had always been a mission attached. Now it was day again, blinding day. He was in rapt elation, pure surrender. He noticed every trigger of experience, air and sweat and wet and cold, and understood that his reactions shaped him. A man's face broke through clouds in the ceiling and told him he was suffering from an infection.

*

They told him it was the closest he'd come to dying. He begged to differ.

A nurse said they knew he'd been sneaking around at night. She told him the roof was off limits, unless he wanted to meet his maker.

For a time he feared he'd gotten Ramiro fired, but then Dub saw him sweeping with what looked like an abashed posture. He didn't stop by Dub's room any longer.

Dub now recognized how different it was, to be back in the arms of a different kind of machine: an institution. All the people who fussed and scuttled nearby, they weren't his friends but they saw him…watched him, cared for him, steered around him, incorporated him into their lives. Such a small thing to notice, such webs. But Dub thought about all the men he'd served with, and his parents' empty house. Common in his mythology of self was that all he'd wanted in the four years since coming home was a quiet room. The antibiotics flushed him clean.

A couple days into this new recovery, a nurse aerated his chest wound but didn't patch him back up, left the spools of gauze and tape sitting on their stainless-steel tray. "Doctor's orders," she said, and left the big purple slash alone, to breathe.

Dub sat up in bed. The evening glided by. He could still wait for hours without moving. Around midnight, he saw Ramiro slinking past his door.

"Hey!" Dub said. "Vato!"

"I'm not supposed to," said Ramiro.

"I know, sorry man. I got sick. It was weak sauce. Did you get in trouble? Hey, I got my bandage off if you want to see. It's sticking to my shirt a little bit."

"That's fucking disgusting, dude," Ramiro said, grinning.

"I can tell looking at your face that tonight's the night. You're going up there right now, aren't you?"

"Sorry, dog."

"Maybe it's something I never learned. Salvation is supposed to be other people. But fuck that noise. Fuck. That. Noise."

Ramiro looked at him funny. Dub climbed out of bed, threw on a robe, and hijacked the little bags of chips and candy he'd hidden underneath the sink in his bathroom. He followed Ramiro to the service elevator with its filthy silver cross-hatched floor. The world was wild and howling up on the roof. There was a blanket laid out on the black tar, a brick holding down each corner. Ramiro reached inside his janitor's cart and came out with a hookah, with three hoses spiraling off into three pipes.

"Ta da!" he said.

A voice behind them scared Dub, saying, "Boys, let's do this thing!" It was Glenn, one of the daytime custodians.

The three of them kneeled around this sculpted brass altar, which looked like a marvelous three-foot-tall candlestick. Ramiro passed around ecstasy hits. Glenn popped open a Shiner Bock. Dub was somewhere between the scandal of teenage rebellion and the helpless pork-wiggle of mindless addiction.

"I got it from this guy," said Ramiro, "he got samurai swords in his shop and he used to work for the CIA. He knows shit about the Kennedy assassination and Watergate and everything."

The other two men performed ministrations on the hookah as Dub watched. This was where he was. Even his own feelings were an unresolved mystery.

Then in a wash of moonlight he saw something on Glenn's wrist. He reached to touch it and the older man showed him: an ancient strip of yellow nylon, with faded black marks. A piece of measuring tape.

Glenn said, "It's stupid I keep wearing it, but maybe they brainwash you a little bit, right? This one shrink at Ferguson, she makes a big production. She gives it to you when you get out."

"Ferguson," said Dub.

"Prison, son."

"…"

"She cuts you off a length and ties it around your…." He waggled his hand. "Nobody says you gotta keep it on. You're supposed to, I don't know, measure the distance between doing right and doing wrong? I can't remember, it's been a couple years."

Dub's mind yelped. The second protestor at the AAA rally on Brodie Lane, the one who saw Dub threatening Jeb Sparks and crossed the street to help. Tarasco. He wore the same measuring tape around his wrist.

"But you do keep it on, Glenn!" said Ramiro. "You're a good boy!"

"What I mean, it's like a graduation present when you get out," Glenn said, and popped the ecstasy home. He drank his beer and splayed on the blanket, big belly double-convex with the half-moon.

*

He found a nurse's cell unattended on a desk, but had nobody to call. Kid was the one with acquaintances on the APD. He thought about Berkshire's number, entombed in the brain of his own phone, but surely the detective had long since ditched any traceable objects. Dub retreated to his room: sober, grinding, electrified.

He said the Pledge of Allegiance. He endured a liberating, yodel-worthy bowel movement.

When Pete Bellingham was spying at Guero's, he thought he heard Sparks ordering hot sauce. But Sparks wasn't saying "Tabasco." No. He was looking for someone who wasn't there. Tarasco.

In the morning Dub decamped. It turned out he was in San Antonio's outskirts. It was April. The Longhorns had made the Final Four, were playing Syracuse tomorrow night. He stole a gray sweatshirt from the lost-and-found, finagled it over his robe and immobilized hand. He put on his blood-spattered topsiders and boarded a greyhound.

You build a city. You build a case. His car had been towed from downtown Austin; he found it, paid the fee, and drove another half-hour out to Dripping Springs. Getting the address for the Easley home there was as easy as a payphone call to 411.

It was a goliath compound off East Creek. There were no visible parked cars, and no police tape or anything else to indicate the APD had dug even half-an-inch further into the case. What Dub noticed first were the dragons: huge bay laurels and privets carved to look like winged reptiles in various stages of combat and repose. They were a bit overgrown, but still recognizable, and they probably delighted young Hunter. Acres of unworked farmland extended behind the house. Nobody answered when he rang the bell. Dub stood sweating in his ridiculous hospital garb, trying to remember what this all was really about. A wonderland for a scion. Pain and chaos. Everything overturned.

He sat beside an open-mouthed dragon whose breast was swelled, as though about to breathe fire. The ground was dry and hard. It was a ceaseless estuarial weave, his power and his powerlessness. He was thinking much more about his parents these days. He tried to imagine what they'd have done had he been killed at age three.

The next morning, he rented an old Bronco with a lifted suspension and big all-terrain tires, then visited the Westlake Hills station and told a new detective just enough to get what he needed. He found Jeb Sparks waiting for reporters alone on a curb at 6th and Lamar, and got the rest.

*

"Do you remember me?"

"Jesus, man. The way you're blocking the sun like that."

"I said do you remember me?" Dub stood against a screen door, peering in. Nathan Tarasco smoked a cigarette at his kitchen table.

"I can't even fucking see you, dude. Come on in."

Dub did. It was a second-floor apartment over someone's garage. The kitchen was carpeted and filthy. Dub didn't know. He didn't know what he was going to do.

"Aw, man," Tarasco said.

"We're going for a ride," said Dub. He showed the grip of the M9 he had tucked in his jeans waistband.

"What?"

"Get up." Dub took a step forward.

Tarasco stood, hands out, placating. "Hey, man. You look like shit. You know that?"

"Downstairs," said Dub. "Now."

They drove west on 290, past Dripping Springs, and kept going. Dub didn't say anything. He tried not to think anything. He tried to believe he was under orders. Tarasco was mostly quiet, shoved up against the passenger door. He still had blond streaks in his dark hair, still wore funky hipster glasses and a soul patch. The air conditioning was on full blast.

They hit I-10. Dub said, "You used to be a gardener."

"Yes," said Tarasco.

"It was you who cut all those bushes into shapes."

"Now I paint houses."

Dub gripped the wheel.

Tarasco said, "What, we're talking now? We're talking like long-lost…? You're bringing me somewhere to what?"

But Dub didn't answer, just kept driving. At Ozona he exited and headed south. In his mind everything was clicked off. There was no thirst, no hunger. Tarasco wasn't arguing, wasn't fighting hard. He wasn't threatening to jump out of the moving truck. Only as the sun skated its arc over them, as other cars grew scarce, as they crossed onto I-90 and skirted Mexico, was Dub's reverie broken by crying sounds. He looked at Tarasco.

"Do you know what they did?" he said, sobbing. "Do you know what those fucking Easleys did to me?"

"I do," Dub answered.

"Almost a year. They locked me up almost a whole entire year just because I talked to that crazy bitch a few times. Because I felt bad for her."

"Angela," Dub said.

"Then she changes her mind, I didn't actually rape her after all. And they let me go. Fuck, I never even touched her, man."

Dub nodded. Even as Tarasco stopped weeping for himself and stared out the window, Dub kept nodding.

The country was now dark red. They passed an airport and Dub pulled off the highway, onto an unmarked dirt road heading south. The Rio Grande was maybe ten miles away, and the terrain here was volcanic. Dub left the road, drove slowly with the suspension jouncing, just kept moving into the sun.

"Please," Tarasco finally said. It was about time.

"…"

"Please, man. You don't have to do it."

"Tell me what you did," said Dub.

"Oh, God, please. Please."

More minutes passed. He saw mountains to the south, figured the bare ground could become impassable any moment. But this was far enough. He took his foot from the brake and switched the engine off.

"It's me," Dub told this kid, ruefully. "I'm the one. If I don't blunder into your protest, you assholes just camp out for the afternoon and then go home. But I push you around and make it seem like you've got the Easleys' attention. Jeb Sparks gets all excited, wants to strike while the iron is hot. He figures he's crawled under Thomas Easley's skin. But he can't leave the protest, it's his baby, so you volunteer. You'll drive over to their house in Westlake and see if Easley wants to negotiate. But things are too crazy over there, right? And you used to be their gardener, so you know about the summer house, too. Why not take a little spin over there, just to check. So you see: I'm the one who set it in motion."

Tarasco said, "You're gonna leave me out here."

"Tell me," said Dub.

"You can't do this."

Dub pulled the gun from his waistband. He pocketed the truck's key, motioned for Tarasco to get out. They walked a half-mile along a scrub wash, hard rock beneath their rubber soles. He wasn't aiming the gun at this younger man, but he had it out. He fingered the trigger obscenely, as in old days. They stopped. It was only April, but it was over 90.

"You don't know me," Tarasco said. "You're doing this to scare me."

". . ."

"You can't just fucking…execute me."

". . ."

"*Do you know what they did to me!*" The words failed to echo. Everything here was rather drab.

"I'll give you the key," Dub said.

"What?"

"I'll give you the key if you tell me the truth."

"You'll…?"

"It was hiring *me*," said Dub.

". . ."

"It was hiring me that fucked everything up."

"You'd die out here," Tarasco said. "You got no water."

Dub pulled out the rental key with its laminated rectangle that read *DC-42*, and tossed it to the younger man.

Heat shimmered in the flatland. From this swell, the mountains were crusts barely visible where the leeched-white sky ended. There was no breeze. Dub saw red sand had already attached itself to his pant cuffs. Nothing alive in this place, no snakes or insects, just the fine-muscle grip of these rocks. He shaded his eyes. Out here, he could make a simple life.

Tarasco put his fist around the key. He looked at the sky. "He was playing outside by himself. I pulled up and whoever had him there…I didn't see anyone else. I knew who he was,

I knew whose kid he was. It went through my head, like, I was about to be a really big hero. All I had to do was take him by the hand, stick him in my car. What a story, right? Where was everybody else? I mean, it seemed like the most fucked-up kidnapping ever, just letting this tiny little kid run around by himself for anyone to see. I started thinking there was probably a reward. But money is what did it to me in the first place, because they've got so much. They can buy off anybody, they can make it look like anything. Are they really gonna let me play the hero? If they could put me away for rape, who says they won't pin me with the kidnapping? It was just one second. I was thinking about *her*. I did it, and I left his body. I ran."

Dub nodded. And when Pilgrim found the body, he figured he'd been double-crossed and set up, so he took Hunter to New Braunfels and buried him there, then flipped out and decided to just kill everyone.

"I mean, I don't sleep anymore, man, the last three weeks."

"..."

"Man, you don't want me to just leave you here."

"..."

"I'm sorry. I'm so sorry. It's just I don't know what to do. What comes next?"

Progress was for fucking *suckers*.

Dub raised the M9 and even with his left hand it was an easy shot. The kid never saw it coming.

ABOUT THE AUTHOR

Christopher Harris is the author of four novels, *Slotback Rhapsody*,
The Big Clear, *War On Sound* and *Tulsa*. He lives in Amherst, MA,
and Los Angeles, CA, USA.